Valiant

A King David Novel
Book Two of the Davidic Chronicles

Greg S. Baker

Valiant

A King David Novel
Book Two of the Davidic Chronicles

by

Greg S. Baker

Independently Published

Copyright © 2018

ISBN 13: 978-1724620989
ISBN 10: 1724620983

First Edition

All Scripture quotations are from the King James Bible.

All rights reserved. No part of this publication may be reproduced or transmitted in any form or by any means, electronic or mechanical, including photocopy, recording, or any information storage retrieval system, without permission in writing from the copyright owner.

This is a work of fiction based on the Holy Scriptures as presented in the King James Bible. All characters and events resembling real people and events outside the Scriptures is wholly coincidental.

Other Books by Greg S. Baker

Biblical Fiction Novels

The Davidic Chronicles
Anointed
Valiant
Fugitive
Delivered
King

The Rise of Daniel
Crucibles of God
Children of the Captivity
Revealer of Secrets
Arising Wrath

Adventure/Fantasy Novels

Isle of the Phoenix Novels
The Phoenix Quest
In the Dragon's Shadow
Phoenix Flame
Rise of the Dragon Spawn
More to come…

Christian and Christian Living

- ***The Generational Warrior*** – *The Battlefield Manual for First-Generation Christians*
- ***Fitly Spoken*** – *Developing Effective Communication and Social Skills*
- ***Restoring a Fallen Christian*** – *Rebuilding Lives for the Cause of Christ*
- ***The Great Tribulation and the Day of the Lord***: *Reconciling the Premillennial Approach to Revelation*
- ***The Gospel of Manhood According to Dad*** – *A Young Man's Guide to Becoming a Man*
- ***Rediscovering the Character of Manhood*** – *A Young Man's Guide to Building Integrity*
- ***Stressin' Over Stress*** – *Six Ways to Handle Stress*

www.GregSBaker.com

To my dad.

*No one is more deserving.
In biblical times, a man was known by
who his father was.*

*I am the son of Keith and couldn't be
more honored.*

Acknowledgments

These novels represent the fulfillment of a burden to create more interest in the Bible and the people of whom it speaks. No work of this magnitude is the sole product of a single individual.

My Saviour, Jesus Christ, is of course the One I believe laid such a burden upon me. I pray that this work exalts His name and helps expand His kingdom.

I am grateful to my beta-reading group. Each person was instrumental in pointing out specifics that enhanced this work. Elizabeth Speers was most diligent in her efforts to help make this novel stand out. Her contributions were immeasurable. Other readers in this group helped as well, specifically my beautiful wife, Liberty, Diane Frazier, and others.

My editor, Linda Stubblefield, has once again been fabulous.

Author's Note about Biblical Fiction

What Is Biblical Fiction?

Biblical fiction can have a variety of meanings, but essentially for my purposes, the genre is similar in nature to historical fiction. In biblical fiction, the author takes the true events and people of the Bible and expands upon them into a fuller story of "what might have happened" that connects separate events into a broader fictional, but possible, story.

In such a novel, I would expand upon the historical facts mentioned in the Bible and present a possible fuller picture of what the Bible describes. An entire novel could be based on those few chapters, filling in fictionally all the blank areas.

For example, David mentions to King Saul that he had killed a lion and a bear. The Bible does not describe those events, so in a biblical fiction novel, I might write the scenes surrounding those events as they might have happened while staying true to the biblical account. This work is not intended to be Scripture or to replace Scripture. Instead, my intent is to bring to life a possible fuller picture of the characters and events that the Bible describes.

This book is similar to what preachers do when retelling a Bible story from the pulpit. They embellish the story, add emotional responses or reactions to the characters, and extrapolate events and actions in ways that depict logically what might have happened or how biblical characters might have felt. Still fictional—but logical fiction.

Scriptural footnotes have been added to show where a biblical fact is anchored in the story.

My desire is to ensure that the biblical facts are the mainstays and core of the story while the fictional aspects are forced to revolve around those facts to bring a cohesive narrative that remains true to the biblical record. I won't bend the facts or alter them to present a more "entertaining" story.

Again, to be clear, this book is not meant to be Scripture or to replace Scripture of any sort. Except for what the Bible says, the rest of what I write is fictional—my best guess based on the information the Bible shares as to what might have happened.

These stories are meant to be fun and adventurous while remaining true to the biblical account. These novels are not children's books, though they are suitable for children. I am writing predominantly for a more mature audience, that of teenagers and adults. I don't sugarcoat the men and women in the Bible. They were often thieves, liars, murderers, adulterers, and bloodthirsty warriors. I decided not to reduce the violence and other horrible deeds that the Bible describes. I aim to present an entertaining story, true, but also one that will hopefully inspire the reader to see Bible stories in a broader sense. These were real people with real problems who made real mistakes but who lived real lives that God wanted us to study and know.

So, enjoy!

Map of Israel

At the Time of David's First Anointing

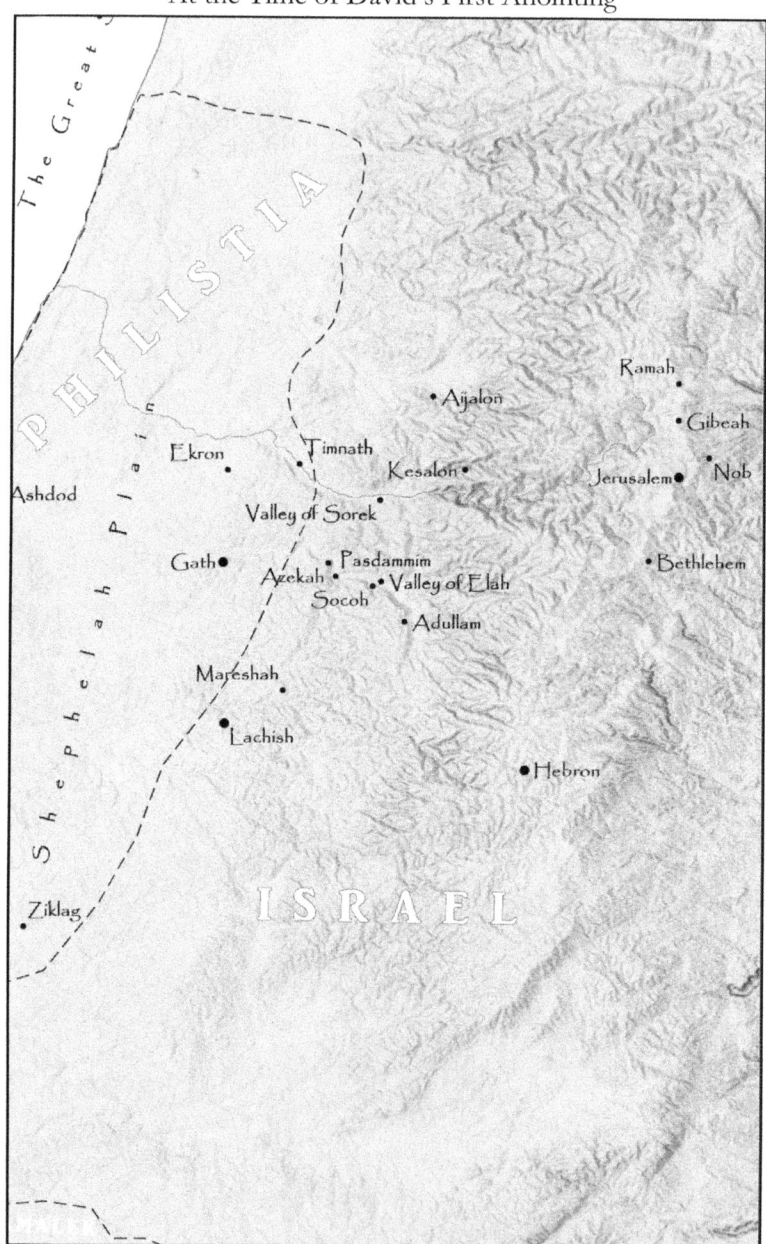

Prologue

Michal watched David closely. Her veiled face reflected a speculative, almost hungry expression that would no doubt worry her father if he saw it. She took in every detail of David's face and bearing. That he sat awkwardly atop one of her father's war horses or that he spent more time trying to keep from sliding ignobly off than he did in acknowledging the crowds thronging the road leading up to Jerusalem hardly mattered. With her attention so firmly set on the new hero of Israel, she scarcely noticed her stately and confident father riding before the shepherd, and she spared only a brief glance at the gory head of Goliath impaled on the end of a long spear and hoisted above the returning army like some macabre banner of victory.

No, her eyes saw only one person. David. The tale of his battle with the giant had passed through the countryside like a fire through a dry wood. The news buzzed from lips to lips across the land and raced far ahead of the returning army. A *boy* had killed the Philistine champion! Singlehandedly. With naught but a sling and a stone. The Philistine army had been routed, and rumor spoke of David leading the charge into the very teeth of the enemy. Apparently, the sight of him had struck such dread into the hearts of the enemy that none could stand before him. Tens of thousands lay dead at his feet—if not directly, Michal figured, then indirectly.

It was truly a tale of legend. David was a hero, Israel's champion. He had saved the nation from the brutality of the heathen

Philistines. Fathers would be spared the sight of their families murdered before their eyes. Israelite women would avoid being raped and abused by grimy heathen hands and profane breath. Children would not be enslaved. Babes could nestle safely in their mother's arms instead of being dashed against walls and their lifeblood spilled upon the ground.

David had saved them all.

And Michal determined to make him hers.

What better match for the daughter of a king? From lowly shepherd to savior of Israel, David had made himself more than worthy to claim her hand. She'd heard the *other* rumors of course—the ones that said that the Great Seer had anointed David to replace her father. In truth, it only fueled her desire to claim David for her own. But even if the rumors weren't true, David had come out of nowhere and had stolen the hearts of the people. With the people behind him, her father would need to tread carefully in dealing with this potential usurper lest they turn against him. In this matter, Michal figured she could help. In fact, it was her duty to do so.

If she was honest with herself, duty in this case was merely an excuse. Looking at David's handsome face and knowing the heroism he had displayed in defeating the Philistine champion had stirred something deep inside of her. Her heart had been stolen too.

Inspired by his heroics, she lifted up a song in praise of David as he rode past on his way toward Jerusalem where Goliath's tattooed head would be hoisted high above the walls of the fortress.[1] She sang and danced for David.

When the women on the other side spontaneously sang, "Saul has slain his thousands," she burst out in echoing chorus that was instantly picked up by thousands of other voices, "And David his tens of thousands!"[2]

So they sang, their voices raised in a great harmonious chorus that seemed to shatter the sky. At the first refrain of the song, David

---

[1] 1 Samuel 17:24.
[2] 1 Samuel 18:7.

looked up in obvious surprise, his face flushing with pleasure. *Good, Michal thought, satisfied. I can use that.* She positioned herself where David would see her, and when he did, his cheeks reddened even further. *Perfect.*

Well over a month had passed since they'd seen each other, but Michal was gratified to know that she'd not been forgotten. That aside, her feelings bemused her somewhat. She'd never felt this way before about a man. She'd always known that her father would give her away to a deserving man—most likely where the union would benefit King Saul and his kingdom. This was the way of things, and she'd long ago accepted the fact that her husband would likely be chosen for her.

But now she wanted David. Besides, what better union to strengthen the crown? What better way to preserve her father's legacy and kingdom? Now she only needed to convince her father of it—and David too.

That's when she noticed that David's eyes weren't directed exclusively at her. Frowning, Michal followed his gaze to another girl standing nearby: Michal's older sister, Merab. Worse, her sister had that absentminded adoring look she got when some handsome face had snared her heart—something that happened all too frequently. Much of her face was hidden behind a thin veil, but Merab somehow managed to find material that clung to her face and outlined her small, perky nose and shapely cheeks on her perfectly oval face.

Michal's eyes smoldered darkly. What was it about small, perky noses that so endeared themselves to men? Michal's own, she knew, was neither small nor perky—more like straight and pointy. An offending mole grew on one side, further marring her overwhelmingly uninteresting nose on a face that was just a tad too wide.

No, if Michal wanted to compete with her older sister in snaring the eyes of men, she would need to bring her hair into the fray. Merab's hair, an unremarkable dark brown, looked coarse and disheveled. Michal's lighter locks, however, looked soft and honied like the rippling silk clothes she wore. Michal's hair, inherited from her mother, had that lustrous look that caused people to do a doubletake to be sure it wasn't really alive. She'd caught the eye of plenty of men—including David. She vividly remembered her first meeting with David in Saul's court when a frightened young shepherd boy had been brought in to play the harp for her father. He had been taken with her, but he had been merely an unremarkable shepherd back then, and she hadn't given him a lot of thought.

Now things had changed.

But Merab could also snare the looks of men. She portrayed a sense of helplessness that sometimes appealed to men, and her almond eyes were like pools of liquid that one could just sink into like a warm bath.

Merab, being older, knew that she would most likely be given in marriage before Michal. Being eldest gave her first rights if she could somehow persuade Father of the merits of the object of her fancy. Her latest fancy had been Jonathan's armorbearer, a man by the name of Adriel, but now she couldn't keep her eyes off David.

And David seemed to be as equally ensnared.

Michal's eyes narrowed. Well, she'd just have to do something about that when the time came. Father wouldn't be too hasty to promise David one of his daughters—not without purpose. So, she had time. Time to make sure that she was the one given to the new hero.

She danced over to her sister and grabbed her hand. "Merab," she said, laughing. "Sing with me!"

Merab's eyes lit up. "Aye, sister!"

Together they sang David's praises. Standing so close together, David couldn't help but look at them both. For the moment, Michal was content with that. Focused as she was on David, she never noticed the look of utter dismay that came over her father's face when he saw her singing of David, and she thus failed to see the dangerous curl to his lower lip that presaged violence and anger.

Michal also failed to notice another man, standing sullenly in the back of the crowd, who also watched David with angry eyes. She never saw him slip away and begin his journey to Gath to report to King Achish, the Philistine lord, of all that he'd seen and heard of this new upstart named David, the son of Jesse.

1

"Slayer of tens of thousands?" Jonathan teased as he eased into a chair next to David. "More like slayer of one underfed and undersized pup."

David threw his friend an incredulous look. "Undersized? You did see the same giant as I, did you not?"

Jonathan shrugged, yawning. "Not worthy of a second look. That's why we sent the shepherd and his sling." He grinned. "Did you think we would send you to battle a man truly dangerous?"

David snorted, scratching idly at his growing beard. It had filled out over the last year and looked fairly respectable at his young age of seventeen. Jonathan, at least ten years older, had his trimmed and full. David felt a bit envious of it.

"You seemed most anxious to avoid the giant," David shot back, also grinning, "standing safe atop a hill while I expended all the effort to bring the giant low."

Jonathan shrugged his powerful shoulders. "Effort? You flung but a single stone. And if the Philistine was indeed a giant as you claim, then you could hardly miss such a large target. Why should a prince do what some lowly shepherd could do half-drunk and half-asleep?"

David barked a short laugh, shaking his head at the futility of arguing with his friend. He loved Jonathan's laconic nature and easy way with words. Already, they were bonding in ways that warmed David's heart. Their blood covenant made on the field of battle after David's victory over the Philistine champion meant the world to him. They were now sworn together in a bond that David suspected would supersede all other human bonds.[1]

If he was honest with himself at all, recent events had him slightly bemused. He had killed Goliath, the Philistine champion, felling the giant with a single slung stone from his sling. That singular event had instantly propelled him to champion status. He could still hear the ringing voices of the women singing his praises. He could still picture the awe stamped upon the faces of the Hebrew warriors. And in his own mind, he could still see himself standing atop Goliath's body holding high his bloody, tattooed head in victory while the Philistine armies panicked and fled.

That moment was the highlight of David's young life. He had fought the enemies of Jehovah Elohim and had defended Israel, his people. He had removed the blasphemous stain and insult of Goliath's words from Hebrew hearts. The king had praised him and honored him, and the king's son, Jonathan, had made a blood covenant with David.

David's head still spun from the wonder of it all. No one, least of all David, doubted that God was with him. Perhaps more than anything else, this thought brought him the most comfort and peace. If there was one thing David wanted to do well, it was to please his God, and the moment he was purified from his uncleanness of having handled the dead,[2] he would offer the appropriate thanksgiving offerings.

Jonathan tapped the table where David's food, a loaf of bread, cheese, and a fig cake—thankfully no goat meat—remained untouched. "Are you not hungry?"

David regarded the food uncertainly. "Your sister brought it," he said as if that explained everything.

"Ah, then it is no doubt tasteless and hollow. Which sister?"

"Merab brought the bread and cheese." David glanced at the flagon of wine. "The wine is from Michal."

"Doubtless weak and tasteless too. And the fig cake?"

---

[1] 2 Samuel 1:26.
[2] Numbers 19:11-13.

1 Samuel 18:10-11

"I know not. They came like a whirlwind, casting frowns and scowls about like spears in battle." David shifted uneasily. "You've never seen such a sight. Did I displease them in some way?"

Jonathan slapped him on the back. David winced. The warrior had a mighty swing. "Be wary, my friend, for when a woman casts such scowls, she has cast her line and expects a nibble." He grinned. "Fear not, their frowns and scowls were not for you."

Well, that's a relief. Saul's battle company had hardly been back at Gibeah for a day, and both of Saul's daughters had taken it upon themselves to serve David hand and foot. David found the whole affair equally flattering and disconcerting.

He wasn't stupid—though perhaps a bit naive when it came to the ways of women. He knew that they were trying to get his attention. All three of them were of suitable marriageable age—or at least old enough to be betrothed. And Saul had promised the slayer of Goliath one of his daughter's hand in marriage.[3] But which one? Frankly, he liked both girls. And under normal circumstances, he would easily consider either of them for his wife. He had reached an age where such things were routinely done and expected. He saw just one problem.

They were King Saul's daughters.

And despite Saul's promise, David didn't truly feel worthy. Slaying one man was doubtless not enough to earn such a reward. To add to the problem, the king now knew that Samuel had anointed David as the next king of Israel.[4] The irony and awkwardness of the situation was not lost on David. Samuel the seer had warned David not to let Saul know of the anointing lest the king seek to kill David, but thus far, King Saul seemed content with the knowledge and had made no overt move to harm David in any way.

In fact, David had saved Saul's life and had become the king's armorbearer.[5] He had gained Saul's trust and found grace in the king's eyes, but none of that necessarily made him worthy to marry one of Saul's daughters. But secretly he wanted it to. To have Jonathan as a brother in more than name was vastly appealing to

---

[3] 1 Samuel 17:25.
[4] 1 Samuel 15:28, 16:13.
[5] 1 Samuel 16:21.

David. And, of course, both of Saul's daughters were very pleasing to the eyes.

Jonathan pointed at the only other object lying on the stout oak table. "What will you do with your spoils of war?"

David glanced at the huge iron sword, Goliath's sword. It would take an immensely strong man to wield it comfortably. Despite its size, he liked looking at it. It reminded him of what Elohim could do with a man willing to submit to His will. His fingers suddenly itched for his harp. The beginnings of a song sprang to his mind.

He dismissed his thoughts, filing them away for later. Instead, he admitted, "I know not, nor do I know what to do with the giant's armor. Your father's armor was too big for me,[6] and yours also fit badly.[7] I am content to return it to you." He looked away from the giant's armor. "I believe Goliath's armor would fit three men together."

Jonathan shrugged. "Give it to my father's smiths. Perhaps they can alter it."

David brightened. "Would your father approve?"

"After what you did? You could ask for anything you want, and he'd give it to you."

David wondered if that extended to the king's daughters—the king *had* promised—but he doubted it. The dowry alone would exceed anything David could come up with, and without a proper gift as a starting point, David's father would not entertain any negotiations that were sure to embarrass the family. David heaved an internal sigh and refocused on the original topic.

"I'd be grateful," David said, meaning the armor.

Jonathan smiled. "It is well then. I will see it done, but I wouldn't expect over much. These smiths of my father are a lazy group and hardly know one end of a hammer from the other."

David smirked. In truth, Saul's smiths were the best in the land. And that was saying something, considering that the Philistines had

---

[6] 1 Samuel 17:38-39.
[7] 1 Samuel 18:4.

once tried everything in their power to destroy Israel's ability to make war by enslaving or killing all the smiths.[8]

Jonathan gestured to the sword. "And what of that?"

David considered it for a moment. "I think I would like to offer it to the priests at Nob. They have no use for a weapon, I know, but it is a symbol of Elohim's greatness. All who see it will remember how the LORD delivered us out of the hand of the Philistines. I say give it to them."

Saul's eldest son looked pleased. "I agree. It will make a good trophy to set at the feet of our God."

"I would, however, be most grateful to continue to carry your sword henceforth."

Jonathan beamed. "Aye, it will bring me honor for you to do so."

David relaxed. Jonathan had given him his sword and bow when they had made their blood covenant. He had no real use for the bow, but the sword—it was made of rare iron. He had no skill in its use as of yet, but that it had come from Jonathan was reason enough to cherish it.

With the matter of Goliath's armor and weapons now settled, David changed the subject. "Have you spoken to your father this day? I thought he would call upon me to attend him with my harp, but he has not."

Jonathan's good-natured smile disappeared to be replaced by a pensive look. "Patience, my friend. My father is still regaining his strength from the long battle—we all are. He will call upon you soon enough. Of this I have no doubt."

"Then you have spoken to him."

Jonathan hesitated. "Aye, briefly."

"Did he seem well? Yesterday, he seemed…distraught."

"Well enough. He has called for a feast this night. We are to rejoice in our victory over the Philistines."

David could sense that something was troubling his friend, but he was too polite to pry, so he turned his attention to the food in front of him. There was to be a feast tonight? Well then, he would

---

[8] 1 Samuel 13:19.

most likely be called upon to play his harp, which meant he would not get much opportunity to eat. He might as well take his fill now. He picked up the fig cake and took a bite of the compressed fruit. It still retained a sweetness that instantly set David's mouth to watering. He chewed it, savoring the taste.

Jonathan grunted as he pushed himself to his feet. "It appears as if you have discovered your appetite. The feast will be held in my father's court an hour before the first evening watch."

David bowed his head politely to Jonathan around a mouthful of fig cake. Jonathan shook his head in mock despair and walked out of the room, leaving David alone with his food.

Now that his mouth had a taste of the food, he didn't mind being alone. He dug into his meal with gusto.

David strummed his harp, letting the shimmering notes dance into the air. No one noticed. A long wooden table heaped high with food and drink had been brought into the court. Most of Saul's family was in attendance. He and his sons sat at the head of the table while the rest of his family found what place they may.

Sounds reverberated around the room in interesting and unfamiliar ways. King Saul's house was a small palace. The outside walls were built of sturdy stone, but the inside walls were built with cedar and oak, a novelty in Israel—and very expensive. In fact, the king's house was the only house David had ever been in that had actual doors on the inside to divide the various rooms. He had never before seen such a thing.

The floor, instead of being hardpacked dirt like in most houses, was paved with cobblestones imported from Moab. A second floor held the various bedrooms for Saul's family, but David had never been allowed up there, so he couldn't testify to its grandeur.

David had been given a wooden seat against the wall, a stool really, where he sat strumming his harp. He kept the tune lively to match the joy and laughter, but, unlike his music, he was in no way ignored. Apparently, his defeat of Goliath had given him a measure of respect even within Saul's household. Several of Saul's sons took time to congratulate David, admiring Goliath's sword which David had brought along and propped up next to him—though Ishui's scowl as he muttered words of congratulation seemed to belie his sincerity.

The women, young and old, seemed quite taken by the young hero, and David found many sidelong glances cast at him, and even a few thankyous for helping to bring their men home safely. It was all gratifying to David, except for one thing: the king would not even look at him.

The young harper worried about this. He could tell that something was bothering his king, and just as clearly, that something had to do with him. David studied the king, trying to discover a clue.

The king's face seemed haggard and lined, but this was to be expected after the many years of difficult warfare. His graying hair gave the king a sense of dignity that seemed right for a king. His muscular frame had not softened, for kings in this day would always be at the forefront of battle. Indeed, Saul's prowess as a warrior was known throughout the land.

The king stood then, looking over his kin with tired-looking brown eyes. He towered head and shoulders above everyone in the room,[9] including his sons. His height had always impressed David as possessing the right mix of kingly majesty and strength—unlike David's average height and reddish complexion.

Saul wore rich robes for this occasion, foregoing his more practical attire that was but one step from being battle ready. He raised his javelin—his staff of office, more like a scepter of sorts—high until all had quieted.

"We rejoice this day in our victory over the enemies of Jehovah," he began, his voice strong, clear and still infused with authority. "Our enemies sought to crush us under their heathen gods, to enslave our women, and to steal our children, but Jehovah fought for us, and a mighty victory was wrought. This day, we sit in safety. This day we feast. This day we enjoy company with our wives and children. This is a day of freedom, a day of rejoicing, of song and dances. Let no ill word be spoken this day or evil deed

---

[9] 1 Samuel 9:2.

performed. Let praises be spoken instead. Come! Eat! Rejoice in our God!"

The men roared their approval, pounding the table with heavy fists. Smiles blossomed on everyone's face and hands darted to the table to begin tearing into the food. Children jostled each other in efforts to claim the choicest of meats, and the adults laughed and joked with each other.

David had stopped playing while Saul made his announcement, but he picked it up again, content with his lot in such an august company. Servants came and went, keeping the flagons of wine full and bringing in more food, which was disappearing at an alarming rate.

Jonathan wandered over to the harper, holding a slab of meat still attached to a few ribs. "Come, David, eat with us! You are deserving of a place at this table."

David saw the king cast a scowl in their direction, but what it meant was beyond David. He got a whiff of the meat in Jonathan's hand and almost gagged. "Goat?" he asked.

"Perhaps once. 'Tis more like undercooked kid by its lack of taste. The cooks have failed yet again, but what matter? 'Tis food. Come eat."

David shook his head. "I think not. You would not like the results of my rebellious stomach. I find goat meat to be most abhorrent."

Jonathan's eyes glittered. "Truly? This meat does not set well with you?"

"Truly," David confirmed. "I am content here, playing the harp."

Jonathan shrugged. "So be it. More for me then." He tore off a huge mouthful of meat, and said while chewing, "Undercooked and utterly tasteless." He grinned as he chewed heartily on his food.

David rolled his eyes in an insulting manner, but Jonathan only grinned broader and strolled away. David figured the cooks were more than safe from Jonathan's wrath.

And then it happened.

No one noticed it at first as everyone was absorbed in eating, but David, with nothing to do but play his harp, noticed. Saul had not eaten. He had not even so much as touched his flagon of wine. He sat hunched over in his chair, his eyes downcast, his body trembling just enough to cause his robe to quiver.

David knew the signs. He'd seen them before. An evil spirit had struck the king without warning, tormenting his body, ravaging his mind, and twisting his emotions.[10]

David gasped and began to let his own spirit fall into the music of his harp. In times past, only his playing had refreshed the beleaguered king.[11] David didn't know why exactly. He only knew that as the evil spirit came upon Saul, he needed to let the Spirit of the LORD come upon him. Somehow, that was sufficient to drive the evil spirit from his master and bring him back to himself.

Eyes and ears began noticing the changing nuances of his playing, and many instantly knew what it meant. Laughter died on suddenly nervous lips as the gathering turned to stare at the king.

Saul sat hunched over, his trembling body growing fiercer. Suddenly he threw back his head with such violence that David started in surprise, and he missed a chord on his harp. As the disjointed note floated in the air, a rattling sound issued from Saul's throat, and he spoke in a voice not his own, "Is Jehovah a man that He should repent?" His voice, though not loud, carried to every ear as if spoken directly to them. The sound raised the hackles on David's neck, and his fingers froze on the harp. "Nay," Saul continued to prophesy,[12] "for He has rejected the son of Kish and shall rend his kingdom from before his eyes and give it unto his neighbor, the son of Jesse, and to his seed after."

And then the evil spirit deserted Saul, but not until a spirit of anxiety and worry had descended on the house of King Saul upon hearing those prophetic words.

The king seemed to gather himself, his body still trembling, and his eyes, as they locked onto David, were red. He rose to his feet then, staring at David in such cold fury that the young harper recoiled as if stung.

---

[10] 1 Samuel 18:10.
[11] 1 Samuel 16:23.
[12] 1 Samuel 18:10.

David didn't know what to do. He sat motionless in a cold sweat, his heart threatening to beat itself right out of his chest. "My lord," David tried to say, his voice sounding hoarse and broken. "I—"

"Nay!" Saul bellowed. "Nay! I will not let you bereft me of mine!" With the speed of a trained warrior, Saul spun his javelin into a throwing grip and hurled it with stunning force straight at David's chest.

David threw himself aside just in time. The javelin's heavy iron head smashed into the wooden wall right where David had been sitting. The force splintered the wood, and the shaft quivered in place like an angry viper robbed of its kill.[13]

David wasted no time. He left his harp and Goliath's sword, scampered across the floor, and flung himself out the court door where an astonished servant stood with it half-open. He collided with the servant, and both crashed to the hard-cobbled floor, food and wine going every which way. David rolled frantically to his feet, keeping his momentum, and raced away, his sandaled feet pounding hard as he ran.

Behind him, the room erupted in an astonished uproar, but David had no intention of waiting around to see how it all resolved itself. The king had just tried to kill him. His life was forfeit if he stayed.

Tears of frustration and hurt mingled in his eyes as he barreled down the hallway. He didn't understand. Saul's prophetic words continued rang in his ears, and he could see Samuel once again anointing him as the next king of Israel. But none of that was his fault! He'd never asked for any of it. He wanted only to serve his king and his God! It was not in his mind or heart to become king himself! Why couldn't Saul see the truth?

He slammed open the main door to Saul's house and fled into the gathering night.

---

[13] 1 Samuel 18:11.

2

"My king!" Abner shouted in confusion, coming to his feet as the javelin slammed into the wall where it stuck fast. Saul cursed under his breath as David scampered away unharmed and darted out the door, like a rat seeking its hole. He cast about for another weapon to give chase when Jonathan loomed up before him.

"Father!" the young man cried, eyes confused and worried. "What are you doing?"

Saul shook off Jonathan's hands and cursed himself for leaving his sword in his room upstairs. None of his other male relatives were armed. Two of the guards were armed with spears, but they milled about uncertainly and obviously would be of little help. He cursed again. David would be long gone by the time he could organize any pursuit. The treacherous shepherd could run like a rabbit.

"Father," Jonathan said again, refusing to budge, "this is unseemly. By your own words you commanded that no evil deed be done this night!"

That rattled Saul. He blinked, trying to focus on his eldest son, and only then realized his whole body was shaking. Saul groaned and slumped back, his son helping him to find the chair. Weakened from the evil spirit's influence, it required his remaining strength to stay in the chair and not slide out onto the floor. He silently cursed this weakness. It would not be well for the others to see him so weak.

"Fear not," he whispered to Jonathan. "I am myself again."

Jonathan hesitated, and his voice reflected his confusion. "The evil spirit compelled you?"

"Aye," the king agreed, though secretly he knew it wasn't true. Killing David had begun to take on a sense of implacable necessity. It had become clear to him that the Spirit of the LORD had abandoned him and was instead with the young shepherd boy from Bethlehem. A shiver of fear coursed through his body.[1] He had to believe that the prophecy he had spoken was naught but a reflection of his fevered dreams.

Only one cure existed for this curse: slay David. If David died, then his problems would be solved. The Spirit of the LORD would return to him, and even the Great Seer Samuel would have to acknowledge Jehovah's favor and return to his place at Saul's side.

Whatever love he had once held for the former shepherd had died with the women's song of yesterday. He knew in his heart that David would one day seek to wrest the kingdom from his hand. This left him with no choice. The harper must die, here and now.

Even knowing that, he realized that he had acted too hastily in trying to skewer David with the javelin. Killing David now would only make the lad into a martyr. The shepherd had become the people's champion. Saul could see the misplaced love even in the eyes of his own servants,[2] and Saul knew that if the people turned on him, he would die as surely as if David had wielded the sword himself. More so even than David, Saul was at the people's mercy. He had to be careful. The entire concept of king and kingdom was new to the psyche of Israel.[3] His position wasn't so secure that he could antagonize the people and expect them to meekly bow to his whims.

No, if he wanted to kill David, he would need to be more subtle about it. A plan began to form in his mind.

Looking up, he glanced at his family who stood watching him like one would watch a rabid animal. He forced a half smile to his

---

[1] 1 Samuel 18:12.
[2] 1 Samuel 18:5.
[3] 1 Samuel 8:4-6, 19-22.

lips. "Forgive me," he whispered, just loud enough for everyone to hear. "The evil spirit has robbed me of my wits it seems." His mouth felt suddenly dry, and he motioned to his wife and daughters. "Attend me," he ordered.

His wife, Ahinoam,[4] rushed to his side, holding out a flagon of wine for him as Jonathan stepped away. Saul drank greedily, letting the liquid ease his throat and dull some of the pain in his mind. The stately woman had stood by his side for so long, and if there existed a person on earth to whom he felt most indebted, it would be his wife. Her unjudgmental eyes were like a refuge into which Saul could retreat. Of all his family, his wife understood him best.

In contrast, Saul's concubine hovered in the background. Rizpah[5] was more attractive than Ahinoam and at least ten years younger. The concubine served her purpose, but it was Ahinoam who Saul turned to most in such times of distress.

Merab and Michal also crowded closer to him. He could read concern and confusion in their eyes. He would need to reassure them. Looking around, he realized he needed to reassure everyone.

He handed the flagon back to his wife and stood unassisted to his feet. He swayed for a moment, letting his strength slowly return. Then he spoke, "All is well, and there is nothing to fear." He glanced at the javelin still stuck in the wall. "Neither has the son of Jesse ought to fear from me. This I swear. The words I spoke were but the dark whispers of the evil spirit, a false spirit. They mean nothing, so let them not find a place in your heart." He placed both hands on the table to steady himself a bit more. "Leave me now and let me regain my strength."

The feast was mostly finished anyway, so his family began to file out. Before Jonathan and Abner could leave, Saul motioned for them to stay behind. On an impulse, he also motioned for his second son, Ishui, to remain. They waited until everyone else had left the room, the guard shutting the door behind the last.

---

[4] 1 Samuel 14:50.
[5] 2 Samuel 3:7.

The king then sat down heavily and sighed long in relief. The evil spirit had sapped him of strength, and he felt as weak as a newborn lamb. "We must speak of David," he told his sons and cousin.

Abner, stern looking as ever, crossed his arms and set his face in one of his patented frowns. "Has the lad done something to offend you, my lord? I heard your words, and I have heard the rumors. Will this be a problem?"

Saul shook his head. "Nay. David is not to be harmed by my hand or by yours."

Ishui's frown rivaled even that of Abner's. "Is such a course wise, my father? Perhaps we should do as you intended and slay the son of Jesse. Such would seem to be the course of prudence."

Jonathan scowled at his younger brother, but Ishui scarcely noticed. Saul shook his head. "Nay. We will not harm him. You will abide by my judgment in this matter."

Jonathan let out his breath slowly, his eyes showing his relief, though he spared one more scowl for his bloodthirsty brother. "Praise Jehovah," he said to his father. "Shall I fetch David then, Father, and return him to your side?"

Saul allowed a small frown to crease his lips. He was quite aware of the growing friendship between his oldest son and the son of Jesse. He didn't approve, but he could do little about it at the moment. No, he had to execute his plan first. If all went well, Jonathan's infatuation with David would come to nothing.

"I think not," the king said. "Perhaps there is more that the son of Jesse could do to serve me than playing the harp. His victory over the giant has proven that the Spirit of the Lord is upon him. Would it not be in our best interest then to give him a command and set him against the enemies of the Lord?"

Jonathan's eyes narrowed fractionally. "You would pit him against the Philistines?"

Saul shrugged. "Is there a reason not to? You saw what happened when he stood against the giant. All Israel loves him and would follow him."

Abner, however, was shaking his head. "It would not be wise, my lord. This youth is yet inexperienced in the ways of leadership. The men would be reluctant to follow him into battle."

"Don't be so sure, cousin. He stood forth as a beacon atop the giant's carcass, and you and I both watched the men rally to him. Without his presence on the battlefield that day, we would still be embattled with the enemy, and the end would still be in doubt." Though Saul hated to admit that truth to Abner, the men *had* rallied to David—not to their king. This fact had smitten his heart. But if his plan to kill David were to succeed, then he would need Abner's support—if not his understanding.

Ishui folded his arms across his chest, his many scars standing out prominently in the lamplight—tokens of his battle prowess that he exhibited with pride. His thin face looked pinched as he tried to think. "Why not send the son of Jesse home? Be rid of him that way."

Saul struggled to keep from frowning. His second son had little imagination, more apt to think with his sword. "Nay, my son. Elohim has sent him to us. It would behoove us then to make use of him."

The general's deep-blue eyes narrowed in thought. "You have something in mind, my lord. Perhaps if I knew your mind in full, I could offer better advice."

Leave it to the highly intelligent man to figure out that something else was involved behind the king's words. "Aye, you are correct, cousin. Two companies of warriors are garrisoned here in Gibeah. I would set him over Jashobeam's company."[6]

Jonathan started, his surprise evident. "The man they call Adino the Spear?"[7]

Abner grunted in disapproval. "That company is made up mostly of the indebted, my lord. They are just this side of being

---

[6] 1 Samuel 18:13.
[7] 2 Samuel 23:8 (Perhaps a nickname. See also 1 Chronicles 11:11.).

criminals. And I know this Adino. He's lazy. Many men have died under his command."

Saul smiled. Neither would say it, but every army needed a captain like that—someone who could command the troublemakers. If they died, it was no great loss. Saul knew that Abner often used them as shock troops, the first company to the battle, so it was of little wonder that many had died. "Then perhaps he needs a new commander, cousin. Set David as captain over this company. Let him lead them. If the LORD is indeed with him as we all believe, then perhaps he can make something useful of this company."

Abner considered the idea. Secretly, Saul was delighted. *This idea is perfect.* He needed to remove the son of Jesse from his presence[8] and put him in danger so that when David was killed, blame would not fall on Saul. *Let the Philistines' hands be upon him,*[9] he thought, satisfied.

Finally, Abner nodded. "I will do as you command, my lord. You may be right. Adino's company could do with stronger leadership."

But Jonathan looked concerned. "Is this wise? Truly, my lord, the LORD God of our fathers is with David, but as Abner has pointed out, David is not experienced in leadership or in combat. You know what he said to us on the day he fought the giant. He would not wear my lord's armor because he had not proved them.[10] We would be putting him in considerable jeopardy by making him captain over this company."

Saul waved away the objections. "He is most eager to serve, and I have no doubt that he would learn quickly. This is the best way, my son. We must put his fate in Jehovah's hands. The Philistine dogs have been driven back to their holes, but they will seek our blood again as soon as they may. The son of Jesse, whether or not he knows it, is now our champion. His name will strike fear into the hearts of our enemies."

---

[8] 1 Samuel 18:13.
[9] 1 Samuel 18:17.
[10] 1 Samuel 17:38-39.

His son seemed on the verge of arguing further, but a tightening of the king's lips quelled his objections. Jonathan bowed. "As the king wishes. Shall I find David and escort him to his new command?"

Saul shook his head. "Find him only and tell him if you will, but the duty of seeing to the command structure is Abner's. Let our cousin confirm the change of command." Another thought came to Saul. "A captain over a thousand should have his own house. Tell David that if he does well, a house will be given to him in the city." That goodwill gesture should placate Jonathan but keep the son of Jesse away at the same time.

Indeed, Jonathan grinned. "It will be done, my lord!"

As he turned to leave, Saul waved an impatient hand toward the wall where David had sat playing the harp. "Take that with you."

Jonathan obviously wasn't sure if the king meant the javelin, Goliath's sword, or David's harp. He strode over, picked up the sword, hesitated a moment and then picked up the harp too. Bowing to his father, he left the room.

Sighing in irritation, King Saul walked over to where his javelin stuck out of the wall and jerked it out. He gazed at it in disappointment, wishing it had tasted David's blood. Instead, the tip had been bent from the impact with the wood. He'd need to have one of the smiths straighten it.

It was just one more thing that the son of Jesse owed him.

King Achish, one of the great Philistine lords, tapped the arm of his throne impatiently. The grand hall where he held audience was filled to capacity. The engraved walls, depicting the journey of his ancestors from across the Great Sea, was partially hidden by the milling mass of humanity.

The buzz of conversation swept over him like a swarm of insects, and he ground his teeth together in irritation. He folded his arms across his fat belly and glowered at the throng. They ignored him for the moment, more caught up in their own despair than in trying to pacify their king.

The cursed Hebrews had scattered the Philistine armies. Not five days ago, the Hebrew army had butchered the armies of the Five Lords and scattered them to the four winds. Bodies, bloated and decaying, still dotted the landscape outside the great city of Gath, Achish's home.

Goliath had been their champion; the god-like man had seemed invincible. How could he have fallen so easily? The ease with which their greatest warrior had fallen bothered Achish to the point that he had eaten only a fraction of his normal daily ration for some days now.

A scout pushed his way through the throng and genuflected to the image of Dagon set up in the corner and then bowed to his king. "O mightiest of kings," he declaimed, his voice ringing through the hallway to still all other conversations, "I bring tidings!"

"Then say on," Achish ordered.

"I spied upon King Saul's armies at your command, O great king, and this I saw. I saw a man riding a horse, the head of Goliath raised high beside him."

"King Saul?" Achish asked.

"Nay, my king, it was a youth. His name is David, the son of Jesse. He defeated the giant and beheaded our champion."

Achish surged from his throne. "A youth you say?"

"Aye, my lord. He is ruddy of complexion and sat a horse poorly."

"And yet he slew Goliath? With but a sling and a stone?"

"Aye," the scout whispered, quailing before the portly king. Achish may not be physically imposing, but at his word, a man could be butchered on an altar to Dagon or Ashtaroth and his still beating heart cast into the fires of their gods.

Many had witnessed the battle between Goliath and the Hebrew champion, but most of the stories varied wildly. Some claimed that the Hebrew victor was as tall as Goliath had been. Others claimed the Hebrew spat lightning from his eyes. *But a youth?*

Merely a youth? Achish could hardly credit the truth. Only the fact that this particular scout was among the most reliable and trustworthy of his spies gave credence to the tale.

He looked at the throng. "This blasphemy shall not go unanswered!" he roared. "To the man who brings me the head of David, the son of Jesse, will I give its equal weight in gold!"

A buzz of excitement zipped through the throng. This was a kingly ransom!

The scout pulled a man from the crowd. Achish's eyes narrowed. The newcomer looked to be a Hebrew.

"I have brought, O great king, one who knows something of the Hebrew David."

"Who is this?" Achish demanded. "And what does he know?"

The young man in question, bowed low. "I am a Hebrew, O king," he said, "but I have deserted my homeland and forsaken the God of Israel to serve the gods of the Philistines. My name is Maon, and I know David the son of Jesse well."

Glee rose in Achish like a child who sees snow for the first time. He rubbed his hands together briskly. "Approach then and tell me all you know."

David lurked deep in the shadows of the city wall, watching warily the guards lounging near the gate that led out of Gibeah. The sun had set, and darkness had descended upon the walled city. The darkness acted like a balm to David, hiding the tears and secreting the pain etched plainly on his face. He had wandered around the city for hours, his mind numb and his heart heavy. He didn't know what to do or where to go. At one point, in a fit of despair, he had decided to return to Saul. If the king wanted to kill him, then was it not his duty as the king's servant to yield his neck to the executioner? But his heart failed him, and he turned away.

Now he hugged the shadows not far away from the closed gate. The city watch would unlikely open the massive gate until morning, so he was trapped in the city. Not that he had anywhere to go. He could return to Bethlehem, but the prospect of facing his father and brothers and explaining what had happened felt worse than the wounds inflicted by claws of the lion he had once fought.[11]

He didn't even have a house of his own to go to. As the king's armorbearer, he lived under Saul's roof and ate at his table. Silently, he framed a prayer toward heaven, "O Jehovah, what is it that You would have me to do? Tell your servant, I beg, for I cannot abide my king's displeasure."

Since there was no priest handy with a linen ephod, David really didn't expect an answer, so when a voice spoke out the darkness behind him, he nearly leaped out of his skin.

"David? Is that you hiding in the shadows?"

David spun around and fell into a fighting stance, his heart in his throat. Then he saw who had spoken. "Jonathan! You frightened me!" He scowled deeply at his friend, trying to regain control of his wildly racing heart. "You speak of shadows when you lurk within such gloom like a bandit seeking mischief!"

But David couldn't keep his anger. Jonathan's grin was infectious. "By Isaac's beard," Jonathan said, "you are not easy to find. I sought you up and down these narrow streets thrice, but here you are staring at a closed gate. Do you seek to leave then?"

David shrugged. "I was of a mind to. Your father seeks my life. I thought there were better places for me to be."

"Nay, my friend. My father no longer seeks to take your life. You know well that the evil spirit drove him to cast his javelin at you."

David's eyes narrowed suspiciously. "It was more than a 'cast'," he muttered.

His friend spread his hands out innocently. "Perhaps, but my father has repented of the deed and has decided to promote you in a small way to thank you for your service."

---

[11] 1 Samuel 17:34-36.

Jonathan fell silent, waiting for David to speak. David remained quiet. The king's son would tell him in his own good time anyway. After an uncomfortable pause, Jonathan frowned, disappointed that David hadn't risen to the bait. He sighed sadly, but David knew a fake gesture when he saw one.

"Very well then," Jonathan began, "my father has made you a captain over your own company of warriors. You will no doubt lead them to inglorious battle."

Not quite sure he'd heard right, David merely blinked, saying nothing.

"That is not enough?" Jonathan hedged, surprised. "Then know, if you do well, my father has promised to give you a house here in Gibeah. We can't have one of his captains living on the streets, now can we?"

David still didn't react. Suspicion filled his eyes and face.

Jonathan's frown deepened. "I can see that you don't believe me, but it's true. You have been promoted to captain and are being offered a house if you prove a capable commander." His eyebrows rose as if daring David to mock his words. "My father, with Abner's agreement, has decided to give you your own command. Seems you are something of a hero these days—though personally, I can't for the life of me see why." His eyes twinkled with mirth.

"You're serious, aren't you?" David sputtered. He was still getting to know Jonathan, and his friend's penchant for understatement was as natural to him as breathing was to other people. But if he was joking, surely he would have let David know by now. This rambling on and on was hiding something else, something deeper.

A lengthy pause stretched out between the two friends. The tension in the air didn't come from David alone. "Aye, I speak truly, my friend." He placed a hand on David's shoulder. "But I fear for you as well."

There it was. Suspicion still clouded David's mind. The promotion was real enough, which meant the house was likely true too, but why? David was still not old enough to be counted among

Israel's warriors. From the time of Moses, a man had to be at least twenty years of age before he could fight,[12] least of all be in command. Something was wrong with all this.

"What is it that you fear?" David asked.

"The company of a thousand you are to command is a mixture of all the tribes of Israel."

That *was* unusual, David admitted to himself. Typically, army ranks were segmented by tribe, and commanders were chosen from the same tribe. This process was a holdover from the time of Moses and Aaron.[13] So to have an entire company made up men from various tribes was strange and only served to deepen David's suspicions. "What is it that you are not telling me?"

"They are indebted," Jonathan said, shrugging casually.

David froze. Indebted men were virtual slaves. They could not pay their debts, so they were sold and bargained for like cattle. King Saul had his choice of men. If he saw a valiant man, he simply took him.[14] But those he took were given places of honor in the army. They were trusted, trained, and uplifted. The indebted were different. They had proven themselves to be untrustworthy. They were often lazy, dishonest, discontent, and possibly criminals.

"He wants me to be their commander?" David threw his arms up in disgust. "What have I done, Jonathan? What have I done to make your father hate me so?"

"You have done nothing!" Jonathan shot back, his face stern. "This is not a punishment. This is an opportunity. No one so young has ever been promoted to such a position. Do you think my father would put you in command of another company? What captain should you replace? What company would follow an untried youth? Is this arrogance or fear speaking?"

David snapped his mouth shut. Jonathan was right. In no way would he be given command of regular troops—not yet, not this young. The only way around it would be to give David command of

---

[12] Numbers 1:3.
[13] Numbers 2.
[14] 1 Samuel 14:52.

the indebted. If he could prove himself to Saul, then maybe he could win back the king's good graces. And ultimately, that was all that David wanted.

Of course, there was another problem. "How can I command these men? I'm just a shepherd."

"Then treat them as sheep." Jonathan's eyes narrowed, and even in the darkness, David could see their intensity. "What better leader than a shepherd? When they stray, bring them back. When they become independent, teach them the importance of unity. When they're wounded, care for them. All the skills you learned of shepherding can apply to men."

For the first time, David began to relax. *Maybe this isn't such a bad thing.* "You really think I can lead these men?"

Jonathan regarded David solemnly for a time, his face wreathed in shadow. "You must, my young friend. You must."

3

Two days later, David went to meet and inspect his men. He rode an ass given to him by Abner. The old creature seemed calm enough, David supposed, but he worried about the type of impression he would make atop the sorry-looking beast. He doubted the ass could build up enough speed to qualify as a trot.

Abner, the commander of all Hebrew armies, rode beside him on a horse that seemed to be bursting with energy. The stallion pawed the ground and pulled against his bit. Abner didn't seem to notice. He rode stiff backed, eyes forward, and with a rigid grip on the reins.

Horses were not often used as individual mounts. Mostly, horses were trained to pull chariots, a better way, it was supposed, to utilize a horse's superior speed and power. Mules and asses were believed to be surer of foot, easier to care for and breed. Horses brought a premium price and were often too valuable to be used as a single man's transportation.[1] But King Saul and the general were exceptions.

Abner, his mind elsewhere, did not notice David's speculative look. Clearly, something bothered the mighty general. "Do you expect trouble?" David asked, not quite sure why Abner had elected to ride out with him.

---

[1] The Bible never directly speaks of anyone ever riding a horse. In nearly every instance, the mount is a camel, a mule, or an ass (donkey).

"Nay. My authority is required to make the transfer of command official."

David thought of several sarcastic responses but decided the stern-faced general would hardly appreciate the joke. David tried a different tact. "What is your impression of these...indebted? As a fighting unit, I mean?"

Abner didn't say anything for a time, and they rode on in silence. David's new company was pitched outside the city to the west. The unit occupied a large meadow—close enough to be called upon when needed and far enough away not to trouble the inhabitants of Gibeah too much.

"They are undisciplined," Abner finally said. "As fighters go, they are better than most," he added, surprising David. "But they lack unity. Their effectiveness is therefore severely diminished."

"I see," David lied. He wasn't a commander—well, not one with any real experience—so he didn't really understand the nuances of what Abner was saying. Then he remembered what Jonathan had advised: *Treat them like sheep.* A sheep's best defense was to stay together when predators lurked nearby. The ones who were separated from the herd were the ones that usually fell prey to jaw or claw. David turned it over in his mind. It was certainly something to think about.

"They will likely be discontent," Abner continued. "Their debts mean they cannot return to their homes and families and must serve at the king's pleasure. After the battle in the Valley of Elah, they came here and have yet to see their wives, children, and kin."

That made sense. Typically, there were two types of Hebrew soldiers. The professional soldier was part of a garrison, usually posted near his house and family. He would be called upon to help quell minor raids and rebellions and do the king's bidding. In general, he was supported by the king, receiving a wage. The second type was the common man who was called upon in extreme emergencies such as the recent invasion by Goliath and the Philistines. These men would be called up from their houses, their farms, and their flocks to serve in the army until the danger was over. They may or may not receive wages, but they would be allowed to return home as soon as it was safe to do so.

But the indebted were different. They existed somewhere between the professional solider and the common solider. Their debts bonded them to the king's whim. They were, essentially, slaves.

David wanted to know more, but the closed-mouth general didn't seem interested in imparting any wisdom to the young captain. David decided to ask nothing further.

Soon, the tents of the camp came into sight. David frowned. The tents were scattered over the meadow in a haphazard manner, as if their owners had simply flung them up wherever they happened to be standing at the time. Weapons and armor lay scattered around the campsite, rusting, unsharpened, and generally neglected.

The men themselves were a slovenly lot. David could see men lounging, playing at dice, sleeping, or brawling. As to the latter observation, he couldn't rightly call what the men were doing as fighting, since the men rolled around on the ground drunkenly more than doing any real damage to each other. Their tunics looked unwashed, torn, and ragged.

Abner seemed neither upset nor surprised by their appearance or behavior, which said little for the character of the men David would be commanding. He swallowed, realizing that the glamorized picture he'd held of being a captain had just been crushed. These ragtag men were hardly battle-ready.

And the smell! Unwashed bodies mixed with poor sanitation procedures produced a rancid odor that nearly caused David to gag as he and Abner rode into the camp. His stomach churned uncomfortably, and he began thinking that herding sheep would not be such a bad alternative to these pathetic examples of humanity.

The general ignored the smell, the men, and the obvious undisciplined setup of the camp. He simply rode toward a cluster of tents that had been pitched in the general vicinity of the camp center.

Men watched them ride by, but they neither saluted their general nor acknowledged him. However, a buzz of conversation followed, and from what little David could pick up, none of it was flattering. His stomach churned again, but this time, the smell had nothing to do with it. He realized that these men had little regard for their own lives, and if so, then what regard would they have for other lives?

He shuddered.

Abner pulled up before a tent that had nothing particularly distinguishing about it, except for perhaps the man who lounged in its shadow. The man looked like some long-legged weasel left out to rot. He sprawled against the tent side with his eyes closed and surrounded by the remains of a small fortune of Elah nuts. A wineskin lay beside him along with a spear that had been propped against the tent. He neither looked up nor stirred at their approach.

"Behold," Abner said, gesturing to the man, "Jashobeam, or as his comrades call him, Adino the Spear."[2]

One eyelid lifted enough so that Adino could regard the speaker. "Abner, you old mule," he drawled, his words coming out as if breath was a precious commodity to hoard. "What do you want here?"

Abner's cheeks flushed slightly, but the general, who under other circumstances might have scourged the offender, merely sighed in resignation. That sigh, David decided, didn't bode well for his future among these men. Abner's resigned face cracked enough for him to add, "I've come to relieve you of command, Jashobeam."

Adino grunted softly, but he gave no other sign of interest.

The general gestured to David. "This is David, the son of Jesse. He is to be captain now of this company."

Adino's eye shifted slowly to take in David. Not to be outdone, David studied the laconic soldier in return. Adino was the thinnest man David had seen in quite some time—even the man's black beard was long and thin. The man's yellowish skin was stretched tautly across his face and body, like a hide stretched over knobby wood.

---

[2] He is called Adino the Eznite in 2 Samuel 23:8, which means literally "Adino the Spear" or the "slender spear." In 1 Chronicles 11:11, his name is given as Jashobeam an Hachmonite or the son of Hachmoni. This appears to be the same person.

He seemed more legs than anything else. His long limbs stuck out of his stained tunic haphazardly, like tent poles. The man's greasy hair had been smoothed back and fell just below his ears, and about a month's worth of dirt and sweat covered the man's exposed skin.

But underneath that grimy exterior, David wondered if there weren't something more substantial to the man. After all, the spearman had, until this point, been captain over a thousand men. There *has* to be some merit to the man, though David couldn't for the life of him determine what it might be.

Slowly, as if unfolding himself, Adino rose to his feet to stand before them. His thinness made him seem taller than he really was, but there was a whip-like quality to his stance. David had the impression that if this man ever did decide to act, he could be lethal. The Spear regarded David with penetrating gray eyes. "He's kinda young, don't you think, Abner?" he asked. The general said nothing, so he turned more fully to confront David. "What did you do to be stuck with us?"

David hesitated. The man's words weren't a challenge. He seemed genuinely interested. People didn't join the indebted unless they had no choice. Despite the friendly tone, David sensed danger here. Some of the men, curious, had begun to gather around the trio, and he could hear them muttering and whispering as they passed the word that Adino had been relieved of command and some youth had replaced him. David's first words would set the tone of his command.

Casting a prayer toward heaven, David slid off the ass's back and shoved the old beast away to give him room. Then facing Adino directly, he grinned. "What did I do?" he repeated, his voice wistful. "I accidently killed a fat giant."

Adino started, blinked, and then barked out a short laugh that sounded more like a dog's yelp of pain than anything containing real mirth. "That was you, son? Thought I recognized you." He reached over and clapped David on the shoulder who had to school his face so as not to wince. There was power in those long fingers. "T'was as good a throw as I ever saw!" Adino added. "That's the truth, I tell you. The whole truth." His eyes twinkled. "Showed up the king, did you? Well, I can see as why you'd be stuck with us then."

David frowned. The man had amazing insight, assuming he was right. Had David somehow embarrassed Saul? Was that why he'd been stuck with these men? It was something to consider, but if true, David vowed to find a way to please his king and restore his favor.

Abner's patience apparently had ended. He turned his horse back the way he'd come. "I'll leave you to your command then, David, son of Jesse." He paused, looking around at the slovenly camp. "Your first order is to whip these men into something that faintly resembles soldiers. If I have need of you, then I want you battle ready. Do you understand, son of Jesse?"

David swallowed hard. "Yes, my lord. It will be done."

Abner didn't look convinced. "Perhaps. I'll send a man to you on the morrow to be your armorbearer."[3] He shook his head and put heels to his horse. General and stallion fled the camp, leaving David surrounded by a motley looking group of would-be soldiers.

David felt exposed suddenly, and he had to clench his hands together to keep them from trembling. This was worse than facing Goliath. He licked his dry lips and looked around. Not a single friendly face looked back, and a malevolent silence had fallen over the entire lot.

Adino suddenly barked at the men, "Away with you, you dead dogs! Your gawking faces is an offense. The captain will call you when he is good and ready and not before. Move or taste my spear!"

His words cracked through the air like a whip. Men started or jumped at the sound, and slowly, grudgingly, they dispersed, except for a group who stood defiantly not far away. Adino gestured toward them, a lazy gesture that promised everything and nothing at all. "Come, captain, let me introduce you to your lieutenants."[4]

---

[3] An armorbearer would be much like a military aide in today's vernacular.
[4] Military divisions in King Saul's time were divided into captains of thousands and captains of hundreds (1 Samuel 22:7). To avoid confusion, "lieutenant" is used in this book in place of captain of a hundred and "captain" is used for a captain of a thousand. I use "general" for Abner who is captain over the entire army.

David followed the man to where seven others stood in a collectively disapproving group. One, a massively built man with arms and shoulders that an ox wouldn't be ashamed of, addressed Adino, "Are you going to allow this, Captain?"

Adino shrugged. "Not captain anymore, Shammah. You heard the general."

The man's frown disappeared into his thick bushy beard. "It is not right," he muttered, glaring at David, who couldn't help but stare back. The man's massive beard was braided at the edges and colorful beads had been woven into the beard to give the man a rakish appearance. To offset the beard, the man's head was completely bald—and it glistened brightly in the sun like a polished bronze shield.

Adino shrugged. "I'll get more sleep."

David raised an eyebrow to cover his nervousness. Adino certainly didn't seem disappointed about his demotion.

The man they called The Spear continued, gesturing to David, "This here is the giant slayer. Our king has put him in command. He's our new captain." He glared at the men. "Be kind to him, or I'll tickle your bellies with my spear." Looking at David, he jerked a thumb toward the group of men. "These are your lieutenants, such as they are. I'll give you their names later if necessary, but it's doubtful that most of them will live long enough to make remembering them worthwhile."

Seven pairs of eyes shifted to look at David's face. For a moment, panic set in. He saw no friendliness in those eyes. He did see hopelessness and despair. He felt obligated to say something, so he cleared his throat. "Men, it is a privilege to serve with you. I—"

One of the men snorted loudly. "There is no privilege here, young one. Our lot in life is to die. That is the only privilege we get."

David's anger rose. It was not of his doing that he'd been placed in command over them. It wasn't his fault that they had to deal with a young, inexperienced commander. He didn't need to take this from them. "I don't take your meaning," David said slowly, his eyes narrowing.

The man, oblivious to David's growing wrath, pushed forward. "Most every man in this company is indebted, boy. We must fight for the king as long as he sees fit. Maybe someday he'll free us and forgive our debts, but not before most of us have tasted the end of a Philistine spear or sword."

David's anger transformed into confusion. "Are you not warriors?"

"No more than that old ass your rode upon is your armorbearer, boy," the man snapped, gesturing to David's aged mount. "Our purpose is to blunt the enemy advance and give the real soldiers an opportunity to do the actual fighting."

The other lieutenants were nodding in agreement. Adino shook his head. "Easy, Mahli," he murmured.

David didn't understand. Hadn't Abner said that these men were better warriors than most? Before he could question this, another man stepped forward. He, of all the men, looked to have kept his tunic and armor clean and in working order. He was of average height and appearance with nothing remarkable to take note of. Even his beard looked average somehow. His eyes took in everyone around him as he spoke.

"I knew this was going to happen," he pointed out, and several of his fellow lieutenants groaned, one calling for him to go soak his head in dog urine. He ignored them. "If you'd have heeded my words, my fellows, we could have prevailed upon the king and found favor in his sight. But all of you were too busy wallowing in your own misery to take heed. King Saul has decided our fate by sending this stripling to us. It is as I foretold."

"You foretold nothing, Eleazar," the one named Shammah snapped. He scratched at his bald pate with both hands. "But there is sense in what you say. King Saul has sent us this boy so that we'll die all the sooner. It is too much, I say."

David cut in, his anger having once again been aroused. "Stop this talk of treason," he said in a soft voice, but one that somehow conveyed his anger. "Our king is Jehovah's anointed. We will not speak ill of him or of our God. Do not defy me in this."

David's pulse raged. His breath came raggedly, but he hoped these men would take it for anger and not the fear it was in truth. He had never spoken to men using such words before—except for Maon, his lost brother, and, of course, to Goliath. But they had been enemies. These men were allies, comrades. He could not guess what they would do, but he wouldn't stand around and let these men speak ill of his king and, by association, his God.

The foremost of the men, Shammah, who bore the same name as one of David's brothers, kept his glare focused on the young captain for a long moment. Then he relaxed, and a half smile appeared on his lips. "Well spoken, lad—Captain. I beg your forgiveness." He looked David up and down. "I know our king placed you in command, and your battle with the Philistine giant was well fought indeed, but I can't but notice that you lack your sling with which you felled the giant." He gestured to David's sword, a gift from Jonathan. "Do you know how to use that?"

The man was calling David's bluff. David took a deep breath and regained control of his temper. "As you say, I am but a lad. My only victory was over a giant, but you mistake. It was not I that felled the giant in valley that day. It was Jehovah Elohim. Our God fought for me—for us—that day. It was His victory to give us. If you permit, I will lead you as Jehovah wills. We will yet win many victories if our God is with us. This I know. For by a single stone, God felled the giant. Tell me, men, when have you ever heard of such wonders?"

They were silent, considering. Finally, Eleazar spoke. "Aye, I have heard of such. Many years ago, in this very field, a troop of Benjamite left-handed warriors helped route the rest of Israel with their slings.[5] I heard tell that they could cut a petal off a flower at a hundred cubits."

Shammah cuffed Eleazar alongside the head. "Stand back, you wastrel. You know not of what you speak."

---

[5] Judges 20:16.

Eleazar glared at the larger man, rubbing his head. "It is the truth. Mark me well."

Adino cut in, yawning. "This is all well and good, Captain. We'll follow you—if for no other reason because our king wishes it. But it would be well if you speak your mind of what is to become of us now that *you* are our captain."

For a moment, David felt as if he'd gained control of things, but with that one comment, his hands clammed up again. He *was* their captain. That meant he had to lead, and despite what Jonathan had said, these men weren't sheep. They were more like wolves. He swallowed as his eyes went from man to man, seeing a mixture of curiosity, disinterest, and hopelessness.

"To start," he said slowly, "we'll move the camp tomorrow."

"Move the camp?" Shammah demanded incredulously. "Whatever for?"

David clenched his shaking hands tightly together and forced himself to look the massive man right in the eyes. "Because you smell like swine. We need a clean camp, a proper latrine, an exercise yard, a central fire pit for cooking, and…" he hesitated "…and someone to teach me how to use my sword."

The shepherd turned captain could hardly credit the words that had come out of his mouth. He expected one of the men to strike him down at any moment, but, he decided, if he was going to be so abused, he'd take it with dignity. He kept his eyes level and his chin firm as he faced the men down.

"Well," Adino drawled, a small smile playing with his lips, "can't argue with that, Captain."

"And," David added as an afterthought, "I'm going to need a tent."

4

David's armorbearer arrived the next day while the Indebted, as David had come to think of them, began the arduous process of moving camp to another of the meadows that dotted the landscape west of Gibeah—a simple task made arduous by the men's constant complaining and procrastinating.

The armorbearer found David standing under a pomegranate tree that overlooked the meadow. An irritated frown decorated the new captain's face. "My lord," the man called as he strode up the slope in immaculate armor, a sword swinging from his waist, and a bulging bag slung over one shoulder, "the king's son sends greetings."

"Jonathan sent you?" David asked curiously, instantly losing his frown.

"Aye, my lord. I am to be your armorbearer. I am Adriel, son of Barzillai."

David felt uncomfortable being addressed as "my lord." He didn't feel all that lordly just yet, but Adriel not only looked competent, he possessed a presence that immediately set David at ease. "What city do you hail from, Adriel?" David asked.

"I am a Meholathite, my lord."

The small town sat near the Jordan River north of the Salt Sea. "Of the tribe of Issachar?"

"Nay, my lord. I am of Manasseh."

"It is well," David said, satisfied. "What experience do you have?"

"I served as Jonathan's armorbearer for the last six years, my lord. I've fought beside him in every major engagement during that time."

"You were with him at Michmash?"

Adriel's eyes twinkled. "Aye. I was very young then."

David was impressed. Adriel was the man who had gone with Jonathan to challenge the Philistine garrison those years ago. If Jonathan had sent him, then David immediately felt that the man could be relied upon. He waved toward the camp and the men slowly breaking down tents. "I am sorely in need of your advice, Adriel. These men are indebted. They have little care for their person or possessions. What do you think I should do?"

Adriel set his awkward-looking bag on the ground and turned to examine the camp, slapping violently at a fly buzzing around his head. He stood several finger-widths shorter than David, and while David was still putting on muscle and filling out in the shoulders, Adriel, in his mid-twenties from what David could tell, possessed a lean, handsome frame that did not lack for well-toned muscles. He wore a sword at his left hip, and he walked as if he knew how to use it. His light-brown hair nearly matched David's in shade and cut, though Adriel's skin color was several tones darker. His brown eyes scanned the camp and the men, and David could see intelligence there as he weighed and evaluated what he saw.

"Take two or three of the worst and scourge them, my lord."

David blinked. "Scourge them?"

"Aye. That usually works to motivate the slothful, but perhaps such a course would do little good with these men."

Intrigued, David gestured for Adriel to continue. "Go on."

"As you have no doubt divined, these men believe they will die before they can repay the debts they owe. Experience has taught them this, and they've learned that no man cares for their person. Fear may motivate some, but these need hope, my lord. They need to believe that they can survive and become free in Israel.

Remember, my lord, they are here because they have nowhere else to go."

David was impressed. The man had barely laid eyes on the company before divining the real problem, one David had only just begun to formulate fully. "And what, pray tell, should I do to give them hope?"

Adriel shrugged. "It's quite easy, my lord. When they are sent forth to die, you need to lead them forth to victory instead. They need to live and believe they will one day be free."

Not so easy as all that, David disagreed mentally. He kept quiet though, pondering his options. At any moment, the king could order his company to move against the Philistines, but as things stood right now, David doubted that the men would fare well in a pitched battle. And truth be told, David doubted he would fare well either. He was an expert with the sling, but these men needed someone to lead them directly into battle—like Jonathan or King Saul. That meant he would need to use a spear or sword.

He sighed, his uncertainty looming large like a tree's shadow as the sun began to set. No matter how he turned it in his head, he saw only one place to start. He needed to at least become proficient with the sword. He'd had some practice with his older brother Abinadab, but if his sparring with his brother had taught him anything, it was that he didn't know much at all when it came to effectively wielding a sword.

"Then there is one thing I need to do," he said almost to himself.

Adriel raised an eyebrow, "What is that, my lord?"

"How competent are you with that sword you bear?"

"I boast of only moderate skill."

David pondered that, toying with an idea. His own sword was with his tent, the only tent to have been moved to the new location some distance off. "Lend me your sword."

Both of Adriel's eyebrows shot up. "Aye, my lord," he agreed, drawing his sword and handing the iron weapon hilt first to David.

"Slaying two or three of your lieutenants would likely get their attention, but—"

David started as he took the weapon, nearly slicing his arm open in the process. He stared at Adriel. "What?"

Adriel nodded as if David hadn't asked a question. "Your solution might work better than scourging, I suppose, but you're going to need to slay someone of importance for the rest to take notice. I've some knowledge of the lieutenants, and if I recall rightly, there is one big one, shoulders like an ox…might I suggest slaying him? That should get everyone's attention, my lord."

"What, by the blood of our ancestors, are you talking about?"

The armorbearer looked surprised. "Why your plan, of course."

"I've no wish to slay anyone!" David huffed. He brandished the sword. "I merely need to learn how to use this, is all, and I…" He trailed off seeing the smirk spreading across Adriel's face. "I should test your blade's edge against your skin," he muttered darkly.

Adriel's grin grew wider. "Forgive me, my lord. I couldn't resist."

"You could teach me how to wield this?" David asked, looking at the sword.

"Aye, but I hear tell there is one Eleazar, the son of Dodo, in camp."

"Aye. There is."

"Then I would seek him. He is a master with the sword, one of the best I've ever seen. His hands are very deft, no doubt leading to his career as a thief and thus one of the Indebted."

Pursing his lips, David returned Adriel's sword and looked back at the camp. Yes, perhaps his new armorbearer was right. David hadn't spent a lot of time with Eleazar yet, but his first impression of the man was one of annoyance. But it would do good for the men to see their captain taking instruction from one of their own. They already believed David to be naught but a tender-eyed youth. Perhaps they would be more receptive of David if they saw his determination to fight alongside of them.

Gesturing to Adriel, David commanded, "Let's find Eleazar."

"Aye, my lord," the handsome armorbearer agreed, slinging his bag over his shoulder and striding off after David.

A short time later, David came to a stop in front of Adino's tent. The man had resumed his former position, lazing in the shade and munching on Elah nuts with closed eyes.

For a second, David wanted to kick the man to his feet, but he held himself in check. "Jashobeam," he said, "why are you not breaking camp in preparation for the move?"

The lanky man cracked open an eye. "Ah, Captain, you do my eyes good. Call me Adino. All do."

"Abner does not," David said.

"True. True." The man frowned and then shrugged ever so slightly. "But he should. Is there something you wanted, Captain?"

"Why have you not broken camp?"

The spearman rolled his eye around to look past David. "The men *are* breaking camp, Captain…as you ordered."

David ground his teeth together. "But why are you not?"

The man gave an ever-so-slight shrug of his shoulders. "It will do no good while the rest of the men are milling around out there like ants, Captain. I'll wait until things straighten out."

David didn't know if he should scream or start kicking. Instead, he took a deep breath and calmed himself. "Very well. Where is Eleazar?"

"Probably breaking camp, Captain."

"And where is his tent?" he asked slowly, closing his eyes briefly.

"Yonder," came the reply as Adino pointed his chin and thin beard slightly to his left. He then opened his other eye and regarded David evenly. "What are you about, Captain, if you don't mind me asking?"

"I need someone to teach me how to use a sword, and rumors claim he is the man to see."

Adino considered this for a moment. Finally, he nodded. "Aye, true enough." He somehow unfolded himself from the ground, picked up his spear, and stood before David. "Come on then. I must see this for myself."

David didn't know if he'd won a victory or not, but he and Adriel followed Adino as he wandered slowly over to another tent. From the snores inside, it was occupied. Adino regarded the tent for a moment and then casually kicked out one of the wooden poles, dropping the tent atop the sleeping man inside.

The man inside cursed and thrashed about, vowing all kinds of mayhem upon his tormenter. The tent material was made of prickly goat's hair, and David knew from experience that the material poked the skin and itched abominably. He winced in sympathy, but Adino simply watched with vague interest, leaning on his spear and half smiling to himself.

When the swordsman did manage to squirm out, he kicked the remains of his tent into a jumbled heap and turned on the three men in righteous indignation. "By Dagon's cursed tongue, what is the meaning of this foul and cowardly attack?" He glared first at Adino then at David, unsure who was the true culprit.

Adino yawned and then spoke mildly, "The captain here wants you to break camp and move. Your snoring fell evilly upon his young ears, so he could not but notice your treacherous lack of obedience to his orders."

"I was not snoring, you miserable excuse for fish bait! And I was planning to break camp just as soon as everyone else got out of my way!" He rounded on David. "Is this how you motivate your men, Captain?"

David tried to hide his grin, but he failed miserably, and Eleazar's scowl grew in proportion to David's grin. David shook his head, figuring he needed to mollify the man. "I sought you for another reason, Lieutenant. I have need of your skills."

Eleazar perked up at that, his scowl falling away instantly. "As I knew you would," he said, standing straighter. "What can I help you with?"

"I hear you are quite skilled with the sword. I wish you to teach me."

The vain man pursed his lips in thought for a moment. He looked hard at David's eyes and then shook his head. "Nay, it will matter little."

David's eyebrows rose. He thought the man would jump at the opportunity. Other men, having seen the commotion were gathering around sensing entertainment, their duties forgotten. David would need to rectify that at some point. But first things first. "Please explain."

The swordsman shrugged. "We'll likely all be dead before I have time to teach you enough not to accidently fall upon your own blade."

This was not how David had envisioned this conversation going. He desperately wanted to build some measure of rapport with these men. If he were to lead them, then they must come to respect him somehow. He had no idea how to put Adriel's advice into practice. What hope or purpose could he give to men convinced their only purpose was to die? Still, he had to start somewhere.

"My brother taught me some," David said evenly, struggling to keep his temper in check. "I think I can hold my own." Which wasn't exactly true. He'd watched his brother practice and had sparred with him on occasion, but that was all.

Eleazar raised an eyebrow. "Is that so? Well then, Captain, I'm not against finding out." He turned and burrowed through his collapsed tent and plucked out two wooden practice swords. "I keep these at hand for people such as you," he explained, tossing one of them to David.

The new captain caught the wooden sword—by the blade, of course—and quickly arranged his grip properly. He brandished it at Eleazar but noticed that the swordsman held his nonchalantly at his side. David's eyes narrowed, and his jaw clenched. "What now?" he asked, noticing that increasingly more men were gathering around to watch.

1 Samuel 18:13-14

"Now we see what you know." The swordsman pursed his lips, eyeing David speculatively. "Attack when ready, but don't hold back." He grinned. "I won't."

David nodded. He expected nothing less. "What about shields? Shouldn't we be using them."

The vain swordsman smiled. "Not necessary for this. What? Are you afraid?"

The young captain clenched his wooden sword tightly, but he refused to be baited. He took a stance his brother had taught him, sword up, feet spread apart for balance. Eleazar, he noted, stood easily, almost casually, his sword held loosely in his hand. He was even whistling! Well, if the man was going to underestimate him, then the man deserved to be smacked upside the head.

David lunged, swinging his sword with enough strength to send his vain opponent sprawling unconscious on the hard ground. But somehow, Eleazar avoided the strike, his body, like a lithe reed, just waved aside, and the blade passed harmlessly by.

Pain exploded behind David's left ear, and he collapsed to the ground, his ears ringing, and the world spinning. He never even saw Eleazar strike. The man was wickedly fast. Nausea gathered in David's stomach, and he had to fight down the reflex to retch.

"You're dead," said a sing-song voice to the laughter of the other men. "Did I not say this would be so?"

David struggled back to his feet and spun to face Eleazar and nearly fell again, but he kept his balance and blinked away the tears that filled his eyes. He would not give up. He would not show weakness before these men.

The swordsman's eyebrows rose in surprise, and he began whistling again, a mocking tune that set David's teeth on edge. David growled, and this time tried to stab straight ahead, but somehow Eleazar wasn't there again. A wooden blade smashed into David's wrist, numbing it instantly. Before David could register the blow, another strike crashed against his left knee. David cried out in pain and collapsed to his knees. Agony shot through his body. He would've never believed the wooden sword could cause so much pain.

"You're dead. Again," came the mocking voice.

David shook his numb hand until tingles of stabbing pain told him that life was returning to the appendage. He then picked up his impotent weapon and used it to help leverage himself back to his feet.

Eleazar was whistling and shuffling his feet in a parody of a dance, but as David stood, the tune changed to one of curious surprise. He regarded the youth with appraising eyes and nodded once to David in respect. "Perhaps that is enough," he said, stopping.

"Nay," David growled, lifting up his sword "it is not enough. Defend yourself!"

He swung again, this time with both hands in a huge overhand blow, trying to take his vain opponent by surprise. Eleazar had to actually parry the strike, but not in a way that David could have anticipated. Instead of stopping David's sword with his own, Eleazar took the crushing force on his sword at an angle and deflected it down and away. Off balance, David had no chance to stop the spinning elbow that smashed into his cheek, sending him sprawling into the dirt once more.

For the second time, David had to clear his ringing head. He spat blood and idly hoped a tooth hadn't been knocked loose. The laughter had died off now, he dimly realized. Maybe watching their captain being beaten half to death held only so much humor.

"How many times must you die, Captain?" Eleazar asked. His tone no longer held that mocking quality, but David didn't really notice. In fact, he could hardly hear above the ringing in his ears.

He was embarrassed and hurt, and he didn't like either feeling. He squeezed a fistful of dirt in one hand and painfully gathered himself. Finding his feet one more time took a lot more than he cared to admit.

Adino leaned on his spear, watching with his usual lack of energy. The other lieutenants had gathered around him. Shammah

1 Samuel 18:13-14

watched with a frown that lost itself in his bushy beard. His huge arms were folded in front of him, but he said nothing. No one offered any help.

Grimacing, every inch of his body on fire, David stood up straight and faced Eleazar, wooden sword still in hand. "I'll die as often as I need," he growled through a pain-filled mouth. "You're my men, and I intend to lead."

Without warning, he threw his handful of dirt straight into Eleazar's face. The vain man cried out and flung up his arm to ward off the surprise attack. David wasted no time. With what little strength he had remaining, he smacked the swordsman upside the head hard enough to knock the man stumbling.

The lieutenant gasped in pain, but unlike David, he didn't go down. Instead, he found his balance and went on the attack. He flicked his sword at David who tried to parry it, but if David's brother, Abinadab, was good, then Eleazar was a master. David never saw the blow that laid him low again. He woke up sometime later to see Adino looking down at him while leaning on his ever-present spear.

"Learn anything?" the lazy man asked.

David wanted to shrug, but the effort required too much energy. "Ask me tomorrow." He thought about it. "Nay, ask me in a week."

Another face filled the sky. This one had a purple bruise on the side of his face. "Seems we're both dead," Eleazar said, smiling. "You have iron in your blood, lad." He looked at Adino. "Did I not say so before?"

"Nay," Adino drawled. "Why don't you help our captain out of the dirt. He may be a fool, but he's our fool."

Grinning, Eleazar bent down and heaved David to his feet. The world spun as if Elohim had decided to use the earth as a chariot wheel. After a few moments, the sensation passed, and David blinked into the sunlight. A few lonely clouds dotted the sky in the distance, he noticed absently.

The pain had receded for the moment, but David knew it would come back with a vengeance once the adrenalin had worn off. He looked around at the men who had gathered to watch the sparring bout. Adriel stood near the lieutenants, his face a mask of concern, but he hadn't intervened. *Good man.*

Someone handed him a wineskin, and he drank huge mouthfuls of the watered-down wine. It helped sooth some of his aches, but only enough to stand on his own.

He looked Eleazar square in the eye. "Listen to me," he said quietly, but putting as much command into his voice as he could. He then took in all the men with a gesture. "All of you, listen to me. I do not intend to bargain your lives for my own. I do not intend to sell your lives to the enemy. We are now brothers. If you are going to survive—if *we* are going to survive—then we must fight as one. If you fight with me, I will see your debts paid and you free in Israel. This I swear by Jehovah Elohim in whom I trust and confide." He paused, looking fierce. "This I swear!"

The warriors stood silently. No one cheered…but neither did they jeer. David had won a victory here somehow—not as he had intended, but he had gained the respect of the men. They knew of his reputation. Many had witnessed him kill the giant with the sling. But with his words, they had witnessed his heart. David had somehow become one of them.

"'Tis a holy vow," Eleazar agreed, smiling. "And I will do my part to help you keep it. I will teach you how to wield a sword, Captain—and I swear not to leave as many bruises about your person."

Adino heaved a sigh. "This probably means you still want us to move the camp, Captain?"

David looked at the man in confusion. "Of course."

The spearman heaved another longsuffering sigh. "Then we should be about it."

He shuffled off, and the other men began to disperse as well. But David noted that they did so with a spring in their step and less procrastination than before. David even heard Eleazar whistling as he went to gather up his things. He hadn't won them over completely yet…but it was a start.

Shammah wandered over, his huge arms still crossed and his disapproving frown still stamped on his face. He suddenly grinned, surprising David. "I've never seen anyone slip through Eleazar's guard before and rap him upside the head. Well done. I think the Spirit of the LORD is truly with you, Captain."

David nodded his thanks, but if the Spirit of the LORD was indeed with him, then why did he hurt so much? He shrugged it off and turned to find Adriel. The man's bag had a bulge in it that looked suspiciously like it came from a harp. It would be like Jonathan to send David's favorite instrument along with Adriel, and right now, David needed the comfort of those harmonious chords. Singing praises to God would be soothing for both his sore body and his apprehensive soul.

5

"What news from Abner?" Saul asked the travel-weary messenger. The runner took a moment to catch his breath.

"The Philistines are stirring, my lord. Abner reports the border towns of Gezer, Zorah, and Beth-Shemesh have been raided."

Saul glanced over at his son, Jonathan, who stood off to one side, listening intently. "It seems the heathen dogs were not so defeated as we thought," he said, letting a hint of disapproval slip into his voice.

Jonathan stiffened. "The death of their champion shook their confidence in their false gods, Father. They have not stirred from their holes in three months, but you know as well as I that they would eventually come forth."

Saul reflected on the truth of his son's words. He did know it. Ever since David had killed Goliath in the Valley of Elah, the Philistines' power had been broken but not destroyed. Enough Philistines had escaped the battle that they remained a very real threat. In truth, Saul was surprised that three entire months had gone by without a raid, but he hesitated to acknowledge this fact. He did not want to credit David if he could help it.

Turning back to the messenger, he asked, "What does Abner request?"

"A Philistine army, nearly a thousand strong, is striking across the northern extreme of their border where our defenses are weakest. Abner believes that King Achish is succoring them from Gath. He requests leave to lay siege to the Philistine city, take it, and raze it to the ground. The Philistines will be forced to recall their army to defend the city, and we can then destroy it there."

Saul almost permitted it. He needed another victory badly, one that would return the people's hearts to him. Even after three months, the story of David's miraculous victory over the giant continued to be talked about throughout the land. David's fame ate at Saul, like termites on wood. Slowly, the hearts of the people were turning against him and turning to the son of Jesse.

A shiver of fear ran up his spine at the thought. He desperately wanted David dead, but the opportunity had not yet arisen to be rid of the treasonous harper. Maybe the Philistines had just provided him with one. Tapping his bearded chin, he cast a sly glance back toward Jonathan. "How fares the son of Jesse with the Indebted?"

"He fares well, Father," Jonathan said, coming to David's defense instantly as Saul knew he would. "David has been able to instill some small amount of discipline within the ranks. He's won them over, and I believe they are a more superior fighting force than before."

Perfect, Saul inwardly crowed. He knew all about David's struggles to wield the criminal company together into a cohesive fighting unit. He also knew that David had far from succeeded, though he had done much better than Saul had anticipated—*curse that boy!* Regardless, Jonathan, unwittingly, had just delivered the son of Jesse up to his death with his praise.

"It does my heart well to hear this," he lied. "Send David to deal with this minor problem. I would not have Abner leave the rest of the border defenseless and be caught in a protracted siege. Nay, that would not be well. Send word to Abner that the son of Jesse will be dispatched with all haste to destroy this rogue company of Philistine dogs that is so plaguing our nation."

Saul could see his son's indecision and instantly divined the source. Jonathan had uplifted David and essentially deemed the young captain's company battle ready when he knew in his heart that

David was anything but. However, retracting his words would shame David. His son was trapped.

The king hated the fact that even his own son had fallen under the spell of the youngest son of Jesse. Why couldn't he see the danger? It made no sense. Soon…soon the harper would be no more, and things could return to normal.

Saul smiled to himself, pleased with his manipulation of events. Perhaps this was proof that the LORD had not yet abandoned him completely.

"What say you?" he asked Jonathan casually.

"You are wise, my king," Jonathan conceded. "Send David. He can swat the few Philistine flies for us." The king's eldest son's eyes narrowed fractionally. "Shall we accompany David, my lord?"

"For what purpose?" Saul snapped back. "Do you think David unable to accomplish this task?"

"Nay. He is able. But—"

Saul cut him off. "Then we will send him. If the LORD is indeed with the son of Jesse, what need for us? You and I will stay here and attend to other, more pressing, matters." Inwardly, Saul gloated. The Indebted were a cowardly lot for the most part, but not so David. The son of Jesse would stand against the Philistines alone if he must—and be cut down. It was perfect. "Call the son of Jesse to attend us here so that I may command my servant." He placed some emphasis on that last word to remind Jonathan of his own place.

Jonathan bowed, hiding his thoughts behind his dark eyes. "As my king commands."

Several hours later, David stood before Saul. The king took some time to study the young captain, to try and gauge the other's mindset before issuing his commands. The lad looked worn, frazzled even. The toll of commanding a thousand men as unruly as the Indebted had taken its toll on the young man. The lad's tunic, though clean, looked old. The boy's face looked thinner than Saul remembered, as if he hadn't been eating enough. The king sent a daily portion of food to the Indebted, but it consisted mostly of watered-down wine, vegetables, bread, and cheese. Saul was loath to send meat to men such as they.

Despite the young man's appearance, he stood straight, eyes level, but unchallenging, ready to obey the king's command. This bothered Saul. He knew David's true heart, the one he hid from all, even from Jonathan. He knew the son of Jesse was in league with Samuel the seer, that they had made a strong conspiracy against him. He knew this in his heart even if he had little proof. It would help if David would be demonstrably more rebellious, thus giving Saul the appropriate excuses to end the young man's life. But when David stood before him, obedient and appearing eager to serve, it made things difficult for Saul. *Curse the boy!* Well, if the need ever arose, he had ways to encourage such rebellious deeds. Hopefully, it would matter little. Hopefully, David would be dead within a week.

"Son of Jesse," the king said, his voice carrying the confidence that comes with years of commanding armies on the battlefield. "The Philistines have risen up once again and have shed Hebrew blood. I require redress for this wickedness. You will be my sword. I command you to go forth to the environs of Ekron, find the company of Philistines raiding thereabouts and destroy them to a man." He locked eyes with David. "Can you do this, son of Jesse?"

The young man nodded instantly, bowing low to the king. "With God's help, O King, it will be done."

Saul nearly flinched at the mention of God. How could this young man have such implicit faith and retain such a secretly rebellious heart against his king? Saul's hand tightened around his javelin, and he had to fight down the urge to throw it at David. No. Not now. Not yet. He steadied himself and said, "Then go, son of Jesse. My eldest son will explain the details to you as you leave. Do not fail me."[1]

---

[1] 1 Samuel 18:13.

Their eyes locked, and Saul thought he saw understanding in the young man's eyes. He understood the warning. Good.

David bowed low one more time and then turned to leave. Jonathan glanced reprovingly at his father and scurried after the young captain. It mattered not. Their friendship was doomed. David would soon die by the hand of the Philistines.

David turned as Jonathan closed the oak door leading to Saul's court. The confident air he had worn in front of Saul melted away as his friend stepped close. "We're not ready," he told Jonathan. "The men aren't ready."

Truth be told, David didn't feel ready either. He had been training nonstop with Eleazar over the last three months to master the sword, and though he could more than hold his own against many of the men with whom he sparred, Eleazar casually defeated him every time. And the Philistines had been training longer and were more comfortable with the sword than were most Hebrews.

Only about three score of his men owned a sword, most having spoiled them from dead Philistines in past battles. The rest of the men wielded spears, and about fifty were proficient with the bow or sling. David itched to use his sling again, but as captain of the company, his place was at the forefront of the battle where the sling would likely be of little worth.

Jonathan put a hand on David's shoulder. "I know," he said softly. He looked back at the oak door and ushered David further down the corridor where their words wouldn't carry. "You'll fare well, my friend. I've seen your work with the Indebted. I don't think they've ever been as disciplined and as ready to fight as they are now."

David snorted. "That doesn't mean they're ready, my lord. I don't have much experience yet, but I've seen the men you command. They could shred my company to pieces without hardly working up a sweat."

Saul's eldest son shook his head. "My troops are among our best, David. You cannot make such a comparison. These Philistines are probably the remnant of those who fled to Ekron after our victory in Elah.[2] They'll not be among the Philistine elite. You can defeat them."

David slid his tongue over his teeth as he considered the words. He had an agonizing feeling that Saul wanted him to fail. He didn't know why, but the feeling persisted. Adino's insight that David might have embarrassed the king by killing Goliath still haunted him. He so desperately wanted to please his king, and that's why he had dared not refuse Saul's order, but by all that was holy and good, these orders could very well be a suicide mission!

Jonathan grinned. "Why are you worried about a few lazy Philistines anyway? Did our land become devoid of rocks suddenly? Where is that famous sling of yours?"

David couldn't answer the grin with one of his own. "I put it aside. The Indebted believe they are going to die, and to become their leader, I must lead. I must be in the forefront of the battle, Jonathan. There is no other way."

Jonathan sobered. "This I know. I'm sorry for my tasteless attempt at humor. I will help you plan to catch these Philistines. Together we'll come up with a way to drive these uncircumcised back into the holes from whence they've crawled."

David let out his breath slowly and offered a prayer of thanksgiving to Elohim for sending him such a friend as Jonathan. "Thank you," he said simply.

Jonathan waved it off. "It is nothing. Come. I have a gift for you that will help."

Curious, David followed Jonathan through the large house. Like many houses, this one was actually several built next to each other. He realized that Jonathan was taking him to his personal house. They exited the main compound and headed into a dusty courtyard that opened up to the main gate, similar to his father's

---

[2] 1 Samuel 17:52.

house in Bethlehem. This one was uncovered, however, but significantly larger.

Adriel stood here, waiting for David with endless patience. Jonathan waved the armorbearer over. "Come, Adriel, join us." He motioned to David, pointing to a nearby, modest-looking door. "My house is right over there."

Jonathan entered without knocking. He left the door open to allow more light in, and unlike his father's house, his had the traditional dirt floor. Jonathan took the other two men to an open room in the back. The common smells of cooking and clean straw soothed David's nose. It was the closest thing to home he'd experienced in a long time.

A woman sat on a stool weaving. She looked up, saw who had entered her house, and quickly stood, bowing her head. "My lord! I did not yet expect you home."

Jonathan went over to her and fondly kissed the woman's cheek. "David, my wife, Naarah.[3] She is the jewel of my life. Too bad that she can't weave or cook."

Her cheeks grew red, but looking around the house, David figured Naarah was an amazing weaver, and knowing Jonathan's penchant for understatement, she was probably an amazing cook besides. She was also beautiful, marred only by a somewhat long and crooked nose.

"Naarah, you've probably heard of David, the son of Jesse, slayer of an undersized Philistine. He and his armorbearer will dine with us this evening."

David started to protest, "My lord, I need—"

Jonathan smirked at him. "I know. I know. You eat like a bird, picking at your food, hardly able to swallow even the smallest of bites. Very embarrassing this is. But I am the king's son, so you will do what I tell you to do, and tonight, you eat with my family."

---

[3] Jonathan had a wife, but her name is never given. Naarah is a fictional name for a real woman.

David took exception to the unflattering description, but a solid meal that wasn't made up of bread and cheese would be a good change of pace. "As you command then, my lord," David said sweeping into his impression of a royal bow. He overdid it, overbalanced, and had to do a hasty dance with his feet to keep from sprawling ignobly onto the floor.

Naarah giggled, and the two men tried unsuccessfully to hide their mirth. The eldest son of the king looked at his wife. "See? Did I not tell you he felled the giant by playing the fool? I was there. Goliath died of laughter. This I swear."

His wife giggled again.

David gave up and joined in the laughter. It felt good to laugh, and Jehovah knew he had precious little to laugh about in recent months.

Jonathan took the other two men to a staircase where they took off their sandals, washed their feet, and ascended to the second floor. They sat on mats around a short wooden table that could seat six or eight people.

"Now," Jonathan began, "while we wait for my wife to bring us the food, let us plan your victory."

So they talked. David gave Jonathan a frank appraisal of the battle readiness of his men, and Adriel added some of his own insights and suggested a marching order that utilized the strengths he'd observed from watching the men drill. Eventually, they hammered out a plan that David felt good about. Perhaps they wouldn't all die, and God willing, he would bring home a victory. Perhaps then Saul would accept David.

Voices from below interrupted their conversation, and Jonathan's smile spread across his face mysteriously. "It seems the food is nearly ready."

David turned toward the stairway, thinking he recognized the new voices. Sure enough, Michal was the first person to ascend, followed closely by Merab and Naarah. David felt a thrill run up his spine at the sight of Saul's daughters. After not seeing them for three months, he was surprised at how beautiful he found them.

His heart began to thump like a galloping horse, and strangely, he felt both exhilarated and trapped.

6

For the eternal passing of a single instance, David could see nothing but the two girls. Michal wore a blue silk halug that fell to her ankles. Her dark curly hair fell thickly to her waist. Her simple veil hung below her eyes, bridging her nose and only partially hiding her shapely neck. David looked into those blue eyes and felt his mouth go dry. He saw desire and determination there. Most women demurely looked down when a man looked upon them, but not Michal. She returned David's stare with frank interest and a question. One of her eyebrows rose, and David was the one who looked away…

And right at Merab. Michal's older sister looked down shyly, but her cheeks rose in a way that suggested a smile behind her veil. The veil itself was decorated with pearls, and a golden tiara held back her dark hair from her white forehead. She stood perhaps two fingerbreadths taller than her sister, which meant she might reach David's nose. She carried a wooden tray of food, and her arms jingled from the myriad of gold and silver bracelets she wore.

Michal was around David's age, though Merab was probably a year or two older. He noticed that both girls walked directly to him, and only Naarah went to Jonathan. David found himself surrounded by female sights and smells. For the past three months, David had been immersed in a man's world of army life, seeing women only from a distance—if that. Now all things female bombarded his senses. He suddenly yearned for marriage. He was nearly the right age, and most young men and women were betrothed by that time, if not already married.

He clamped down on his emotions. As much as he yearned for a household of his own, it would unlikely be with one of the king's daughters. He wished now that Saul would have kept his promise to give his daughter to the slayer of Goliath. He sighed. He was just a simple shepherd, and he could not afford the dowry that Saul would no doubt demand for one of his daughters.

Michal beat her sister to David and set the platter of food before him. Merab tsked softly, and one of her eyes twitched in irritation, but she smoothly turned to Adriel and, as if that had been her intention all along, set her tray before him. David noticed that his armorbearer had been struck speechless by Saul's eldest daughter, obviously smitten. A surge of possessiveness rose in the young captain's mind, and he felt momentarily resentful that Merab had so easily switched her attention to someone else.

As beautiful as the girls were, the smell of boiled meat wrested David's attention from them. Having lived off Saul's daily portion of meager food for the last three months meant he'd eaten little meat of any kind until now. His father, Jesse, had delivered supplies—including meat—at his request, but he had parceled that out to the men first. His stomach growled embarrassingly, and he thought he heard Michal giggle softly. David's cheeks burned, but Jonathan rescued him by saying, "Let us wash."

Michal hastened over to a large basin set in a corner and picked up a heavy pitcher of water. The men lined up, and Michal poured water into Jonathan's hands who scrubbed them clean as the water fell into the basin. David and Adriel followed. The women washed last. Then standing around the low table, they waited piously as Jonathan gave thanks for the meal.

Seated once again upon his mat, David almost jumped in surprise as Merab sat gracefully beside him. He hadn't expected her to sit so close. Typically, the unmarried women would sit opposite the men, though there was no custom or law against doing so. Her nearness caused a rather strange mix of emotions to rise within him.

Unsettled and uncertain, he swallowed and offered her a smile. She lowered her eyes, but her veil couldn't hide her obvious returned smile.

"My father was wise to make you a captain," she said softly. "I pray to Elohim every night that He will protect you and bless you."

The words warmed David's heart and set off another scrimmage of warring emotions. He beamed at her, but then caught Michal's cold eyes. He froze. Michal's hard eyes bore into her sister like an awl through leather. She spotted his stare, and her eyes changed so quickly to friendliness that he couldn't be certain of what he'd seen. Another pitched battle took place in David's heart.

"Indeed," Michal agreed loftily from her sister's other side. She picked out a few grapes from the platters of food and rolled them between two delicate-looking fingers "Our father is wise, but the son of Jesse is also wise." She looked at David with those captivating eyes. "Is this not so? I have heard marvelous things of the work you have done with the Indebted. Everyone speaks of it. They say you've quelled their baser instincts and have forged mighty men of valor to fight alongside of you."

People speak of me? Once again, warring emotions launched a quick raid against each other in his mind and heart, unsettling him. "I wouldn't say that their instincts are completely quelled, my lady. And I've not yet had opportunity to test their valor. I admit, for the time being, my own valor is in question."

"Perhaps," Michal conceded softly. "But does not the answer hang above the gates of Jerusalem?"

The young captain's mind pictured Goliath's head as it swayed gently on the spear above the gates of that massively fortified city. And he smiled at her in thanks.

Something in her eyes threatened to draw him in and drown him, so he snatched one of the slabs of mutton and began to eat. He stared hard at the meat, trying to keep his focus and balance as he considered her words further. He hadn't realized that he was being so closely watched. It made him feel decidedly uncomfortable…and proud. These conflicting emotions raged through him, and in a moment of desperation, he yearned for the days when he could sit in anonymity where his most weighty task was to prevent sheep from straying.

Fortunately, Jonathan came to his rescue again. Perhaps he noticed David's uncertainty. "Pay my sisters no heed," he said, frowning at the girls. "They like to tease. Perhaps Father was unwise to withhold them from marriage for so long. They need husbands to keep them from mischief, I fear."

Merab's eyes fell with those words, the bracelets on her arms twinkling as she clasped her hands together. Michal, however, refused to lower her eyes, and one thin eyebrow arched up challengingly. "Oh?" she asked, her voice silken. "And do you have someone in mind for us, brother?"

Jonathan leaned back a bit and gave his sister a frank appraisal. "Well now," he said, "such a man would hardly need to be strong of body or sound of mind to be worthy of you, dear sister. Your timidity is legendary as is your humility. I suspect just about any man would do…if he could pay the dowry—but then most men might think the price beyond reason, wouldn't you?"

From what little David could see of Michal's face, she reddened under the mocking and biting onslaught. The message was clear. She'd gone too far and needed to back off. To her credit, she finally looked down. "I must apologize, my lord," she said glancing to David. "I overstepped. It is unforgiveable."

"Hardly that," David hastened to say. "Please think no more of it."

"Then I will do as you command," she said, and David was sure her smile had rematerialized behind her veil.

Merab surprised everyone then by softly asking, "Brother, don't you think you're being unjustly harsh?"

David blinked. This was perhaps the first time he'd heard her openly disagree with anyone. Jonathan's frown looked strange as he chewed his food. He swallowed his mouthful of bread and said, "Perhaps my sister speaks rightly. I was the one who spoke too

1 Samuel 18:15-16

hastily. This talk of marriage is unseemly at the dining table. Forgive me."

Adriel, who had sat silently until then, grinned. "I most strenuously disagree, my lord, what better place to speak of marriage than when food is at hand to distract the mind and eye?"

Jonathan laughed. "Oh? And would you take my sisters to wife seeing how they laid out this repast for our enjoyment?"

"Both of them?" Adriel asked, his face speculative. "That is some offer, my lord. To be the king's son-in-law twice over would be a mighty privilege indeed."

David cut in hastily, "He wasn't offering, Adriel!"

Both men looked at David, their amused smiles like slaps in the face. *Oh.* They'd only been teasing. David's face flushed, and he looked around at the girls to see how much damage he had done, but strangely, both girls looked rather satisfied with themselves, like cats with a mouse pinned beneath their paws. David didn't know exactly how to interpret such expressions.

Not knowing what else to do, David continued to eat, wishing he'd just kept his mouth shut. After a long moment, Adriel whispered loud enough to make sure everyone heard, "But if your offer still stands, let me know." He then looked meaningfully at Merab.

Saul's eldest daughter blushed while her sister looked faintly amused and decidedly content. Jonathan barked a laugh. "Well said! But I suspect my father will have the final say in the matter."

"Still," Adriel added with a shrug, "a good word from you would go far."

"Indeed," Jonathan said cryptically.

Thankfully, the conversation then shifted to other matters. Both girls bantered lightly with David, asking him questions, praising his work with the Indebted, and asking him to retell his encounter with the giant, Goliath. David enjoyed their attention and felt disappointed when the meal ended. He'd just started to relax.

David and the others washed their hands once again to remove the grease and other food remains and then stood while Jonathan spoke the grace after the meal[1] and then recited the Shema.[2] Every time David heard the words, his heart and mind became settled. The phrase, "Hear O Israel: The LORD our God is one LORD," stirred something inside of him, and in the face of impending battle with the Philistines, he renewed his love for his God—to love Him with all his heart, soul, and might. The words always stirred up his sense of purpose and renewal.

Hearing another speak the words was significant to David. It felt different to hear the words spoken by another than it was to recite it to himself. Hearing Jonathan speak the words in his deep resonating voice made it seem more real, more personal. It allowed him to dwell on each word and hide them away in his heart.

As the women gathered the platters to head downstairs, Jonathan gestured to David. "And now it is time I give you my gifts, my friend."

Jonathan beckoned to David, and together, they walked to the far corner of the room where a blanket covered a mysterious pile. Jonathan ripped the blanket aside revealing a suit of bronze armor that gleamed in the lamp light. "Behold," Jonathan intoned, "your armor, Captain."

Dazzled, David reached down to pull up a mail shirt and admire the overlapping links designed to turn away a sword edge or to blunt the power of a stabbing spear. "It's wonderful," David breathed.

"Don't be too sure of that," Jonathan remarked. "It's as thin as parchment and will likely fall apart the first time you attempt to put it on, but I can't have you go into battle looking like a plucked sparrow."

The young captain fingered a shield in wonder. "This came from the giant?" he asked.

"Not unless the man was made of bronze," Adriel quipped.

Ignoring the armorbearer, Jonathan nodded. "I had one of my father's smiths forge it into something smaller. Truth to tell, we

---

[1] Also known as the Birkat Ha-Mazon and based on Deuteronomy 8:10.
[2] A prayer that recites parts of Deuteronomy 6, 11, and 15.

forged nearly three entire suits of armor out of it. I sold the other two. I put the gold in a pouch for you there." He pointed to a leather bag next to a helmet.

"Thank you, Jonathan," David breathed.

"Think nothing of it.

David hefted the mail shirt again. "This is a princely gift, Jonathan. I am not worthy."

"It was yours already, fairly won. And you are worthy. My sisters were right. You have done more than passingly well with the Indebted. If you are to lead them, you are to lead them as their captain and armed with the spoils of war." He indicated the armor.

David looked around. "And what of Goliath's sword?"

"I did as you bade and delivered it to the High Priest at Nob. It is in his care now. The sword I gave you was once mine, and I hope seals the covenant we made upon the field of battle."[3]

"Aye, I remember."

"I may not go with you, David, but I pray these will help keep you safe."

David clasped Jonathan's shoulders. Tears swam in his eyes as he realized that deep down, his friend was saying goodbye—just in case.

"My life is in Elohim's hands," David said hoarsely. "It will be He, more than the sword, that keeps me safe. But as you say, brother, your sword is a symbol of our covenant. It shall not leave my side, and it may be Elohim's instrument of deliverance."

Tears in his own eyes now, Saul's eldest son nodded. "Aye, and I will give peace offerings every day you are gone. This I swear."

"Then it shall be well."

The friends fell silent, unsure what more to say. Adriel broke the silence with a longsuffering sigh. "I suppose it will fall upon me to bear this armor."

David smirked at his new friend. "Are you not my armorbearer?"

---

[3] 1 Samuel 18:1-4.

"Aye," Adriel agreed heavily. "'Tis true. 'Tis sad, but 'tis true."

Jonathan's eyes danced merrily. "Perhaps another arrangement would suit Adriel better. I have no doubt that we could prevail upon my sisters to bear your armor, David. That would relieve our friend here of the burden."

Adriel pursed his lips together in confusion. "Do you truly think they could carry both me and the armor? The armor looks quite heavy. Perhaps, for the sake of their fairer arms, they could just carry me."

"I said nothing of carrying you!" Jonathan sputtered, taken aback.

"Aye, you did," Adriel pointed out smoothly. "Did you not tell them to carry the bearer of arms?"

"I did not!"

"True. You did not. For they are not here to tell. Wait but a moment, and I, your humble servant, will go inform them for you." With that, Adriel disappeared down the stairs where David and Jonathan could hear him greeting the women. He didn't seem to be giving them any commands about carrying anyone or anything.

"He's not coming back, is he?" David asked, his voice resigned.

Jonathan hesitated, listening. Then he shook his head. "Nay, he is not."

David began to gather up the armor, grunting as he straightened. As heavy as it was to lift, he didn't relish having to wear it into combat. "I think this Adriel fellow is too clever by far."

"Aye. He is that. But he is a good man. Trust him. He served me well for many years."

David agreed. He liked Adriel.

Jonathan's voice dropped. "Adriel has for some time wished to become my brother-in-law. He has eyes for Merab to be sure, and if I remember aright, she has been in favor of the union in times past."

David hesitated. He understood. "You have two sisters," he pointed out, also dropping his voice.

"Aye, but Merab is eldest."

That made sense. The oldest daughter was often given in marriage first[4] and usually went to the man most in her father's favor. If David could take Merab to wife, then he would know for certain that he stood in good stead with the king. In addition, Merab was very pleasing to the eyes, and he felt confident that she would make an ideal wife. "Do you think your father would see his way to accept me as a son-in-law?" He hesitated. "The king promised her to the one who slew Goliath."

Jonathan nodded. "Aye. That he did. I will speak to my father. Adriel is a good man and a good friend, but I think my father delights more in you than in he—as do I."

Maybe, David thought. He wasn't so sure. Why had nothing further been said of Saul's promise? Still, Jonathan's faith in him meant much. He shared a relieved grin with his friend, slung the armor over his back, plopped the helmet on his head, and picked up the shield. "I will take my leave of you, my brother. Thank you for all you have done."

"May you walk in peace, brother."

Little chance for that, David thought sardonically. Still, with his spirits renewed, he turned and headed for the stairs. He would need to rouse his men and prepare them to march. All too soon, they would be plunged into battle, but David felt better for having spent time with Jonathan. Elohim would succor him and deliver the Philistines into his hand. Of this, he was certain.

He put all of that aside for the moment to focus on a more pressing task. Somehow, he had to convince his armorbearer to actually bear the armor back to their camp.

---

[4] Genesis 29:26.

7

The narrow ravine funneled the sound of running water to David's ears. He paused, breathing heavily, as he surveyed the forested mountains that lay between the valley of Sorek to the west and the valley of Rephaim to the east. The stream below wound its way through the treacherous ravine on its way to the coast of the Great Sea.

David, along with a thousand armed men, stood atop the northern ridges, just south of the small town of Kesalon. David, Adriel, and Shammah had climbed to an outlook that gave them a panoramic view of the country to the west—the direction the Philistines were coming.

"This place is not fit for a battle," Shammah muttered, rubbing his bald head. The man had re-braided his beard and had woven in small bones of some animal. Every time he moved his head, the bones banged together producing a dull knocking sound. "The slopes are too steep and the forest too thick." He scowled as he squinted into the distance. "But, Captain, if you just want to prevent the heathen dogs from coming any farther, this is as likely a place to see it done as any. They would not willingly face us in such treacherous terrain. We could hurl insults at each other until they get bored and go home."

"That is hardly a victory, Lieutenant," David pointed out.

The huge man shrugged. "Any battle where I retain life and limb *is* a victory."

1 Samuel 18:15-16

"We aren't commanded to stop them. We're here to destroy them. That is King Saul's task for us."

Shammah hefted a huge club wrapped in iron bands and studded with blunted iron spikes—his own invention he claimed. "I'm not against bashing some Philistine heads, but look, the Indebted are not men of valor. They'll run the moment things turn ill."

In his heart, David agreed with this assessment. Over the last three months, he had established some measure of discipline with the men. He had chosen ten lieutenants to command squads of a hundred men each and let them choose their own sergeants. David then enforced proper camp sanitation and had even prevailed upon his father to add some mutton and wine to the men's diet. He even convinced the men to begin military drills.

Most of the company was made up of spearmen, that being the easiest weapon to produce by the few smiths remaining in Israel. They were divided into seven squads each with a lieutenant in charge. Adino held commanded over all seven squads and would personally lead one of them himself. David had yet to see Adino fight or drill with his spear, but Eleazar had assured David that the thin man was an expert with the weapon and had rightly earned his namesake of The Spear. David took his word for it. He didn't really have any choice. Trying to motivate the lazy man into any sort of action, sparring or otherwise, seemed beyond David's abilities.

Eleazar commanded two squads of swordsmen. Most of these wielded captured Philistine swords—long tapered double-edged blades with a midrib running down the center. They worked better as thrusting weapons and were ineffective against a stout shield. Eleazar had pronounced the men, one and all, as he put it, likely to be slain in the first ten heartbeats of battle. Clearly, he was the optimist of the army.

Shammah commanded, strangely, a squad of bowmen and slingers. The man himself couldn't hit a target to save his life, but his bellowing voice and vicious warclub could galvanize the most lackadaisical solider into action—except for Adino, naturally. In addition, David had discovered that the huge man had an eye for battlefield tactics and knew precisely where the bowmen and slingers could be best utilized.

Adriel, as David's armorbearer, completed the inner circle of lieutenants. David discovered that not only was the man a competent warrior in his own right, but he understood the management of men and the subtleties of leadership. Already, David had learned much from him.

David pointed toward the winding river and the route the scouts reported the Philistines were following. "Do you see any advantage in terrain we could use?"

The large man squinted into the distance for a time, his eyes roaming over the terrain. Finally, he grunted. "If I was leading this walking massacre, I would go there." He pointed. "See that small lea or meadow right before the stream turns?"

David looked and finally spotted it. "Aye."

"It is large enough to give our men room enough to maneuver and small enough to keep the enemy from forming ranks and slaughtering us. We can hide my bowmen on the two slopes and hit them hard from the flanks as they march into the meadow."

David frowned. "Don't we want to keep them from getting into the meadow?"

"Nay. They'll simply retreat, and our chance to destroy them will end. They aren't stupid. They won't walk into a killing field. They'll send scouts ahead to be sure all is well. We'll need to lay in wait out of sight among the trees of the slopes to lure them in. Once about half their force has gained the meadow, we attack. That way, they won't be able to retreat through the narrow pass or bring their full force to bear on us. This has to be an ambush."

"Or they'll retreat and raid elsewhere," David finished, understanding.

"Or they'll wipe us out," Shammah muttered. He shrugged. "They won't have chariots down there—praise Elohim. So we don't need to worry about that. Mostly, we'll be fighting their infantry."

"What about their bowmen?" David asked.

1 Samuel 18:15-16

"They'll probably be placed at the rear of the column. If we time it just right, they won't be able to get into position through the narrow pass before we crush their advance forces."

David nodded. Not having a better plan himself, it would have to do. "Then let us be about it."

Three hours later, they made it to the meadow, and nearly a thousand men moved into position—minus the thirty men David had left with the baggage and supplies atop the ridge just south of Kesalon. Each man had brought enough water and food for two days. The scouts estimated that the Philistine raiders would come through the pass around noon the following day.

David made sure to instruct the men to stay out of the meadow and to avoid leaving evidence in the tall grass that a large body of men had recently passed through. Because the stream cut close to the northern slope, David decided to post only bowmen on that side. The stream would act as a formidable barrier to prevent any counterattack in that direction. So the men made their way up the steep slopes on both sides, fading into the shadows and clefts afforded them.

Adino wandered over to where David sat shivering on a rock overlooking the empty meadow as daylight slowly faded, casting everything in deep shadows. Adino carried his spear cradled in his arms and used the blunt end to help balance his way across the steep slope. "Chilly," he offered, sitting down next to the young captain, allowing his long legs to splay out haphazardly in front of him.

"Aye," David replied, keeping his voice soft. "Winter is approaching." Although, David suspected his shivering had less to do with the cold and more to do with the fact that his stomach was all tied up in knots.

The laconic man met David's eyes and understood. "This feeling is normal, Captain. Did you not feel fear on the eve of battle when you faced Goliath?"

David shook his head. "Not like this. I was nervous, but I knew I would be victorious. It was as if the Spirit of the LORD came upon me and guided my hands to send the stone that felled the giant."

"You do not feel the same here?"

The young captain considered his words carefully. He did not want to discourage his second-in-command, but he felt no one would better understand than the thin spearman. "I have doubts," he admitted quietly. "How do you think the men will perform in the battle tomorrow?"

Settling back into a more comfortable position, the spearman gave a halfhearted shrug. "I suspect most will die—or run."

Deflated, David sagged against the rock. "That is what I fear as well."

Adino raised an eyebrow. "I did not claim this to be a fear, my young captain. I merely stated what I suspect will happen." He rolled an eye to encompass the men hiding nearby. "King Saul has always thrust the Indebted into battle first. We stand and fight because if we run, we will be cut down by our own countrymen. These men do not want to fight. They want to survive. They do not see themselves as warriors. Most simply want to return to their families and farms, so the moment the battle looks like it is going ill, they will run—and many will die. It has always been thus with the Indebted. But that is not what I fear."

Surprised, David took fuller note of his lieutenant. "What then do you fear?"

"That I will run with them," he said simply, yawning.

"I do not understand."

The spearman dug into a leather pouch and produced some Elah nuts which he popped into his mouth without first prying the nut out of the shell. He crunched loudly, causing David to wince. He spat out the broken shells and chewed slowly on the nut while he considered his reply. Finally, he looked David in the eye. "You are a good captain, my lord. You have tried to give us purpose and hope, but it is not enough. We have nothing we believe is worth fighting for—or dying for. This is true for me as well. I have nothing to fight for, so fear comes easily. I fear I too will flee. It is the most prudent of courses, I assure you."

David was aghast. "But we fight the enemies of Jehovah Elohim."

"And does not King Saul have warriors? Could he not fight this battle?" He popped another nut into his mouth, crushed the shell, and spat out the broken pieces again. "I hear the words spoken by the men. They believe we have been sent here to die. Elohim has never been with this company of thieves, beggars, and indebted. Just ask Eleazar what he thinks."

David already knew what the skilled swordsman thought. Everyone did. He constantly prophesied everyone's inevitable death to anyone who would listen. David wanted to shove the man's sword down his throat just to shut him up. He'd tried ordering the man to stop, but outside of an incredulous look, David had been ignored, and since he needed the man's skill and experience, he was uncertain how best to exert his will upon the man.

The young captain tried a different approach with Adino. "But if the Philistines overthrow us, they will enslave us, take our land, our cities, and our women. This cannot be allowed."

"Then why send us?" Adino countered. "If King Saul truly wished to avoid this fate, then where is he with his thousands? Where is Abner, the son of Ner, captain of the host?"

David fell silent. He didn't have a response to Adino's fatalistic perspective. The vice-like grip on David's stomach agreed with the spearman's assessment.

After a lengthy silence in which Adino appeared to doze, David asked, "Is there not a way to strengthen the hearts of the men?"

Without opening his eyes, Adino said, "It is beyond simple men such as you and I. Tomorrow we fight. Only the gods know what will happen."

"There is no God but Elohim," David replied automatically.

The spearman cracked open an eye. "Then perhaps He knows."

David considered those words. He longed for a priest so that he could inquire of the Lord, but the king's command had required haste, and David hadn't gotten a chance to seek one out. It worried him, not knowing, not having the assurance of the Lord's will. The burden of command, the imminent battle on the morrow, and the fears of failing both his king and his God weighed heavily on his young shoulders.

Not knowing what to do, he began chewing his fingernails as he tried to think of something that would bring heart to his men. He tore off the ends of the nails with his teeth and spat them out beside the Elah shells that had begun to litter the ground around Adino. Finally, he could stand it no longer. He had to ask the question that was eating away at his sanity.

"So what do we do?"

Adino barely shrugged. "We wait." Then he seemed to drift off to sleep.

But sleep would not come to David that night.

8

The birds had long since fallen silent, disturbed by the men huddled under the trees. Only the faint rustling of a breeze in the upper boughs of the trees reached the ears of David and his thousand. The Indebted were poised along the ridge slope, waiting for the word to attack. Tension and uneasiness filled the mind and muscles of each man.

The order of the day was absolute silence and stillness. Shammah had promised to flay the man who betrayed their presence to the enemy. David thought that the rat skulls he'd woven into his braided beard had done more to drive the point home than anything else. The man was positively scary when he set out to be. To himself, David wondered about the man's heritage. Surely, he wasn't a pure-blooded Hebrew!

Whatever the means, it worked. Not a man so much as twitched a muscle as four Philistine scouts made their way through the tall grass of the meadow below. The plan was to wait for the main body of Philistines to reach the choke point. Then the Hebrews would spring their ambush.

The enemy scouts paused at the near end of the meadow where David's men had crossed the day before. David held his breath. If the scouts determined that a body of men had moved through the area, then everything would be for naught. But after a brief consultation, the scouts moved on, disappearing around the bend.

Twenty minutes later, Philistine warriors began to emerge into the meadow from downstream. Heavy infantry moved in first. David peered closely at the warriors. He had only ever faced one Philistine, but Goliath had been an anomaly—not truly of the Philistine race. Until now, David really hadn't had the opportunity to study the enemy or see them up close. Right off, he noticed that the typical Philistine's armor varied vastly from Goliath's. Perhaps the giant's size had necessitated a different form of armament, or perhaps Goliath had taken a fancy to a more Canaanitish style of armor. Regardless, these Philistines were dressed different.

For the most part, they carried round bronze or iron shields covered in leather. Religious images had been painted on the shields as prayers to their various false gods. David couldn't decipher what any of the illustrations meant. The soldiers carried the typical, long, double-edged tapered sword that they favored. Ribbed corselets made of striped metal or leather were wrapped around their torsos in lieu of the mail shirt that some men favored. They wore a brightly colored feathered headdress in the form of a crown that probably represented to which Philistine tribe they belonged. The headdress was securely fastened by a leather chinstrap. In this case, David could make out at least three different styles and colors, which might mean that the warriors below ascribed to three different Philistine tribes. They each wore a heavy kilt-like garment that covered the thighs almost to the knees. Some had attached small metal studs to their armor. A few men had tassels that hung from the bottom of the kilt or wore armbands around their upper arms that might depict various officers or commanders.

The Philistines themselves had sloping foreheads and high cheekbones that gave their faces a somewhat pinched or pointed look. Many had tattooed their faces with symbols of their gods, giving them a fierceness that surprised David. Goliath had tattooed his face, but a giant is a giant and would always look menacing regardless. Like Goliath, these men had mingled their blood with the Canaanite descendants of the region, and David could pick out the Canaanite aspects in their varying height and hair color.

2 Samuel 23:8 & 1 Chronicles 11:11

Without hesitation, the heavy infantry began to march through the meadow. The light infantry, most carrying two throwing javelins instead of a shield began to file into the meadow from behind.

David tensed and looked over at Adino. For once, the lazy man looked intent, his eyes boring into the enemy below as they waited for the signal. David had left it to Shammah to begin the battle. When the huge man deemed that enough of the enemy were exposed, he would lose a flight of arrows and stones into their midst, singling the attack.

David's grip on his sword tightened. His palms were slick with sweat, and his heart pounded in his chest. The moment right before a battle was the worst, Adino had assured him. He glanced left to where Eleazar waited with his swordsmen. Each man wore a shield and either a mail shirt or leather armor adorned with metal studs to help deflect weapons. The man caught David looking and sardonically saluted him with two fingers. David had no idea what that meant.

Then arrows filled the air like a swarm of angry bees and stones snapped through the sky. Philistines cried out in shock and pain, and more than a few fell to the grass writhing in agony or never to move again.

The signal! David charged.

The steep slope provided momentum as he ran and slid to the base. The Philistines had instinctively turned toward the other slope from where the arrows and stones had been released. Indeed, another flight of arrows stabbed out at the Philistines even as David reached the bottom of the slope, creating confusion within the enemy ranks.

The ambush worked perfectly. The enemy had their backs to David's main force. Jehovah was with them! They would win this fight! With a roar of victory, David swung his sword at the nearest enemy warrior. The man only partially turned, and the blade slashed across the man's ribs. The metal corselet he wore deflected much of the blow, but that first slash knocked him off balance enough for David to stab the man in his unprotected belly.

The Philistine gasped in shock and slid back, his life's blood pumping out of the angry wound. David blinked and froze, staring in fascinated horror at the bright-red blood. He'd been training to fight all his life it seemed, but this was the first man he'd ever killed up close. He'd killed Goliath from a distance, and despite having cut the giant's head from his dead body, watching the light and life bleed out of a man was a new experience. The Philistine's blood stained his sword, and he couldn't stop staring at both the dying warrior and his stained blade.

David would have died then. His hesitation, often fatal in battle, nearly cost him his life. Another Philistine, seeing the frozen captain, thrust his spear at David and only Eleazar's timely intervention kept David from being skewered. As it was, the swordsman succeeded in only deflecting the spear, not stopping it, and its sharp edge cut a line across David's right forearm, leaving a trail of blood.

With a gasp, David came back to himself.

"Many more are in need of slaying," Eleazar yelled, stabbing the offending Philistine smoothly and then kicking the body aside. "You came to fight, so let's be about it, Captain!"

Adriel appeared on David's other side, sword and shield at the ready. Galvanized into action, David stabbed a second warrior and shoved the groaning man aside to get at another. He blocked a spear with his sword and hacked off the spearhead, leaving the enemy warrior with naught but a long wooden pole. The warrior immediately twirled it around presenting the sharpened butt end to David. But the captain pushed forward, crowding the warrior up next to his fellows. David found another opening and slashed the man across the throat.

The battle descended into chaos then, and David lost all sense of what was happening in the larger view. He somehow became separated from Adriel and Eleazar, but from what he could tell, their ambush had worked. Nearly eight hundred Hebrews had smashed into the disorganized enemy ranks. Many of the Philistines were killed in those first few seconds, and the momentum clearly favored David and the Indebted.

David fought viciously, if not with any great degree of skill. Mastering a weapon took years, but with adrenaline coursing through his veins and his zeal to defeat the enemies of the LORD, the captain became a terror on the battlefield. He ignored his own minor wounds as he cut down four or five more men. Then he ran into a shield wall, and his momentum was dashed like a wave upon rocks.

The initial surprise had worn off, and the Philistine commanders had brought their ranks back into a uniform structure with heavy infantry out front, supported by the lighter infantry behind. Several squads of light infantry charged across the stream to the north, forcing David's bowmen to engage or retreat. With the cypress trees in the way, he couldn't tell which. Regardless, no more arrows were fired at the Philistines from that direction.

David nearly got killed again as a javelin stabbed out of nowhere from behind the Philistine David was fighting. David yelped in surprise and hopped back, but his opponent, seeing an advantage pressed forward, and David found himself fighting desperately for his life.

Every time he tried to swing at the Philistine, the warrior blocked with his shield and struck back with lightning-fast reflexes. David used his own shield to block, but he also had to worry about the man lurking behind his opponent who would jab his javelin at David whenever an opportunity arose. His newfound skill aside, David had never before fought against two men at once, and he didn't have the reach to menace the javelin wielder.

All along the scrimmage line, the same thing was happening. David's men were being pushed back, and many were taking wounds or being killed by thrown javelins. The enemy saw an advantage, and as the leftmost flank began to yield, David's lines were turned upon themselves, creating confusion and panic.

Hebrew warriors ran into each other, and in some cases, they even attacked one another in their panic. Disorganization became chaos, and chaos led to panic. True to Eleazar and Adino's predictions, the Indebted broke and began to run heedlessly away, throwing aside weapons and armor as they fled.

With the lines jumbled, David managed to extricate himself from his fight and fall back. He barked orders, trying to bring order to the chaos. But no one gave him any heed. He shouted and screamed, pushed and shoved, but it was like trying to stem a waterfall. The press dragged him back even further. He fought desperately to hold his ground, trying to rally several men who, wide-eyed, were frantically trying to get around him. One of them even swung his spear at David. He deflected it, barely, but that gave the men opportunity to literally run him over.

He fell into the thick grass, all sense of orientation lost. He yanked his shield over his head, and men stepped on it or tripped over it in their haste to get away. Heavy kicks bruised and battered David, but all he could do was huddle in a ball until the last man passed.

The moment enough space cleared around him, he leaped to his feet and found himself the sole Hebrew in the center of the meadow, facing an angry army of Philistine warriors. Everyone else had fled the field, and just as Adino had predicted, the spearman had also fled when the Israelite lines had been broken.

For a few heartbeats, no one moved. David faced nearly four hundred Philistine warriors with another four hundred still trying to move onto the battlefield. About twenty cubits separated David from the nearest Philistine. Why the enemy simply didn't charge him, David would never know. Perhaps they feared another ambush. Perhaps they wanted their own ranks in order before pushing on. Regardless, their hesitation allowed David a slim opportunity to escape.

A Philistine thrust his way forward, an armband circling his right arm and his red headdress waving above his head. "Hebrew!" he shouted at David. "You who are about to die, tell us your name."

Slowly, David began to edge backward. He dared not turn to run lest a well-aimed throw send a javelin through his back, so he took slow, careful steps backward toward the east side of the

2 Samuel 23:8 & 1 Chronicles 11:11

meadow to where his men had fled through a narrow opening. If David could reach that point, he could make a temporary stand since only a few men could come at him at a time. It might give him a chance to escape.

And escape was the only thing on David's mind. He had failed. His men were broken and scattered. His lieutenants had abandoned him to the mercies of the enemy. Adino, true to his own fears, had fled. Eleazar had disappeared as well, and David had no clue what had happened to Shammah. David's own armorbearer had also fled the field of battle. Worse yet, David had failed both his God and his king.

Bitterness replaced his fear. He knew, looking into the hateful eyes of the Philistines, that they fully intended to kill him, but death suddenly became the lesser of David's fears. His desire to escape faded and was replaced with the fear of having to report his failure to King Saul. *Better,* he decided, *to die here.* Decision made, his resolve returned. He wouldn't flee. He would stand and fight until his hacked body lay lifeless on the ground.

Glaring at the Philistine captain, he shouted back, "I am David, son of Jesse!"

A murmur rose from the Philistine ranks, and David heard the name of Goliath mentioned not a few times. The Philistine captain nodded, his eyes alight. "Our gods have delivered you into our hands, Hebrew. Your body will be offered to our gods and your head spiked above the gates of Gath!"

David chuckled, thinking such a fate ironic. "Come, Philistine dogs! Come taste my blade and the wrath of my God!"

The Philistines let loose with a roar and charged.

Taking a gamble, David spun and ran toward the ravine mouth, zigzagging to avoid the few spears flung at him. He reached the narrowest spot and turned back around to face his end. His breath came harshly as his body tried to fight off exhaustion and the debilitating effects of his various wounds.

The Philistines' charge was blunted by the narrowing and steep slopes, and the first man to reach David died with a shout to his false god on his lips. The young Hebrew captain, stepped back, wanting the body of the fallen Philistine to help trip the next man in line, but he knew in his heart that his fight was hopeless. He called upon Jehovah Elohim. He wanted the last thing to pass his lips to be praises to the God he loved.

He brought his shield and sword close, calmly preparing to meet the headlong rush of the next two or three men. They would find a different warrior, one who died in the name of the only true God. Resolved to sell his life as expensively as he could, he braced himself for the next enemy warrior.

But he never got the chance to engage.

A blur of leather armor leaped passed David and smashed into the first two Philistines. One, the Philistine captain who had demanded David's name, fell dead, the other tripped and was also quickly dispatched by a lighting fast strike with a spear. And Adino the Spear entered the fray. David stood in stunned silence as his lieutenant became a one-man army unlike anything he'd ever believed possible.

What happened next would be something that would forever be burned into David's mind. He watched in awe as Adino singlehandedly faced down eight hundred men[1] and wreaked destruction upon them with his spear.

The man moved like a cat, leaping, spinning, and stabbing with such speed that David couldn't consciously follow him. Much of what he did wasn't humanly possible. It couldn't be! The thin man never stood still. He never gave the enemy a chance to focus on him or direct a concerted attack. He was like a whirlwind, and he tore into the Philistines, leaving a trail of dead and dying behind him much like a reaper harvesting wheat. He used both ends of his spear, stabbing forward with the spearhead and then stabbing backward with the iron spiked end.

---

[1] 2 Samuel 23:8.

2 Samuel 23:8 & 1 Chronicles 11:11

Then Adriel appeared next to David, his chest heaving as he fought for breath. He watched the spectacle that was Adino, and his jaw dropped. "Impossible," he breathed. "That is not possible."

David didn't respond. He would witness Adino's valor, his redemption, for deep down, David knew that this was what it was. Adino was infused with the Spirit of the LORD. Something within the man had changed, and the hand of God was upon him strongly.

Then Shammah appeared next to David. He paused, surveying the field. "He has them on their heels," he said almost reverently. "By all that is holy, he has them on their heels!"

With a roar that nearly set David's ears to ringing, the huge man charged after Adino, his war club swinging back and forth like a smith's hammer. Then in ones and twos, a few of the braver of David's men returned, paused as Shammah had to witness Adino's lethal dance, and then charged back into the fray.

David wanted to run back into battle as well, but he was rooted to the spot of the ravine mouth. He lifted his sword, stained with the blood of his enemies high, like a banner, like Moses's arms when he held them aloft as Joshua led the Israelites into victorious battle.[2]

The Philistines couldn't stand before Adino. Superstitions fear overcame them. They called out that their gods had abandoned them, that the Hebrew God was stronger this day. The fools. The Hebrew God was always stronger! David's eyes glittered with satisfaction as he watched the enemy melt away, routed by a single man.

In a handful of moments, the meadow was empty except for the dead, the dying, and a handful of Hebrew warriors. The foremost of them, covered in blood, stood straight with his spear held aloft in salute to David.

Exhaustion filled every bone of David's body, and he almost staggered to his knees, but he refused to go down. He would stand and honor Adino the Spear whom the LORD had used to bring about so great a victory.

---

[2] Exodus 17:10-12.

With Adriel by his side, David walked onto the field of battle, and saluted Adino. "Well done," he said. "You are well named, my friend. Adino the Spear is how you shall be known from henceforth."

The lanky man brought his spear back down and shoved the butt into the ground, leaning wearily against it. "I know not what overcame me or how this came to be," he admitted, his voice adopting that tone that bordered on boredom. "I fled with the rest of the men. I saw no sense in dying for naught."

"But you returned," David pressed, trying to understand. "Why?"

The lanky man stood in deliberate thought for a long moment. "When I saw you standing alone before the host, something changed within."

David didn't have the courage to tell the spearman that his stand had been more accidental than deliberate. So he asked, "What changed?"

"I found something worth fighting for—and perhaps dying for."

Unsure if he should intrude into the man's private and obviously enlightening experience, David hesitated. But he had to know. If he could discover what had so inspired his lieutenant, maybe he could win the hearts of the rest of the men. "What did you find that was worth fighting for?"

"*You*, my lord. I'm not sure I can explain it. I just know I did the right thing."

David nodded as if he understood, but truthfully, he didn't. Adino's answer baffled him. He suspected that Elohim's hand had been most responsible, but he had no way to quantify it. But for the first time, David felt a connection to his men, the Indebted. They had bled together, and when people shed blood for the same cause, it does something. It changes them. Bonds them.

"Is there anything you need, Lieutenant?" David asked.

Adino nodded. "Aye, my lord. I request, humbly so, for a few Elah nuts. I've seemed to have run out." With that said, the spearman's eyes rolled up in his head, and he collapsed to the ground, unconscious.

Only then did David notice that not all the blood covering the lieutenant was the enemy's. "Adriel! Attend!" He rushed over to the prone man, fell heavily to his knees, and placed a hand on the man's chest. It rose and fell slowly, but it moved. He was still alive.

Adriel fell to his knees beside David. The armorbearer's voice was thick with emotion. "He saved us," he whispered. "If I hadn't seen it with my own eyes...he slew three hundred men, my lord. This I swear. At least three hundred."[3]

"Aye," David agreed, glancing over the battlefield. Bright red stained much of the browning grass, and the field took on a mystical quality for David. He looked at the fallen headdresses that dotted the landscape, like colorful flower clusters in a brown field. The grass, though trampled badly, also hid much of the horror of death, and the splashes of color seemed almost beautiful. Only in this case, each one represented a fallen enemy soldier.

The LORD had given them a mighty deliverance this day. David had not failed his king, and neither had he failed his God. He paused then, reflecting. That wasn't quite right. It wasn't that David had not failed. Truth be told, David had done very little this day. No, God had not failed, for this time, God had fought for Israel.

This was the LORD's victory.

---

[3] 1 Chronicles 11:11. The 300 here seemingly conflicts with the 800 mentioned in 2 Samuel 23:8. It is possible he faced 800 and killed 300. This is how I chose to tell the story. (See the after-story notes on the timeline for more information.)

9

The scout rose from a stiff bow and then shifted uncomfortably under the king's hard gaze. Saul searched his memory for the scout's name. It came to him slowly. "Be at ease, Joel. What news?"

The scout shuffled his feet, eyes darting about as if seeking escape. The scout had been dispatched to keep an eye on David's company and then to bring back word of the young captain's defeat at the hands of the Philistines. That David would be defeated was expected, indeed a foregone conclusion. What Saul desperately needed to hear was that the harper had fallen in battle as well.

Jonathan and Saul's two daughters had followed the scout into the court. Saul could see that all three of his children were anxious to learn of David's fate. He found it frustrating how easily his children had fallen under the traitorous shepherd's spell. Why was it that he alone could see the evil within David? For a moment, anger flashed through his mind, like a spike driven into rock. Regaining control of himself slowly, he nodded to the scout who continued to shift from foot to foot, looking first at the king then glancing sideways at Jonathan.

Enough. Saul stood, commanding the scout's attention. "Say on, scout. What news?"

The man swallowed hard and cleared his throat. "The Indebted met the Philistines below the valley of Rephaim and fled before them. Many Hebrews were slain."

Saul stifled a smile. *Praise Elohim!* He saw Michal's eyes widen at the news, and Jonathan's face settled into an expressionless mask that fooled no one. A small smirk of satisfaction did reach Saul's lips at his son's discomfort. "And what of my servant David?" he asked, looking the messenger in the eyes.

"He alone stood before the Philistine host, my king. He stood and quelled the tide. The Philistines broke upon him and fled the field of battle." A note of admiration seeped into the scout's voice. "Your servant David lives, my lord. And the Philistines are defeated."

Saul was struck speechless. *No!* It took everything he possessed not to leap forward and strike the offending scout down for his treacherous words. *David survived? Victorious? This cannot be!*

Jonathan stepped forward. "David yet lives?"

The scout's eyes shifted to the king's son. "Aye, my lord. He returns with the survivors. Some two hundred Hebrews lie dead, but more than five hundred Philistines lay slain and broken. The curs have fled back from whence they'd come."

"Then Elohim has wrought a great victory by David's hand!" Jonathan yelled. He spun to look at his father. "The people must hear of this. There must be a feast to celebrate. Your faith in David was not misplaced, Father. Your wisdom has carried the day once again! It is well that you sent him."

Saul couldn't speak. He knew that if he did, the rage that boiled barely below the surface would explode out of him. He nodded in recognition of his son's words, feeling only slightly mollified that his son had attributed David's victory to Saul's wisdom. That had not been the plan, however. David's survival had not been intended. He was supposed to fall upon the field of battle!

A thought struck him with the force of a spear in the gut. Perhaps Elohim was indeed with the son of Jesse. If so, then was the Spirit of the LORD truly gone from Saul? He shuddered, and his rage turned to fear.[1]

---

[1] 1 Samuel 18:15.

Unfortunately, the scout wasn't finished. "The people have already learned of this victory, my lord Jonathan. "The inhabitants of Kesalon even now rejoice in the son of Jesse. They have laid out a great feast for the victorious company and word spreads like wildfire. Within the span of a day, all of Israel will have heard and will rejoice. The people love David, my lord."[2]

Saul glowered at the scout, but the man wasn't even looking at him; his eyes were still on Jonathan as he expounded upon David's victory. The king had to smother this enthusiasm…this love for the shepherd. If what the scout said was true, then he would need to be extra cautious in dealing with the traitorous son of Jesse. Clearly, David meant to take the throne. He and Samuel had conspired together, and somehow the two had persuaded Jehovah to bless their treachery. The situation was intolerable!

Looking back, Saul wondered where things had gone wrong. True, he had made a mistake in offering a sacrifice without an attending Levite, but that had been an honest mistake, made in his zeal to have Elohim bless him.[3] And then there was the whole debacle over the destruction of the Amalekites.[4] What should it have mattered that he had spared some of the best for the LORD and for His people? Samuel's reaction had been overblown and unworthy of the prophet. But none of those mistakes should have driven Samuel to such treacherous lengths! To anoint another to replace Saul was the height of disloyalty.[5] It must be undone.

For just a moment he toyed with the idea of sending his elite soldiers to Ramah and sacking the city if only to see Samuel die. But no, such an action would be unwise. Facing Samuel would ensure that the people would rebel against him. Above all else, Saul could ill afford to turn the heart of the people away from him.

The best way to set things right was to kill David. Perhaps then Samuel would see the errors of his ways and intercede with Elohim

---

[2] 1 Samuel 18:16.
[3] 1 Samuel 13:8-14.
[4] 1 Samuel 15.
[5] 1 Samuel 16:1-13.

1 Samuel 18:16-18

on Saul's behalf. If the Great Seer[6] had done that to begin with, then none of this would have ever happened.

"Father," Jonathan said, eagerly turning to face the king, "what reward should we bestow upon David?"

The question caught Saul off guard. "Reward?"

"Aye, Father. This victory is of Elohim by the hand of David—your servant. Should not such a servant be rewarded?"

He should be dead! Saul shouted in the vaults of his mind. He turned away to hide the struggle of trying to calm himself lest his words and actions betray him. He dared not lift his own hand against David—not yet—not until there was some justification, some action of David's that was untoward, something Saul could use to righteously slay the son of Jesse. *But what?*

The silence was distracting. He needed noise, so he began drumming his fingers on his javelin, listening to the staccato rhythm of the soft sounds.

Then Jonathan broke the silence. "What about a union of our two houses?"

Saul's eyes instantly turned to his two daughters. They had both perked up at this idea, for it was clear that bringing David into the family would mean giving the young captain one of his unwed daughters. The idea appealed to the king, and he began to see a way to bring about David's destruction. It could work. It *would* work.

But which one? He studied his two daughters. Merab's eyes fell to the floor. Saul knew that men found her beautiful, and she would be the easiest to manipulate. He could dangle her in front of David for as long as needed.

Michal, on the other hand, looked at him with fierce eyes that gave not a hairsbreadth when he locked eyes with her. She nodded ever so slightly to indicate that she was willing. *Interesting.* Michal was also a woman of beauty but not so much as her sister. Michal also had an inbred and well-honed sense of duty, which made her likely to obey her father and desire to preserve the kingdom.

---

[6] 1 Samuel 9:9.

Decision made, he smiled and turned back to his son. "Your words carry much wisdom, my son. We should reward the son of Jesse as you suggest. When he arrives, call him to stand before me. Indeed, the time has come to bind him to our house." He glanced at Merab and spoke to her. "I would offer you to him to wife, Merab. Do you find this agreeable?"

Merab straightened in muted delight, but her eyes slid to her sister first, which earned a frown from Saul. Michal stood stiffly, her eyes glaring daggers at her sister. That could be a problem. Saul wanted David dead. He didn't want his own house divided. He would deal with Michal later.

Merab looked away from her sister and focused on her father. Saul raised an eyebrow to indicate he wanted an answer from her. She clasped her hands together, her many bracelets tinkling. "Aye, Father. It is a most advantageous match. I am agreeable."

Of course, it mattered not if she was agreeable, but it was better that she acquiesced willingly.

Jonathan loved the idea. "Father," he said, a smile spreading across his face, "this is a wonderful reward and a good match. Merab is perfect!" That remark produced a glare from Michal which he failed to notice. "Again, your wisdom is to be praised."

Saul held up a hand, frowning. "I did not say I would *give* your sister to him. I said I would 'offer' her to him."

Now Jonathan frowned, his enthusiasm squandered. "I do not understand."

"This is apparent, my son. Your sister should not be casually given to any man. What dowry should the son of Jesse give for her?"

"But, Father—" Jonathan began.

Saul cut him off. "The son of Jesse has naught but what his father possesses. Do you truly believe that all Jesse possesses would replace the loss of a king's daughter? She would become part of their household."

"You are king," Jonathan agreed. "You would gain a son-in-law who has served both God and you well."

"There is that," Saul conceded. "However, it would be unseemly to give her away for naught. I will have the son of Jesse pay her dowry with the blood of our enemies."

"Has he not already done this? He slew the giant—upon whose body you did already promise the hand of your daughter—and he defeated the Philistines just now. What more could he do?"

Saul frowned. He didn't like to be reminded of the promise he'd made. "I will keep my promise, my son, but there are battles yet remaining. The Philistines esteem us lightly and will return. If the LORD is with David, then the son of Jesse will be our sword, our might. In this, he will surely pay adequate dowry for your sister." To forestall any further objections from his son, he demanded, "Do you think the son of Jesse unable to perform such a task?"

Jonathan hesitated. Clearly, he understood that only one answer would be acceptable. "Aye, my lord. David will prevail."

Ignoring the ambiguity of that last statement, Saul said, "Then it is so commanded. Call forth the son of Jesse to stand before me when he returns. Let us see how David feels on the matter."

Two days later, David presented himself before his king. Saul had rehearsed this moment in his mind, so he was able to check his fury and speak amicably to the son of Jesse. "You are well come, my son," he began. "I would hear of your victory."

David seemed to swell under the praise, and a smile spread across his lips. He bowed to Saul again—perhaps the third time in as many minutes—and told the story. Interestingly, David did not claim all the glory. He spoke of Jashobeam and his mighty deeds in felling many of the enemy warriors alone and with but a spear. Saul could hardly credit the story. Three hundred slain by one man? Such a thing had not been seen in Israel since Samson had judged the people.[7] He spoke of Adriel, Shammah, and someone called Eleazar.

---

[7] Judges 15:15.

Of these men, Saul knew only Adriel, Jonathan's former armorbearer. Clearly, his eldest son had sent the talented man to aid David.

David himself seemed changed by his experiences. He appeared harder, less naive about the world. He had grown too. His body had filled out even further, and his beard, once scraggly, was now full. His skin had darkened under the sun, and he'd lost that once ruddy appearance that had so endeared itself to Saul. Good. David sported any number of wounds, testament that he had been in the thick of the fight and not just a spectator as his words seemed to suggest. He carried himself with more surety and he had an air of command that he once lacked. Grudgingly, Saul admitted that David had grown well into the position laid upon him.

When David finally wound down, Saul put on his most serene face and said, "You have served me well, my son. What would you that I do for you?"

David's pompous response was expected. "I need no reward, my king. I am your servant, and my duty is to you and our God."

"Well said, my son. But such valor as yours should not go unrewarded. It is in my mind to promote you in a special way." He gestured, and Merab stepped forward from where she had been standing next to her sister. "Behold my elder daughter, Merab. I will give her to be your wife."[8]

David looked appropriately stunned by this revelation. Saul leaned forward in his chair to hear the harper's response. The son of Jesse looked at Merab for a long moment, a smile creeping onto his lips, and then, incredibly, he glanced at Michal and recoiled slightly. Saul's eyes flickered in that direction. *Curse that girl,* he raged inwardly.

Michal resembled a thunderstorm for all the calm she projected. Her clenched fists and narrow eyes bled disapproval in waves. The girl was threatening to undermine everything. Saul stood

---

[8] 1 Samuel 18:17.

then, forcing everyone to look at him. "Well, son of Jesse? What say you?"

"Who am I, my king, and what is my life or my father's family in Israel that I should be son-in-law to the king?"[9]

Perhaps not quite the response Saul was hoping for. He gave it a moment's thought and decided that David was worried about the dowry. He'd planned for that. "I seek only that you be valiant for me and fight the LORD's battles,"[10] he told David. "You will be as Jacob when he sought the daughter of Laban to wife.[11] Fight for me, and in a time appointed, I will give Merab to you to wife. Such service will suffice, my son."

Saul hoped the reference to Rachel would hit a nerve. Everyone knew that Rachel was buried outside of Bethlehem, David's hometown.[12] The connection should appeal to David.

It worked. David's eyes cleared of confusion, and he stood straighter. "Then I am your servant, my lord. I will fight the LORD's battles and bring honor to your name."

Saul swallowed a grunt and said, "See that you do then, my son, and know that I am well pleased. I will think on the details of this blessed arrangement and will in time call your father to confer further."

The dismissal was obvious. David bowed again, though perhaps with not enough deference to suit Saul, and left. Merab looked at her father, her eyes asking a question. He sighed and gestured his permission. She hesitated a moment and then hurried after David.

Wryly, Saul thought his daughter's infatuation a good thing. Any hook into David's spirit would just hasten the wicked shepherd's end.

---

[9] 1 Samuel 18:18.
[10] 1 Samuel 18:17.
[11] Genesis 29:18.
[12] Genesis 35:19.

David's spirits soared as he left Saul's court and went out into the hallway. Adriel awaited him there, and the moment he saw David's smile, he matched it with one of his own.

"Our king was pleased?" the armorbearer asked.

Not able to wipe the grin off his face, David nodded. "More than that, my friend. The king has offered me his eldest daughter to wife!" David's enthusiasm could not be contained, and he slapped Adriel on the shoulder. "Is this not a joyful occasion?"

Adriel's face had stilled, but David didn't notice. The door to King Saul's court opened and the subject of their conversation stepped through, softly closing the door behind her. David couldn't help but admire Merab. She was truly a woman of great beauty, and the idea of being wed to her thrilled him. Along with nearly every available male near King Saul, he had harbored the hope that he would be able to become Saul's son-in-law, but he had never really thought it would happen. He didn't really know how it could be done, seeing as his father's house was so far removed from the power center in Gibeah. But then Saul had changed all of that with but a few words.

Merab stood meekly before him. Her eyes flickered to Adriel, and David detected a measure of desperate pleading in them. He wasn't sure what it meant, but he did remember Jonathan warning him that both Merab and Adriel had sought for the union to which David now laid claim. He gave his armorbearer a suspicious look, but the man's face was impassive, his eyes distant.

Merab's eyes shifted back to David. "My lord," she began, "I hope you find this arrangement acceptable." There was a questioning note to the statement.

"Aye, Merab. I find it most pleasing. Do you think your father would have us wait long to betroth us?"

She gave a small shrug that caused her jewelry to dance, reflecting the light from the oil lamps in the hallway. "I know not. Father appears to want my dowry paid in the lives of the Philistines. It would seem he has left this in your hands, my lord."

1 Samuel 18:16-18

"Then I will be most zealous in its fulfillment," he promised, knowing in his heart that fulfilling Saul's requested dowry could take years.

Common betrothals often lasted a year, but that happened only after both parties agreed on the dowry and the future husband had paid the dowry in full. King Saul's reference to Jacob and Rachel was prophetic. Jacob had worked fourteen years in the end to wed Rachel. David sincerely hoped it would not take that long.

He cleared his throat. "But what of you, Merab? Do you find this union acceptable?"

"Aye, my lord, I do," she said. "You are now the foremost warrior among my father's servants. All of Israel looks to you. You will bring much honor to my father and his house."

Perhaps David wished for a more…enthusiastic response, but marriage was rarely about love and more about mutual advantage for the two families involved.[13] For David, he would become the king's son-in-law, and for Saul, he would gain a loyal warrior tied to his house forever.

Merab continued, "I will be most anxious to present myself to your family, my lord. Is your mother well?"

This pleased David. "Aye. My mother is well, and she will doubtless be agreeable to our match as will my father and brothers."

Merab smiled and bowed. "I look forward to our betrothal then, my lord, and will pray for your speedy fulfillment of the dowry."

She whisked off, leaving David standing in the hallway with Adriel. Both watched the girl leave, but both had extremely different thoughts running through their minds.

Adriel turned slightly to address David. "Did the king set a dowry price then?"

David shook his head. "Not exactly. He ordered me to fight the LORD's battles, and Merab would be given to me at the time

---

[13] See story explanations on marriage at the conclusion of the novel.

appointed. He appointed no time. Perhaps he wishes to bargain over the details with my father."

Adriel snorted softly, his version of a short laugh. "Saul is king. Your father will agree to whatever conditions he states."

True enough. David sighed. "Then I must be strong. I fear that the king will send us forth once again to fight the Philistines."

Now Adriel sighed. "Indeed."

The door opened again, and another girl planted herself before David. Michal's small eyes were flinty. "Are you well pleased?" she spat out.

"Pleased?" David asked, confused. It was the wrong response, but in his defense, David had little experience with angry females.

"About my sister!" she shouted. "Is my lord happy with his purchase? Does she please you well?"

"I—I…" David trailed off realizing he had no good response to that question. Instead, he said, "It was your father's idea, Michal."

She ripped off her veil, causing David to flinch. Married women would often go about without a veil and some unwed girls as well—usually of the lower class—so seeing a woman's face was not all that unusual, but he had never before seen Michal's face. He gaped at her, realizing she was very pretty. Even the mole growing on the side of her nose looked endearing.

"Do you find me displeasing, my lord?" she asked without any semblance of modesty in her voice.

"Nay," he whispered, feeling his blood pound in his veins.

Her eyes softened some. "Then mayhap you can think on that." She reattached her veil and walked calmly off, her anger abating as quickly as it had surged.

"Did you understand any of that?" David appealed to Adriel as he stared after the retreating girl.

"Aye, my lord. She wishes you to think on that."

David sighed. "You are doing that on purpose!" he accused. Grumbling to himself, he gestured curtly. "Come, my friend, let us leave lest any other women come forth from those doors."

Together they hastened away.

10

King Achish walked up the stone steps of the temple of Dagon, his mind wreathed in turmoil. He desperately needed some assurance right then for word of his army's defeat at the hands of the son of Jesse had reached him.

The huge temple, carved out of stone, was the most prominent structure in Gath. It faced west, toward the sea to the west, and indeed, from its lofty height, the Great Sea could even be seen on a clear day.

Behind him trailed his ceremonial guard, their red headdresses fluttering in the breeze that blew in off the Great Sea. Among those who followed was the one called Maon, the young man who claimed kinship with David, the son of Jesse.

At the top of the temple steps, Achish turned toward the rebel Hebrew. "Join me, Maon."

Tentatively, the young Hebrew climbed the steps to stand beside the king of Gath.

"Have you ever been in the temple of our god?" Achish asked in a pleasant voice.

"Nay, my king, I have not been permitted."

Achish studied the young Hebrew speculatively. Unlike most of the Philistines, Maon's head was straight, not sloped, and his brown eyes lacked the darkness more common to the Philistines. Maon's hair had grown out some since he had arrived, the brown locks tied in a Philistine style that looked odd on Hebrew features.

He was shorter than the average Philistine, but from what Achish understood, this was of average height for the enemies to the east.

The Philistine lord waved for the Hebrew to follow. "Then come and witness the true might and strength of the Philistine race."

Achish marched to the polished gold doors of the temple where two priests, warriors in their own right, stood guard. The two guards shoved the huge doors ponderously open.

The temple inside was a buzz of activity. An altar stained with the blood of its latest victim stood before the pedestal of Dagon. Upon the pedestal was a statue of the god Dagon. Half-man, half-fish, the idol rose high into the air, dominating the temple.

"Behold, Dagon, your god," Achish said, bowing low to the idol.

Maon hastily followed with a bow of his own. "Am I not permitted to worship Ashtaroth?" he asked as he straightened.

"Of course," Achish agreed, "the Queen of Heaven is always worthy of worship and service. But do you know why we serve Dagon?"

"Nay, my king."

Achish walked over to the wall, careful to avoid treading on the threshold of Dagon's pedestal,[1] and ran his hands over the carvings that showed the Philistines emerging from the sea onto the land.

"Dagon brought us forth from the sea to find a home here," he explained. "Legend says that life started in the sea, and Dagon is master of the sea. When we came to this land, Dagon was here already and gave us mastery of the people here before us. We owe him much."

Maon's eyes gleamed as he listened. "This is a marvelous tale, my king."

"It is more than a tale," Achish corrected, smiling. "It is our history, our way of life. We defeated all our enemies, conquered a fertile land, and even prevailed against the Egyptian gods." His smile disappeared. "Until the cursed Hebrews boiled out from the east like

---

[1] 1 Samuel 5:5. This likely carried over to other temples of Dagon as well.

a plague, slaughtering everyone and everything before them." He glanced at Maon. "The one called Joshua tried to take our lands, but he failed.[2] We have been at perpetual war since. The Hebrews have ever been a thorn in Dagon's side. Did you know that your ancestor, Abraham, once walked our lands as our guest?"[3]

Maon looked surprised. "Nay, my lord."

"We have many legends, many tales of the Hebrews and their God from long ago. Always Dagon has prevailed, but I tell you truly, the Hebrew God has grown in strength in recent years. First Saul came and stirred up our ancient enmity when peace had at last prevailed between our two people. And now there is the one called David. Have you heard of our recent defeat at the hands of your brother?"

Maon stiffened. "Call him not my brother, I pray. I am stricken from books of the house of Israel, and I call no Hebrew my kin."

Achish nodded. "That is well. Howbeit, you know him. Do you think we can entice him away from King Saul? Or must he be slain?"

"You must slay him, my king," Maon said slowly. "He will not be enticed away from his God."

Achish sighed. "That is regrettable. His skill in battle has been noteworthy, and with him at my side, I think I can easily quell some of our more rebellious nations."

Maon shook his head. "He will not be enticed. This I swear."

"Then he must be slain." Looking over at his guard, Achish motioned to a swarthy-faced man to approach. The man had remained concealed among the soldiers, unobtrusive. The Philistine Lord noted that Maon flinched in surprise at the man's sudden appearance. *Good.* "You know my will?" he asked the man.

"Aye, Lord. David, the son of Jesse, will be slain. This I swear." The man beat his chest with a fist in an odd salute.

"Then go," Achish said, grinning, "and bring me his head. You will have twice its weight in gold as a reward."

---

[2] Joshua 13:2-3; Judges 3:1-4.
[3] Genesis 21:24.

1 Samuel 18:15-16

The dark-skinned man didn't so much as crack a smile as he turned and slipped silently out the temple doors. The highly trained assassin was their best. David was as good as dead.

David's top lieutenants clustered around him on the hill slope, overlooking the camp preparations of the Indebted. They met openly like this at least once a day to discuss strategy and plans for the company. It did the men good to see their commanders working on their behalf.

Shammah, large and foreboding, and wearing a perpetual scowl regardless of his mood, predicted, "We'll be prepared to march within two hours." His bushy beard was braided at the edges and interwoven with red beads. David still hadn't mustered enough nerve to ask the man what the beads meant or why he sometimes chose bones instead of beads.

"That is well," David said. In fact, it was excellent. Not so long ago, the men would have taken much longer to break camp, complaining and arguing with each other every second of the way.

Eleazar broke off his soft whistling long enough to ask, "The king's command is pressing then?"

"Aye," David answered. "Abner reports that the Philistines are stirring around Lachish and Mareshah."

"And he wants us to defend the cities," Eleazar finished.

"More the region," Shammah interjected. "The Philistines probably won't try to take the cities directly, but they will likely raid, stealing sheep, cattle, and razing fields."

Eleazar traced a scar on the back of his hand, one earned during the battle in the ravine meadow. He viewed it with distaste as he said, "Winter will be upon us soon. Is it wise to be marching out now? Surely the Philistines will wait until spring to continue their depredations. I'm not all that keen on camping in a tent all winter."

Neither was David. As a partial reward, Saul had officially given him a house in Gibeah. He would've liked to have spent at least one night in the house, but that was not to be. He shuddered, thinking about the cold nights to come.

"And what about supplies?" the vain lieutenant continued. "Are we to rely upon Lachish or Mareshah to succor us? I tell you, they will take a dim view of such appropriation. They will have enough to feed themselves through the winter and spring, but not if they have to feed an additional thousand men."

Adino, looking like he was half-asleep as he leaned lazily against his spear, rolled one eye toward the swordsman. "We'll just have to raid Philistine cities for the supplies we need."

"In winter? My friend, that last battle has rattled your wits. The weather is too unpredictable in winter. I told you what would happen when we last fought the Philistines, but no one listened. Perhaps you will listen now."

David grinned at the swordsman. "You speak witlessly. We won the last battle—unlike your prediction."

"Adino won it. The rest of us ran—as I foretold." The plain-looking man frowned, thinking. "Not all ran," he corrected, glancing sheepishly at David.

The young captain acknowledged the concession with a slight nod. "Jehovah-jireh[4] will provide," he stated pointedly. "When has He not?"

The swordsman frowned and rubbed his arms as if already feeling winter's cold bite. "Aye, that is true. I just hate relying upon an unknown. Can you not inquire of the LORD and ask *how* He plans on preserving us through the winter?"

"I did seek the LORD," David answered, thinking back on the LORD's words. "I know only that I am to yield to my master's command. Saul sends us forth, so forth we go."

"That is not all that comforting," Eleazar grumbled.

David shrugged. "How are the men's spirits?" he asked, looking at Shammah. The huge man had a better connection with

---

[4] The name Abraham gave to the place where God provided a ram to sacrifice in place of his son, Isaac (Genesis 22:8, 14).

1 Samuel 18:15-16

the men than the other lieutenants. Eleazar was too aloof, and Adino too lazy. Shammah, however, loved interacting with the men and felt most at home among them. David, as their overall commander and something of a legend, was still trying to find his own place with them.

"They are well, my Captain," the huge man rumbled, rubbing a hand over his bald scalp. "The meadow victory did much for them. Most were shamed that they ran. They know you stood alone to face the enemy, and they love you for it. They are more willing to fight, and they are more active in their training. Even Eleazar must agree."

"Nay, I do not," the swordsman snapped. He hesitated. "But, aye, it is true."

Shammah reached into a pouch and pulled out a small bottle. He poured some of the containing oil in his hand and then began to rub it into his scalp.

David watched in astonishment. "What are you doing?" he demanded.

The big man eyed David. "I rub oil into the skin once a week."

"Whatever for?"

"It promotes hair growth," he replied.

David chuckled in disbelief. "Your head is still bald," he pointed out. Looking at the man's massively bushy beard, he added, "Behold, your hair has fallen through your face!"

The bald man adopted an injured look. "It hasn't had time to work yet is all."

"And how long have you been doing thus?"

Adino who, around chewing on his ever-present Elah nuts, answered. "Years."

Shammah scowled at his fellow lieutenants. "It will work! It but requires more time."

David looked at the man's head, now glistening brightly with the oil and then at the man's huge clenched fist and decided to leave well enough alone. "We'll take the road to Socoh," he said. "Have the men ready to march in two hours." He thought of something.

"And what of our numbers? How many men can we array for battle?"

Shammah broke into a grin. "That's the good news. We are at full strength. Volunteers have been trickling in for weeks now."

"Volunteers?" David echoed, shocked.

"Aye. They heard how Elohim delivered us in battle. Everyone believes the hand of Jehovah is upon you, so we're getting volunteers. If this keeps up, we will no longer be the Indebted."

This was amazing news, and David felt some tension bleed out of him. Most of the Indebted were simply biding their time until their six years of service was up,[5] but the attrition rate was so high among them that few ever lived that long, so anything they could do to stall the inevitable they did. But with volunteers, the whole dynamic and spirit would change. This was indeed good news!

Adino, who still appeared to be half-asleep, spoke up. "We've got company."

Everyone looked around and saw a group of men heading toward the camp from Gibeah, walking slowly. The leader was obviously Adriel, but the others were still too indistinct in the sun's glare. They all waited a moment as the men drew closer, and then David let out a whoop of delight and charged down the slope to meet them, leaving behind his bewildered lieutenants.

David had recognized the white-haired old man following his armorbearer. Jesse, his father, had come.

He intercepted them and fell into a tight embrace with his father. Tears graced both cheeks as he kissed the aged face and hugged him tightly. "Father, I am most joyful that you have come to see me."

Jesse's wrinkled face looked a bit more haggard than David remembered, and he seemed to lean more heavily on his walking staff than in years previously, but the sparkle in his father's eyes brought peace to David's heavy heart.

---

[5] Deuteronomy 15:12.

He glanced at the other men, his brothers, and smiled even broader. "Eliab, Abinadab, is it well with you?"

His two eldest brothers nodded, smiling. "It is well with us," Eliab said. "Shammah[6] sends greetings, but he remains in Bethlehem to tend to his wife and newborn son."

That thrilled David. "He has another son then! What did they name him?"

"Jonadab.[7] He is a goodly child, and Shammah is most pleased as is his wife."

"This is indeed good news! But come to my tent, and we will talk."

David led his family into the camp. As they passed through the tents, the men bowed or nodded deferentially to David. Abinadab, ever the warrior, looked about with approval. "You run a good camp, my brother. You have done well."

"Thank you," David replied, pleased.

"Your men appear somewhat unfit, however," his lithe brother added. "I mean no disrespect. Simply an observation."

"No harm done. You are correct, however. Most of these men are untrained and indebted. My lieutenants are working hard to prepare them, but the road is long. Any suggestions would be gladly accepted."

Abinadab looked around again and nodded. "I will speak with your lieutenants before I leave. Perhaps there are a few things I can suggest."

"I thank you, my brother."

They reached David's tent, which, fortunately, was larger than the tents the common solider owned, and they all stooped inside and sat in a circle. Adriel remained by the entrance where he could see to any needs.

David passed around a wineskin to quench everyone's thirst and then turned eagerly to Jesse. "What bring you here, Father?"

---

[6] Not David's lieutenant, but David's third eldest brother (1 Samuel 17:3).
[7] 2 Samuel 13:3 (Shimeah is the same as Shammah.).

"King Saul summoned me to stand before him and speak my mind concerning the matter of his daughter being given to you to wife." He smiled. "I wanted to speak to you first, my son, and know your mind."

Eliab gave David a half smirk. "Imagine our surprise when Saul's messenger brought word. My brother—my *little* brother—is to be the king's son-in-law. As this concerns the whole family, I decided to attend Father on his journey and hear of the matter myself. Tell us how this miracle came to be."

"Do you know of our victory over the Philistines?" David asked.

Abinadab nodded. "Aye. Who has not? It is being talked and sung of far and near. They say you slew five hundred men, David."

As ever, David was amazed at how rumor could bloat itself, like a dead animal lying long in the sun. He shook his head and smirked. "Nay. I slew few. One of my lieutenants, Jashobeam, son of Zabdiel,[8] slew at the very least three hundred."

"I know of him. Is he not called Adino the Spear?"

"Aye. He slew with the spear in his hand." David leaned forward. "I have never seen the like, my brother. He was like the whirlwind. Anytime the Philistines attempted to trap him, he would spin away, confusing them. I wonder if many were killed by the hand of their own countrymen as they tried to catch him. I but watched."

Abinadab nodded slowly. "But word says that you faced the enemy host alone."

"For but a moment, brother. I slew perhaps two before Adino intervened. The victory surely belongs to Elohim. The Lord's hand was upon Adino, for surely he would have been slain otherwise." David looked at his father. "But this battle and victory is what persuaded Saul to reward me and to offer Merab to me to wife."

Jesse leaned back a bit, considering. "And what dowry does the king wish?"

---

[8] 1 Chronicles 27:2.

"It is a dowry of service, Father. I am to fight the LORD's battles, and at the time appointed, Merab will be betrothed to me."

Eliab clapped David on the arm. "For surely this betrothal could not take place before your battles, eh? Else you would not go forth to battle."

"Aye. The betrothed must not go into battle,"[9] David agreed, having not seen the sense of this before. In fact, newly married men were not required to go to war for at least a year,[10] but this last was considered less vital than the betrothed not going into battle. So it made sense that Saul would wait until the dowry service was complete to finalize the betrothal. "But no time has been appointed, Father."

Jesse laid a comforting hand on his son's arm. "I sense your disquiet, my son. Fear not. I will speak to the king, and we will appoint a time."

David's muscles relaxed under the sound of his father's voice. "I thank you, Father."

For the next twenty minutes, their talk centered about family. David learned that his nephews had all vowed to become warriors and join David's company after hearing of his victory, and the thought of Joab and his brothers one day fighting alongside David warmed his heart. He missed them.

No one mentioned Maon, David's missing brother. Maon had been cut off from Israel after his betrayal and blasphemy. His name had been stricken from the family records, and he was to be treated as if he'd never been born. David knew that his father grieved over Maon, but their culture would not permit him to do so openly.

Finally, David rose to his feet and bowed to his father. "Thank you for coming to see me," he said. "But forgive me, for I must beg your forbearance. We are under the king's orders to garrison at Lachish for the winter. It seems the Philistine dogs are restless."

---

[9] Deuteronomy 20:7.
[10] Deuteronomy 24:5.

His father and brothers also rose to their feet. They exchanged kisses on both cheeks, and Jesse promised to offer a sacrifice on David's behalf. His brothers murmured parting words and promised to offer prayers on David's behalf as well. Being the youngest of eight brothers, David had never been particularly close to his older brothers, but he was gratified by their words.

Abinadab paused at the tent entrance. "I will speak with your lieutenants and offer some advice in preparing your men for future battle. I hope it will help."

"I'm sure it will, brother. Thank you."

After they had departed, David turned to Adriel. "Let's break camp. We've got a long march ahead of us."

The armorbearer put on a wistful expression. "I have need of Shammah's club then."

"What?"

"It's probably the easiest way to break the camp," Adriel said, deadpan.

11

David's arrival in Lachish, a small walled town at the edge of the fertile Shephelah plain[1] and to the southwest of Gibeah, set off a two-day celebration.[2] The elders invited David and his chief lieutenants to a feast held in their honor. The rumor-mill had already spread the details of David's exploits throughout the region—and some of the rumors were even true, but most exaggerated David's role, particularly in the meadow battle.

If Adino the Spear felt any angst over the downplaying of his incredible feat in singlehandedly killing roughly three hundred Philistines, he didn't display it. The lanky man showed little interest in the feast until a bowl of Elah nuts was produced. The thin man spent most of the evening stealing what he could to replenish his dwindling supply. On the whole, Adino was perhaps one of the most egoless men David had ever met.

The elders fully expected David to rout the raiding Philistines who were rampaging throughout the countryside and to protect the coming spring crops. He felt a little out of his depth. He had no idea if he could be what everyone expected him to be. Even the men of his command had begun to believe the rumors. There was a swagger to their walk that hadn't existed before. Their confidence in David

---

[1] Called the Plain of the Philistines in Obadiah 1:19, Shephelah is the Hebrew pronunciation of the lowlands that lead to the Mediterranean Sea and primarily occupied by the Philistines.
[2] 1 Samuel 18:16.

had grown, and his name was uplifted in drink around cooking fires, and at least twice, David had to send a drunken Shammah to his tent before his boasting got out of hand about how David would personally skin every Philistine alive. The bald man's descriptions of how to skin a human being had left David feeling somewhat nauseated. The man liked his strong drink too much, and once he had a flagon or two, his tongue loosened beyond his ability to control.

David's presence in the region did have an immediate effect on the Philistines. The raids dropped off significantly. Whether this was due to David's growing reputation or a turning in the weather as winter had finally arrived, he could not guess.

But he still worried. The young captain found sanctuary in Jehovah Elohim, knowing his God would see him through the battles ahead. Only one other thing helped. Now that Saul had offered him his eldest daughter to wife, he felt certain he'd gained the king's favor. This relieved a lot of pressure from the young captain's shoulders and gave him a measure of confidence he sorely needed.

Winter settled in and the temperature dropped—not enough to snow but enough to bring discomfort to the men encamped outside of Lachish. David's greatest challenge became finding ways to keep his men active—and warm.

One of the first things David implemented was to set up a series of outposts all within sight of each other. If the Philistines stirred in the immediate region, signal fires could be lit, and David would know of the enemy's movements within moments.

Unfortunately, few relished the idea of being isolated out in the cold wilderness and saw outpost duty as a form of punishment. Displeased by the complaining and grumbling, David set out to dispel that notion, so he often trekked out to the watch posts in an effort to raise morale.

So it was on a freezing, blustery afternoon that David trudged out to make one of his informal inspections of the watch posts.

"It's cold, my lord," the man trudging beside him complained.

1 Samuel 18:15-16

David wrapped his fur-lined cloak tighter around him and shivered. "Aye, that it is, Machbanai," David answered the young man at his side as they wove their way up the hillside to the third of the outposts northeast of Lachish.

Machbanai, perhaps four years older than David, grumbled something under his breath that the wind whipped away before David could hear it.

"What was that?" he asked his companion.

"It is nothing, my lord," the man spat out louder. He truly looked miserable, hunched over and shivering into the freezing wind.

"Take heart," David said, trying to ease his companion's misery. "This is the last outpost we will visit this day."

Machbanai grunted. "That is well. I find this cold weather abominable."

David wanted to remind the man that he hadn't been required to come, but he knew that wasn't precisely true. His lieutenants would not let David make these inspections alone, and the young captain guessed that Machbanai had been unlucky enough to have been chosen. Either that or he'd lost at dice playing against Shammah.

The third of a series of five watch posts northeast of Lachish had been constructed atop a lonely hill that overlooked the Shephelah plain to the east. "Construction" though was perhaps an exaggeration. The post consisted of a tent raised in the lee of hill to try to reduce the effect of the wind and a wooden platform at the hill's apex. Perhaps the height of two men, the platform would be easily visible by the next watch post to the southwest if set on fire.

One man huddled next to a campfire just below the tent when David and Machbanai walked up. "My lord!" the scout shouted, jumping to his feet when he saw David.

"Be at ease," David said, huddling up to the fire. Machbanai sighed deeply as he felt the warmth of the fire, causing David to grin. "I came to see if you needed anything," he continued. "This is a lonely post to be sure. Where is your companion?"

The scout pointed to the top of the hill. "He's watching the plain for signs of the Philistines, my lord." He shrugged. "They probably have no more liking for this cursed cold than we do."

David's grin broadened. Scouts were often an outspoken bunch, for they more than others lived in constant peril. The closest Philistine stronghold was Gath almost due north, but the Philistine raiders had been attacking more from the west and southwest in recent months. David believed that Abner's main army to the northwest was the reason why the raids had shifted farther south. His scouts were the first line of defense many of the southern cities had.

David gestured to the hill. "Well, call him in then. Let him warm himself by the fire while we talk."

"Aye, he'll be sore glad," the scout replied, echoing David's grin. He faced the hill and shouted, "Pelet! Get your rotting carcass down here! Captain's here to scourge you for laziness!" The scout looked apologetically to David. "He needs motivation, and this is the whole truth."

David nodded, suppressing a smirk. They waited, but Pelet didn't emerge from whatever spot he had found to keep an eye on the plain below.

"Perhaps he heard you not," Machbanai suggested, edging even closer to the fire.

The scout frowned. "The wind is blowing most fierce, but still…" he trailed off, looking at the crest of the hill.

David looked regretfully at the fire and rose to his feet. "Come, let us find your companion."

"He had better not have fallen asleep," the scout said darkly.

"In this weather?" David asked mildly.

"True."

Machbanai didn't volunteer to walk with them to the crest, and David didn't have the heart to pull him away from the comforting heat of the flickering campfire. So David and the scout walked stiffly toward the top. The moment they crested the hill, the wind grew even more forceful, whipping the leafless tree branches and dead grass violently. David leaned into the wind to keep from sliding back down the hill.

Mutely, the scout pointed in the direction toward a huddled form next to the tree. Tears stinging his cheeks from the cold, David squinted into the wind and frowned. The bowed figure beside the tree wasn't moving.

And that's when he saw the blood.

For a moment, David froze, and that probably cost the life of the scout standing next to him. A shadow detached itself from other shadows gathered beneath the platform of the unlit signal fire and hurled itself at David.

He saw the flash of sunlight off a knife blade, and he flung up an arm in a desperate effort to ward off the attack and barely managed to knock aside the stabbing knife—right into the chest of the scout standing with David.

The scout gapped in stupefied horror at the knife blade sticking out of his chest, and his eyes lifted pleadingly to David's. The shadow holding the blade cursed in the thickly accented language of the Philistines.

Roaring in anger and with a surge of adrenalin lending him strength, David punched out at the assassin even as his attacker jerked his knife out of the scout's chest. David's blow glanced off his assailant's shoulder but succeeded in knocking the other back a step or two.

David instinctively turned to the scout to lend what aid he could but saw he was too late. Blood poured out of the man's mouth and his eyes dimmed as he collapsed to the ground dead. Then the assassin attacked again, and David narrowly avoided a similar fate. The cold and gusty wind impeded the Philistine's movements, and that alone doubtless saved David. The lunge missed, but the young captain had no intention of letting the assassin try again, so he leaped on the Philistine, and the two hit the ground hard.

For long moments, they grappled thus—the assassin, older and stronger, trying to plunge his knife into David's body, and David straining with all the strength he could muster to keep the bloody blade away from his body.

The assassin rolled atop David, pushing his knife inexorably toward David's heart. The swarthy face of the Philistine grinned as the young captain's strength began to fade. "Our gods will be avenged upon you, son of Jesse," he hissed. "The blasphemy of your existence will be expunged from the earth."

Panicking, David called upon Elohim, "Jehovah! Help me!"

The Philistine assassin's grin broadened. "There is none who can help you, no god to save you."

And for a moment, David felt sure that the assassin was right. But motion caught the Philistine's attention and he whipped his head up to see Machbanai charging up the hill, sword held aloft and face set in determination.

Cursing viciously in his native tongue, the Philistine jerked his knife up, ripping away David's already weakening grip to free his hands, and then from his kneeling position above David, he threw the knife at Machbanai in a smooth, practiced cast. David watched helplessly as the knife rammed hard into Machbanai's stomach. The injured man staggered back, his face turning unnaturally white. He slipped, fell, and rolled down the hill where he lay quite still, one hand holding the hilt of the dagger imbedded in his stomach.

Angry now beyond thought, David jabbed stiffened fingers into the assassin's exposed neck. The assassin gagged horribly, his eyes widening in shock and pain, but the wily and experienced assassin rolled away before David could attack again.

They climbed warily to their feet, facing each other like two male tigers contesting over territory. The assassin held his ruined throat with one hand, his face pale, and his labored breathing testifying to the injury David had inflicted. Grimly, David drew his sword, noticing without remorse that the assassin had no other weapon.

The Philistine's face began to turn blue as he struggled to breathe, but David would give him no chance to recover. He leaped forward as Eleazar had taught him in a quick strike that took the assassin full in the heart.

David left the dead assassin and stumbled quickly down the hill to where Machbanai lay. The young man was still breathing, but his eyes were closed and his lips blue from cold and shock. David dared not remove the dagger, knowing that doing so would most certainly kill the Hebrew solider before help could arrive.

"My lord David?" Machbanai whispered.

"Aye, Machbanai, I am here. Still your tongue and conserve your strength. You will need it."

"I failed you, my lord."

"Nay," David whispered, tears streaming down his cheeks. "You did not. Pray to Elohim."

"I go to His embrace," the young man whispered. "I feel my spirit departing, my lord. Bless me before I die, I beg."

"Blessed is the True Judge who will embrace you this day, my friend."

Machbanai nodded one final time and whispered before he died the concluding phrase of the blessing, "This is also for the good."

David held the dead man for a long time, his tears freezing on his face. At length, he rose, returned to the dying campfire, took a still inflamed brand, and strode back to the top of the hill where he lit the signal fire, calling for help. The help, though, would come too late.

The assassination attempt on David's life sobered the company of Indebted, but the winter passed with little in the way of any further activity to mark it. The Philistines, despite David's forces in the region, did raid a few times, striking and then melting back across the border before David could catch them. Upon the advice of his lieutenants, David countered these depredations by raiding into the enemy lands himself. They burned a few villages, killed the inhabitants if they were too slow to escape, and left a message that the Philistines couldn't ignore. Soon, both sides fell into an unspoken and uneasy truce. If the Philistines didn't raid, then neither did David. Both sides knew, however, that come spring, things would change.

The winter was mild, for the most part. It rarely snowed in the Shephelah plain, but the chilly nights did create a certain amount of unrest with David's troops. Whereas most of the Hebrew army returned to their homes and families during the winter, David and his men were offered no such option. This was the price the Indebted paid—among other things. So to boost troop morale, David sent word out that the families of his men were welcome to come to Lachish. This consideration only enhanced David's reputation and increased the love that his troops had for him. That winter, the city swelled in size to accommodate the increased population, which naturally presented another problem.

How was David to feed everyone through the winter? Fortunately, his father's wealth helped. Jesse was able to send several relief caravans to Lachish at David's request. In fact, his father made a tidy profit off the venture, and everyone went well fed through the cold season.

The only bit of bad news came from David's father, Jesse. The elderly man had tried to establish the dowry terms to be fulfilled by David's service, but nothing had been set. King Saul would commit to nothing. Eventually, Jesse had returned to Bethlehem with only vague promises of settling the terms of the dowry in the spring.

David fret about the matter, but his duties as captain kept his mind occupied for the most part. He felt confident that things would be settled—eventually.

When spring arrived and the farmers began tilling their fields in preparation of the spring planting, David knew that the raids would resume. The fertile ground of the Shephelah plain offered the greatest bounty of the region, and if possible, the Philistines were determined to deprive the Hebrews of this resource.

And by mid-summer, the raids had increased to the point where David and his men were in the field nearly every day—including the Sabbath, for the Philistine dogs had no respect for Jehovah's law. More often than not, just showing up on the field of battle caused the enemy to melt away, but by then the Philistines had accomplished their main objectives. A farm or a field of crops had been destroyed, and black smoke rose to the sky as a testament to the Philistines' deprivations. Some battles were fought in which men on both sides died, but overall, everyone found it a frustrating experience. He couldn't pin down the Philistines long enough to drive them back permanently. He and his men longed to entrap the raiders and destroy them.

Two more assassination attempts were foiled during that time, and David learned of the price on his head. His men thought it flattering and often teased David that his head was more valuable to others than to himself. He found little humor in it himself.

Everything combined to wear David down. He desperately wanted some sort of conclusive battle to end this attrition that bled both sides dry. And that was why David and his men rushed to Pasdammim[3] when they learned of a Philistine raid developing in the Elah Valley on a gloomy, overcast, summer day.

Eleazar cursed as he watched the smoke rising high into the sky, the grayish smoke mingling with the gray clouds. "They're burning the fields," he reported.

David looked on, his face schooled into a hardness that hadn't existed in him a year ago. He'd already seen too much bloodshed, seen too many friends and companions die. "Typical Philistine raid," David muttered. "Slay the farmers if you can and burn the fields."

"We'll need those crops come next winter," Shammah rumbled from the other side of David. The big man glanced at his captain. "If we don't stop these raids, a lot of people will go hungry come winter. What think you? We have, at last, position over the Philistines. We

---

[3] 1 Chronicles 11:13. Also called Ephes-dammim in 1 Samuel 17:1, it is located in the valley of Elah.

could entrap them, crush them, and send a message that they would not soon forget."

"Aye," David agreed.

The three of them had concealed themselves in the shadows of the hilltop trees. From their vantage point, he could study the terrain ahead. To the east, he could see the place where he had slain Goliath. The Elah Valley stretched out before him running east and west, but turning north for a ways just a bit to David's left. As David had already learned, the valley was an obvious invasion corridor that allowed the Philistine chariots freedom of movement. But thankfully, David could see no chariots with the raiders below. Chariots weren't part of the Hebrew forces simply because they did not work well in the more mountainous regions that Israel controlled, but David dreaded fighting against them. So far, his men had yet to face enemy chariots, and David prayed to God that it would remain so.

A troop of Philistine warriors were marching up the valley, their distinctive headdresses looking like a cluster of flowers from this distance. "How many men do you think they have?" David asked.

Eleazar squinted, trying to see in the gloom. The overcast sky muted everything in darker shades, and rain threatened to fall at any time. "Looks like no more than a couple hundred," the lieutenant guessed. "We should be able to overrun them easily, but I must warn you, we don't have much experience fighting in the rain. Doing battle while wet is a bad omen. Our men will shy from it, I tell you." Then almost to himself, he added, "Besides, my sword gets rusty after a rain. Do you know how long it will take to file all the rust off?"

"It's not raining yet," David pointed out.

"*Yet*," Eleazar echoed ominously.

"Do you ever have a good word to say?" Shammah asked.

Eleazar blinked. "I always have a good word to say."

David shook his head. As the spirits of his troops had risen, so had their casual banter. "Enough. Should we take our entire company into the battle?"

Shammah frowned. "Perhaps not. Philistine raiding parties often break up into these smaller groups. There may be another up ahead. I recommend splitting our forces and sending half around the hills to the east while the rest of us take on the foe before us. If there is indeed another troop ahead, we'll be able to trap them between us once we have dealt with yon interlopers."

The plan had merit. David glanced back down the hill and waved for Adriel to attend him. The armorbearer hurried to David's side, weaving through the trees smoothly and with little sound. "Take word to Adino to split the company," he ordered when Adriel arrived. "I wish for him to take half and circumvent the valley from behind the hills to the east. He is to look for any other Philistine raiding parties beyond."

Adriel nodded. "I shall, my captain. I will then hasten back to your side."

"Nay," David said, holding up a hand. "I wish for you to go with Adino. I will take Shammah and Eleazar into battle with me. I trust you four the most and would have two there and two here."

"My place is with you," the armorbearer argued.

"I have greater need of your able assistance with Adino."

Adriel hesitated, but decided that arguing with David further would accomplish nothing. That was a relief. Ever since Saul had offered Merab to David to wife, Adriel had been acting different—not enough for David to comment on, but enough to be a minor source of irritation in the back of David's head, like an itch he couldn't scratch.

David didn't fear to have his armorbearer fight at his side. Adriel was a worthy companion, but in this case, he truly wanted Adriel to help Adino. As skilled as the lanky spearman was, he didn't have much of a head for tactics, and his laziness could get a lot of people killed if someone wasn't there to keep him motivated. Adriel was an able commander, and Adino respected him enough to listen to the armorbearer's advice.

Adriel bowed and hastened down the slope to relay David's orders to Adino. Five hundred men separated themselves from the men below and began moving eastward. The others climbed up through the trees to join David. They sneaked over the top of the hill, using the trees to prevent their silhouettes from being visible against the sky. Not that such would be a problem with the darkened sky and haze from the approaching rain.

Even as he thought it, the first few rain drops began to splatter around them. Eleazar glared at David. "Did I not warn you?" he muttered.

David chuckled. There was no pleasing the man. "Heed me, my lieutenants. We will move down to the valley as subtly as we can. I would that the enemy not know of us before we can cut off their retreat."

Shammah unlimbered his fierce war club and then stroked his massive beard with one hand. David noted that the large man had woven a pair of bird skulls into his beard this day, and with his shinny bald plate, he looked otherworldly. Perhaps the superstitious Philistines would think the same thing.

"We are ready, Captain," the man said, gesturing for David to take the lead.

David drew his sword and began a slow walk down, slipping from tree to tree in an effort to break up his outline and remain unnoticed. Five hundred men followed. The jingling of their armor and weapons mixed with heavy breathing were the only sounds to be heard. The men had learned a greater degree of discipline over the last six months, largely due to Abinadab's advice to David's lieutenants.

They worked better as a unit now, and David felt confident they could rout the enemy this day. They emerged onto the valley floor near some burning crops. It looked like the field had once contained barley or lentils—or both, as they were frequently grown next to each other. The smoke helped conceal the Hebrew warriors for a bit longer as they spread out across the valley floor, and then they began a quick march toward the enemy.

David led the center with the handful of swordsmen. The wings consisted of spearmen, and a troop of archers followed directly

1 Samuel 18:15-16

behind. The plan was simple. When they got close enough, the archers would unleash a couple of volleys to thin the enemy ranks. Then David and the swordsmen would smash into the disorganized ranks at their center, while the wings outflanked both outer edges and crushed the Philistines between them like the jaws of a lion.

The rain began to fall harder now, and despite Eleazar's qualms, the rain was a blessing as it would impede the Philistines' attempts to burn the Hebrew crops. Unfortunately, it would also hamper the archers since wet bow strings made shooting arrows difficult. The strings had been waxed, of course, to prevent this, but it would still be an issue and would likely provide only a couple of shots before the bows would be largely useless. David hoped the battle would be over before the rain could really affect the outcome.

The Philistines finally noticed the charging Hebrews, and they quickly turned around to engage, but their ranks were disorganized and confused.

David blinked some of the rain out of his eyes and then raised his sword in a prearranged signal. They were close enough. Fifty arrows arched overhead and fell among the Philistines. Cries of pain and fear emanated from the enemy ranks, and perhaps less than score of the enemy crumpled, either dead or wounded.

Another volley followed, cutting down more of the Philistines. The enemy bowman did manage to get off a hasty shot, but most overshot or were deflected by Hebrew shields. David ignored the few cries of pain from his own soldiers, knowing that the time to see to the wounded would be after the battle had been won.

Then the Hebrew soldiers crashed into the ranks of Philistines, and thunder, as if God was personally watching, rolled out over the battlefield in concert with the initial impact. David cut down two men, archers who couldn't get their other weapons to hand soon enough and punched his way deeper into the enemy ranks.

Eleazar followed at his side, his sword a blur as he cut down man after man. The lieutenant then took the lead from David, leaving in his wake a trail of death and destruction.

"I hate fighting in the rain!" the swordsman shouted as he cut down another Philistine, kicking the man's body away so he could get at the next warrior. "You owe me for this, Captain!"

David grinned. "Aye! On my word, Eleazar!"

The swordsman grunted in reply and kept up an amazing display of swordsmanship. Somehow his blade could weave around shields, parry thrusting spears and swords, and find vulnerable points in the enemy armor.

And then it was over. David's extended wings collapsed on the enemy's flanks and drove them together in a horrible slaughter. Some of the Philistines, perhaps less than a hundred, managed to break free of the trap and fled west down the valley, but they left over a hundred of their countrymen dead and dying on the field.

A cheer rose from the mouths of the victorious Hebrews, and taunts followed the fleeing enemy as they disappeared into the rainy haze.

David fell silent. He wiped rain from his face and peered into the gloom. Something felt wrong. He glanced to the east but saw no sign of Adino and the other five hundred men. Perhaps they too were battling a troop of Philistines farther up the valley.

Shammah and Eleazar joined him. They stayed silent, each looking steadily to the west where the remnant of the Philistines had fled. The rain and haze cut visibility to a couple hundred cubits, but all three sensed something coming from that direction, something that had them on edge.

"What is it?" David whispered.

Perhaps sensing their leaders' worry, the rest of the men also fell silent. A few, knowing their task, went to the wounded and began the process of preparing them for transport if they could not walk themselves, but the rest, shifted uneasily and faced west, each man staring into the rain.

Shammah clutched his war club tightly, the rain washing the blood and gore from the blunted metal spikes and hard wood. "Something is coming," he said ominously.

1 Samuel 18:15-16

Indeed, finding his eyes to be useless, David listened. A rumbling sound could be heard, one that David had dismissed as distant thunder, but could not be. It rolled toward them slowly, growing in power.

The young captain knew that sound. So did his two lieutenants.

Eleazar spoke first, his voice a hiss of tension and fear. "Chariots!"

A fearful muttering rose from the men and they began jostling each other as they tried to back up. Facing chariots was an Israelite warrior's worst nightmare.

"Hold!" David yelled, turning to glare at his men. He knew by now that if he couldn't keep firm control of the soldiers, they would break and flee. "They come to mock our God and our people! They will destroy our land and starve our wives and children! Shall we then let them?" He put scorn into his voice, trying to shame the men into action. "Form ranks! Bowmen to the rear; spearmen to the front. Javelin throwers behind the spearmen. Ready shields! Prepare to repel the invaders!"

Typically, the bowmen would be their best defense against chariots. They would target the horses, knowing that once one or two were injured or killed, the powerful chariot would be useless. But the rain had finally soaked into the bow strings, rendering the weapons ineffective. The javelin throwers would be their next best option—depending upon the number of chariots they faced.

The men reacted in moderate discipline, shoving into position, setting shields, preparing spears to the front, and hefting javelins for a cast. But then out of the gloom to the west and north the thundering charge of hundreds of chariots emerged. The Philistine battle cry rose into the air, joining with the rain and thunder.

And David knew they were doomed.

12

"Loose!" David shouted, and dozens of javelins shot into the air to rain down upon the charging Philistine chariots. A few horses were struck and went down squealing in pain, but the Philistines had armored their horses, and most of the javelins either missed or were deflected harmlessly away.

Two horses drew each chariot bearing three warriors, a driver and two warriors. Because of the rain, they carried no bows, but spears and javelins, and as the chariots neared the Hebrew lines, enemy spears shot forth and slammed into the hapless Israelites, and then the chariots struck the Hebrews.

The devastating attack literally crushed David's lines.

Men fell by the score as they jumped out of position to avoid being trampled by the horses. David barely avoided the same fate, dodging to his left just as one of the chariots barreled by. He tried to stab one of the warriors riding in the chariot, but the man blocked with his shield and was gone before David could react further.

Again, David had to dodge by flinging himself aside to avoid another chariot. The young captain rolled across the grass in jarring fashion, the heavy armor preventing him from quickly regaining his feet. When he did pull himself upright, he found himself in the midst of chaos.

2 Samuel 23:9-12 & 2 Chronicles 11:12-14

David's men had panicked and broke.[1] Most fled to the east in a wild and fruitless attempt to escape. A few, clearer headed perhaps than the others, tried to escape to the hills north or south where the chariots could not follow, but the Philistine line swept the width of the valley, cutting them off and leaving them dead in the wet summer grass.

"David! Here!" Eleazar ran up to David, a bloody streak smearing his cheek already being washed clean by the heavy rain. He pointed back toward the west. "More coming!"

Looking in that direction, David saw Philistine infantry emerging from the rainy haze, marching in strong lines toward the remnant of David's men who had survived the chariot attack. Bruised and battered from his heavy fall, David staggered toward his lieutenant. "We need a defensible position," he yelled, his throat dry despite the rain.

"Where?" Eleazar shouted back.

Most of the chariots had overrun them, moving deeper into the valley and harrying David's fleeing men. This left a space between the two Philistine forces which the young captain and his lieutenant now occupied. David would need to do something quickly before the chariots turned around and trapped them.

Shammah appeared as if from nowhere. His chest heaved as he grabbed David and spun him to face east. "There!" He pointed to a barley field with half-grown crops. "The plowed earth is too soft for the chariots, especially in this rain. They'll have to come at us on foot."

David knew it wasn't ideal, but it was the best option available to them under the circumstances. "Let's go!"

The three of them plunged toward the barley field. A few of the Philistine chariots had already tried to cross the soft earth and had bogged down, their crews furiously trying to free the entrenched vehicles.

---

[1] 2 Samuel 23:11; 1 Chronicles 11:13.

David looked around for any more of his men, but they had all fled. Grimly, he uttered a prayer for their safety, knowing most would be killed if the Philistines were not turned back. And right now, only three of them remained to do so. Not very good odds.

They ran into the field, and the ground squished under his sandals and mud squeezed in between his toes. The grass-like crop would bend and support some weight, but not the weight of a heavy chariot. No chariot would be able to plow through this muck.

The three of them plowed their way to the center of the field and saw an adjacent field of lentils, the shrub-like crop grew low to the ground and was more spaced out, meaning the ground would likely be muddier. They hurried to where the crops met. This would be the best defensive position they could find.

Shammah pulled David close, his wet beard plastered to his face and neck. "Back to back," he explained. "We'll not sell our lives cheaply, Captain. We'll teach these dogs what it means to be a Hebrew warrior!"

Eleazar grunted. "Did I not warn you that the rain would spell our doom? Did I not?"

David opened his mouth to chastise the pessimistic man. This was no time for such words, but the thief turned swordsman forestalled him with a sudden grin.

"Death is one way to pay my debt, I think. Still, I wish it wasn't raining." He turned away from David, taking a position just inside the barley portion of the field.[2]

Shammah turned away and trampled some of the lentils[3] into the mud, creating a small patch that gave him room to maneuver without being hampered by the mud overmuch.

David took up his position in the back-to-back triangle, holding his sword before him as Eleazar had taught him. He had a foot planted in each crop and found that he could move well enough by

---

[2] 1 Chronicles 11:13-14.
[3] 2 Samuel 23:11.

following Shammah's example of trampling the crops into a mat beneath his feet.

The rain let up then, turning into a light sprinkle, and he looked up to behold the approaching Philistines. They looked endless, filling the valley from side to side—rank upon rank of infantry marching directly toward David. Over his shoulder, he saw a few of the chariots pulling around to take a run at David and his lieutenants, but they seemed hesitant. They knew the softer ground would impede their chariots.

And then something came over the three men, harried and stalked by death itself. A certainty descended upon them, a premonition, not of death, but of victory. They knew God would deliver them this day. They felt it in their hearts.

More so, David felt himself filled with the Spirit of God. Samuel had not anointed him to be a mere captain over a thousand.[4] God had yet a purpose for David, and that purpose would not be denied, no matter how many enemy warriors were flung upon David's sword.

"We shall not die here," he announced into the sudden silence. "We will place our trust in Jehovah Elohim, and like Samson of old and our friend Adino, God will deliver us from the hands of these uncircumcised. The battle is the LORD's—not ours."

Strength and clarity flooded their bodies and minds. David saw Shammah straighten from a crouch, his eyes bright and clear. Eleazar stood easier, lighter, like a dancer preparing to perform before an enraptured crowd.

Shammah raised his war club into the sky and roared, "Well said, my Captain!" He then faced the Philistine and pounded his chest, slapping the heavy leather that protected his torso and heedless of the metal studs that no doubt stung his fist. "Come, children of false gods! Come, dogs of the sea! Fight with us and know your betters!"[5]

---

[4] 1 Samuel 13:13-14, 16:13.
[5] 2 Samuel 23:9, "They defied the Philistines."

Eleazar picked up the taunts. "Shall your gods deliver you from our hands? I think not! Come, you uncircumcised pigs, and feast upon the iron of my blade!" Then, quite incongruently to the situation they found themselves in, the swordsman began to whistle a happy tune.

The Philistines broke rank. Incensed by the taunts and determined not to let three men blaspheme their gods, they charged in an unorganized mass, their faces contorted in rage, their colorful headdresses limp with rain.

Fortunately, the enemy was hampered by the soggy earth, so the charge turned into more of a plodding trot, their feet making sucking noises as they jerked each foot out of the mud in their haste. Not a few became entangled and fell, but enough made it to David and his lieutenants that he had no time even to rejoice in the enemy's difficulties.

The first man that came at David misjudged his speed. He leaped forward intent on stabbing David with his spear, but the mud, like clutching hands, pulled the warrior up short so he fell heavily to his knees before his mark. David planted one foot on the man's spear and then stepped forward, sword stabbing. The man grunted, and his eyes glazed as he stared stupidly at the length of iron embedded in his chest.

David backed up, knowing that he had to keep his position in the triangle. Ribbons of blood fell from his sword, and the light rain, like a woman irritated at the uncleanliness of her home, began to wash away the stain. But as Eleazar had predicted, David's iron sword already looked stained with rust.

Then David parried frantically as two men, working in concert, thrust their spears at the young captain. He got his shield around to block their second thrust, and a counter stroke sent one man falling away, his hiss of pain piercing the air.

The second man would've skewered David then, seeing that he was off-balance, but Eleazar somehow appeared as if from thin air, parried and then struck with lightning-fast reflexes. The man never even cried out as he collapsed, and the former thief let loose with a questioning whistle of mockery before reverting to his joyful tune.

Indeed, the man seemed happy. Eleazar fought with a finesse and artistry that defied description. Wherever he appeared, men fell with throats cut, stab wounds, or their stomachs disemboweled. He took hits here and there, mostly minor cuts as he weaved his athletic body out of the path of spear or sword.

And the whole while, he continued to whistle.

If Eleazar was a picture of finesse, Shammah was the epitome of brutal destruction. He roared his battle cry, smashing aside anyone who came close to him. His brutal strength could crack shields, bend swords, and smash spears into splinters. He didn't bother trying to get behind the enemy's defenses. He simply crushed them.

David saw one of the Philistine spearmen lift his shield to deflect Shammah's powerful overhand swing, knowing that the large man would leave himself off-balance and open to a spear thrust. But the heavy war club crushed the shield and snapped the arm holding it, driving the man to the ground in an explosion of agony.

Shammah didn't bother finishing the man off. He stepped on the downed man's head, driving his enemy's mouth into the mud and continued his attack against the next warrior in line.

And so the battle went. David had no idea how long they fought, the three of them. The Philistine dead piled up around them, like cords of firewood, but strength continued to infuse the three Hebrew warriors. They did not flag, and their ability to anticipate the next attack never wavered. They fought as they have never fought before, here on this ground of Pasdammim,[6] and it went on and on.

At last the Philistines had had enough. No one could stand before these three mighty men. Philistine blood soaked the ground, fertilizing the very crops they had set out to destroy. The dead lay in piles around the field as David and his two lieutenants had slowly been moved from place to place. There would be much weeping among the Philistine women this night.

---

[6] 1 Chronicles 11:13.

First one, then by twos, then in a flood, the Philistines retreated, leaving their dead and wounded behind. They ran in terror of the Hebrew God and the mighty warriors that He had used to save Israel by a great deliverance.[7]

The rain stopped completely then, leaving the three men standing amidst the ruin of their enemy's attack. David fell to one knee as his strength left him all at once. Breath came hard, and he sucked it in greedily. Beside him, Shammah collapsed to a sitting position, his head hanging.

Only Eleazar continued to stand. The swordsman held his sword with both hands, and he stared at it in absolute wonder. David tried to stand, but he had no strength, his wounds suddenly painful in their need to gain his attention. He waved a weak hand at his standing lieutenant. "It is enough, my friend. The enemy has fled. The LORD has delivered us. Put up your sword. You have no more need of it this day."

The lieutenant turned slightly to face David. "I would, my captain, but I cannot. My hand will not release its clasp."[8]

Curiosity overcoming his deep weariness, David forced himself to his feet. He sheathed his own sword—it took him three attempts—and then moved over to his lieutenant. The man stood with the sword in both hands as if still preparing to do battle. David reached out and peeled Eleazar's left hand off the hilt. The man grimaced in pain, his hand immediately making a claw as if trying to grasp the sword again. The right hand looked as if it had molded itself to the hilt.

David took hold of it and tried to peel back the fingers. Eleazar grimaced. "Careful, my lord. I am over fond of my skin and wish to retain it."

The young captain stepped back puzzled. He'd never seen the like before. It was as if Eleazar's hand had molded itself onto the sword hilt. He gave his lieutenant an inquiring look.

---

[7] 1 Chronicles 11:14.
[8] 2 Samuel 23:10.

2 Samuel 23:9-12 & 2 Chronicles 11:12-14

The former thief shrugged warily. "I could not let go," he tried to explain. "It is as if Jehovah Himself held the blade in my hand. Even now, I do not know if I *can* let go."

David smiled. "It will pass. Perhaps a bit of Shammah's oil will release the sword from your hand."

"Aye! That it might!" The swordsman turned to the large man, who was already offering the small flask.

"Take it and welcome," the big man rumbled. "You fought well, my friend."

The two men had never really gotten along, but the bond of battle transcended all differences. David took the flask and carefully poured some of the olive oil on the hilt and over Eleazar's clenched hand. The action felt holy somehow, as if David was anointing his lieutenant.

They waited a moment and then David tried again to free the swordsman's hand. This time, he succeeded in peeling Eleazar's fingers off the hilt. The sword fell to the blood-soaked mud, and immediately the swordsman gasped in pain as his hand clenched into a fist, cramping badly.

"Thank you," he hissed in pain. "'Tis better."

David patted the man on the shoulder and then went to Shammah to assure himself that the big man wasn't unduly injured. The man was covered in twice the amount of blood as the other two combined it seemed. "Are you well, Shammah?"

"Aye, Captain, that I am. The wounds I sustained will heal easily. Mostly, I am weary." He ran a hand over his scalp, smearing mud and blood over his head in long streaks. David shuddered and looked around. His eyes beheld a wonder. Only Adino's mighty battle could compare to the devastation that now surrounded the three men.

As if thinking the man's name conjured him, the lanky spearman appeared out of the gloom from the east, leading five hundred of David's men and those he had gathered up from the remnant of his destroyed command.

The tall man strode slowly through the field, his surprised eyes surveying the ruin around the three men. Adriel trailed after, his face looking both troubled and awed. Both men clamored over the Philistine corpses and came to a stop before the three weary warriors and bowed. "Well met, my lords," Adino drawled. "I regret that I am so late in coming. Please forgive me."

David grinned then, relieved beyond any measure. "It is good to see you. Both of you. And you are not late. The LORD has delivered us with a strong hand."

Adino appraised his captain and swept his eyes around the field, taking in the hundreds of dead Philistines. He then slowly raised his spear in a salute of profound respect. Adriel hesitated only a second before drawing his own sword and lifting it high.

Behind them, over five hundred men raised their weapons into the sky, and a cheer broke forth from their mouths that filled the valley with its strength.

It went on and on, and David knew that his reputation this day would grow even greater. These men would spread rumors that would exaggerate the deeds done this day. They would seek to be the ones to tell the story, as if by telling it, they were somehow part of the victory. David's instinct was to try and stop it, but he might as well try to stop the sun from rising.

Instead, he turned to Eleazar. "The spoil is yours, lieutenant.[9] Take the men and gather the weapons and anything else that might be of use. Destroy any chariots and kill the horses. I would not that they be used against us in the future." Chariots would be worthless to the mountain-dwelling Hebrews, and they had no time to deal with the Philistine-trained horses.

The lieutenant nodded and walked slowly off, but he did begin to whistle again, a soft melody, one that reflected his weariness and relief.

---

[9] 2 Samuel 23:10.

2 Samuel 23:9-12 & 2 Chronicles 11:12-14

David then took Shammah by his huge shoulders and helped the man to his feet. "We will look after our wounded," David told him. "And bury our dead."

"Aye," the bald man agreed, his voice tinged with sadness. "It is only right." Shammah's stomach rumbled in hungry protest. "But first, if my lord wills, perhaps I could eat something."

David smiled. "Aye. It is only right."

13

King Saul enjoyed the sun's warmth on his skin as he walked along the dusty lane that led to the gates of Gibeah. He had been spending too much time in his house these last few years, something unlike him. He was used to long marches, lonely camps, cold meals, and short nights.

What happened to me? He pondered the question as he walked. Two of his sons strode along behind him. Jonathan, strong, stalwart, and courageous, walked with the easy stride of a warrior. Ishui, Saul's second-born son, strode along with equal grace, but with less presence. Ishui's long, dark hair, framed a thin, if grim, face. His beard, cut short and trimmed around the edges, only enhanced his thin appearance. But the number of scars he bore gave testament either to his prowess in battle or lack thereof. Impetuous and irritable, Ishui seemed to find a fight where ever he went—which may have accounted for the plethora of scars.

Both young men walked quietly behind their father, obviously unwilling to break the peace of the day. Saul appreciated their discretion, but he could sense that Ishui bore disturbing news. Still, the autumn air felt good on his skin along with the sunlight, and he wasn't quite ready to hear what his son had to say. This was the month Ethanim,[1] the holiest month of the year,[2] and for some reason, Saul felt right with the world, more at peace than he had in a long while. He wanted to enjoy it.

Behind his sons, Abner and a small squad of men marched, keeping their distance to afford their king a measure of privacy while scanning the countryside around them uneasily, ready to defend their king if anything untoward were to happen. Abner had also been spending more time at Gibeah in the last two years than ever before, and the general had been vocal to Saul about his discontentment. He too was a warrior, more comfortable on the field of battle than in a bed. But these days, Saul had need of surrounding himself with those most loyal to him. And that, generally speaking, meant family—despite Jonathan's friendship with perhaps the most dangerous man that Saul had ever met. Saul's mood soured instantly with the thought. The issue of Jonathan's loyalty should've been cared for years ago!

Irritated, he decided to get the bad news out of the way. "Speak, Ishui. What news?"

Ishui cleared his throat. "The son of Jesse has once again prevailed, my king. The Philistines have been routed. David's messenger reports that he has secured two of the five Shephelah valleys from further invasion." His son hesitated. "He has done well, Father."

Saul ground his teeth together. And there lay the crux of the problem. For nearly three years now, David had continued to win victory after victory against the enemies of Israel—while avoiding who knows how many assassination attempts. Saul had counted on him falling in battle so that his own hand would not be against the shepherd.[3] Clearly, that strategy had not worked as planned.

---

[1] 1 Kings 8:2 ("Tishri" is another name for this month, more common today.).
[2] The seventh month (September/October) begins with the Feast of Trumpets (Leviticus 23:24); the tenth day is the Day of Atonement or Yom Kippur (Leviticus 23:27), and the fifteenth day is the Feast of Tabernacles (Leviticus 23:34).
[3] 1 Samuel 18:17.

Jonathan, blind Jonathan, spoke up. "Indeed, he has, Father. Has he not fulfilled your dowry of being valiant and fighting the LORD's battles? Should he not be given his reward?"

"You speak as if your sister is so much cattle to be sold," Saul snapped.

"Merab is a daughter of Israel," Jonathan pointed out. "And she favors the union. I do her no disservice."

Saul looked over his shoulder in time to see Ishui scowl at his brother. "It is not your place, brother," the younger son said, "to teach our father his duty. Hold your tongue."

The king stopped and turned to face his sons. "Enough. Both of you." They fell silent as the king thought. An idea began to form. He looked at Jonathan. "Tell me, my son, do you not have a man within David's ranks?"

"You speak of Adriel, David's armorbearer?"

"Aye, the very one. Is he still loyal to you?"

"I would not doubt it. Forgive me, Father, but what is the purpose of these questions?"

Saul let a small reassuring smile play on his lips. He needed to be careful here, for he didn't doubt for a second that Jonathan would object if he knew his father's thoughts. Merab had once spoken of Adriel, son of Barzillai, in a favorable manner. He made an undecipherable gesture to his son. "Adriel has served David well?"

"Aye," Jonathan said, warming up to the subject. "They have become like brothers over the last few years. They have fought well together and serve my lord the king well."

Saul pretended to muse on that. "Was Adriel with David at Pasdammim?"

"Aye, Father."

Everyone had heard what had happened two years ago when David had defeated the Philistines with just two of his men in a barley field. It had been a great victory, one that still irritated Saul to this day. Why wouldn't the treacherous shepherd die? It was so frustrating. The men Saul had given David should have failed. They all should've been long dead by now. Instead, the young captain had somehow wielded the Indebted into an effective fighting force. In fact, some of those men were approaching the end of their indentured service, and Saul would be obliged to let them go free. Not that such was a problem. He could always contrive some reason to indebt the men again if necessary.

No, the real problem lay with David's uncanny ability to survive when he should not. Clearly the LORD was with David, and that fact alone sent a chill of fear down Saul's spine. Saul yearned for the days when the LORD had been with him, when the Great Seer Samuel had stood by his side! But Samuel had betrayed him, and David lurked greedily at the edges of his throne.

If the Philistines could not do the job, then perhaps there was another way to see David dead.

"I would that you call Adriel to stand before me. I would like his assessment on all that David has done. Indeed, it sounds as if the son of Barzillai also needs rewarding. Do you not think so?"

"Adriel has done well, Father. I would be pleased to see him rewarded. I will send a messenger immediately. Does this mean you are thinking of bringing David back to Gibeah? It has been over two years since he last stood before you."

"It is. As you say, David has done well. Even Abner agrees." Which was a point of contention between Saul and his cousin. Of course, Abner hadn't known the real reason why Saul had given command of the Indebted to David. Jonathan's smile was positively beaming. Saul wanted to knock it off. *Why can't he see how dangerous David is?*

"This is good news indeed!" his oldest son said. "I will look forward to seeing the son of Jesse."

Ishui snorted. "Who is this son of Jesse? He has done no more or less than any other captain. Why honor him, Father?"

Saul wanted to grin. At least one of his sons saw things properly. But he needed to set the stage of David's downfall carefully, so he said, "The son of Jesse has done more than you think, my son. He has been ever victorious, and the Philistines have begun to fear him."

"I could do as much," Ishui boasted.

"With the Indebted?" Saul raised an eyebrow. "And what think you of the bounty upon the son of Jesse's head? Rumor, like a dog in the refuse heap, says that the Philistines will offer gold equal to his entire body weight. Could you so bestir the enemy?"

Ishui hesitated and licked his lips. "Given enough time," he amended, his words sounding weak.

Saul gave his son a fatherly smile. "I believe you can, but it is David who has done so, and so David must be rewarded." He glanced at Jonathan. "I would hear Adriel's account first, however. Call him. Once I am satisfied with his testimony, we will call upon David."

Five days later, a travel-weary Adriel stood before King Saul. The court was lit with extra lamps this day, the fumes stronger and more pungent than usual. Saul, dressed in his battle armor for effect, chose to stand so that all must look up at him. Behind him, the banner of the tribe of Benjamin dominated one wall.

Jonathan stood with Ishui and Saul's two daughters, Merab and Michal, against the wall. All was ready.

He watched as Adriel bowed low to him. "My lord," the armorbearer said, "I am come as you have commanded."

Saul nodded respectfully. "You are well come, Adriel, son of Barzillai. I have need of your thoughts. Tell me of David. How fares he, and has he remained valiant for our people?"

Without hesitation, Adriel responded, "He fares well, my lord, and he remains valiant as you have commanded him. The people love him, and the Philistines fear him."

"And why do the people love him?" Saul asked, curious. It seemed like an odd thing to mention.

The armorbearer thought for a moment. "It is because he comes and goes before the people.⁴ All Israel knows that David is fighting the LORD's battles, and as such, he is protecting them."

So, Saul's plan had backfired. Not only had David not fallen at the hands of the Philistines, the people had come to love him—a direct result of what Saul had commanded the former shepherd to do. Growling internally like a dog robbed of his meat, he wondered what more could the young man have but the kingdom? "My choice then was a wise one," Saul nearly spat out.

Adriel was oblivious to Saul's cutting tone. "Your wisdom is of God, my lord."

"And what of you, son of Barzillai? Have you not done well?"

The question obviously caught Adriel off-guard. He shifted uncomfortably. "If I have found favor in your sight, my king, then I am pleased."

"You have," Saul said as emphatically as he could. "I doubt not that your advice and skill in combat was key to David's many successes."

Adriel opened his mouth to protest, but Saul held up a hand, forestalling him. Saul glanced sideways at Jonathan, but his son held his peace, watching curiously. *Good.* Jonathan needed to stay out of this.

"It is in my mind to reward you, a loyal son of Israel. Tell me, of which tribe do you hail from?"

"I am a son of Manasseh, my king, a Meholathite of Abelmeholah."⁵

"The place of the plague?"⁶

Years ago, a plague had wiped out most of the inhabitants of the community near the upper Jordan River. It was interesting to find a survivor.

"Aye, my king. Of my family, I alone survived. I have vowed never to return for it is a cursed place, abandoned by God."

---

⁴ 1 Samuel 18:16.
⁵ 1 Samuel 18:19; 2 Samuel 21:8.
⁶ Meholah means "weakness or sickly." Such a plague *could have* happened.

Perfect. Saul stepped forward until he was a cubit or so away from David's armorbearer. "It seems then that an obligation has inadvertently been thrust upon me, one that I take great joy in fulfilling." He turned to his eldest son. "What say you, Jonathan? Should such a man as this have his name forgotten in Israel? Should his inheritance fall to another?"

"Nay, Father. It should not," his son agreed gravely.

"The duty of a king is to preserve the inheritance of Israel's children," Saul said, turning back to Adriel. "Though you have vowed rightly never to return to Abelmeholah, I would not have your inheritance there bestowed upon another. You must raise up sons, Adriel, son of Barzillai."

"It has been my own thought, my lord."

"Let it not be a thought any more, my servant. I would reward you with a wife. However, it would be untoward of me to give you another man's daughter. A king should not do so. But am I not your king and do I not have two daughters? Therefore, I give you Merab, my own daughter, to wife."

A collective gasp filled the room. All knew that Merab had been promised to David two years before. A promise of betrothal was precious but was not sacrosanct. It could be violated if the betrothal had not taken place. Neither was it an unheard practice, particularly if a man could not fulfill the dowry price. And it was this that gave him leverage to annul the promise to David. Still, Saul doubted that anyone had expected this turn of events, and if the cloudy face of his eldest son was any indication, then this new plan would work perfectly.

Adriel had paled under the words. His eyes drifted to Merab who stood uncertainly against the wall. Her father's words had doubtlessly shifted her entire world. Saul noted that her eyes kept flickering from him and then back to the armorbearer. And, thankfully, she did not protest.

Jonathan clearly felt no such restraint. "What folly is this?" Saul's son exploded. "You promised her to David!"

Saul spun on his son, allowing his own face to slip into a mask of anger. "You would do well to keep your tongue still, my son. I will not tolerate any disrespect in my court!"

Jonathan, taken aback by Saul's sudden rage, swallowed and stepped back.

Saul nodded. "Is David and Merab betrothed?" he asked those in the room. It was a rhetorical question. "Has David yet taken her to wife? I think not. Has the son of Jesse paid her dowry in full?" He glared about him, daring anyone to contradict. "No, he has not!" he shouted. "Aye, David has done well, but it is men such as Adriel who have guided David's hands, fought his battles. Men such as Adriel have been the key to David's success. Why should I reward the son of Jesse before these men? Such a thing ought not to be done in Israel."

In truth, the argument was weak, but it mattered not to Saul. He simply needed a reason to goad David into doing something rash—something Saul could use as justification to kill him. Once word of this reached David, Saul doubted not that the son of Jesse would behave unseemly enough to justify killing his former armorbearer.

Saul placed his hands on Adriel's shoulders and kissed the man's cheeks, a fatherly gesture. "My son, what say you to this?"

Adriel couldn't help but look at Merab with longing clearly showing in his brown eyes. Still, it did the man credit that a guilty cast came over his handsome face as he no doubt realized what this would mean for his friend, David. "My king, I—"

Saul cut him off. "I would have you as my son-in-law, Adriel, son of Barzillai. Do not lightly cast aside my gift to you."

The handsome man looked once more at Merab and then fastened his eyes on Saul. "I would gladly have your daughter to wife, my lord. It would be a great honor. But, my king, I have nothing to pay the dowry. My inheritance is forlorn, and there is no man to till the ground. I have no riches to compensate you for the loss of your daughter."

"Fear not, my son. Your deeds these last three years in guiding my servant David and removing the Philistines dogs from the lands of our people have been dowry enough. If you think that insufficient, then know that your service to my son Jonathan beforetime must be attributed. You have served us well, my son. Have you no token to give my daughter, nothing to seal a betrothal?"

Adriel glance at his hands. He had several rings on his fingers, plunder from various raids against the Philistines—raids led by David. Saul knew this, and the sensation of provoking David into a rage warmed Saul's heart. He had heard too much of David in recent years. The time had come to shake the young captain to his very core.

Adriel pulled a gold ring off his right hand. Swallowing hard, he moved over before Merab. They looked long into each other's eyes, and Saul was pleased. His daughter favored Adriel, and though Saul would have little in return for her, it was more than worth it if David's death was the result.

The armorbearer held out the ring to Merab. His hand trembled, no doubt as the realization of what this all meant hit him. "By this token," he said slowly, "you are set apart for me by the law of Moses and of Israel."

Merab's thin hand reached out and took the ring. "Then I am yours, my lord," she whispered, "forever more."

"It is done!" Saul cried. He moved over to the couple and placed a hand on their shoulders. He spoke the traditional benediction on the betrothal, "The LORD make my daughter as Rachel, which did help build the house of Israel."[7]

Customarily, the wedding wouldn't take place for another year, but Saul felt certain he could hasten the timeframe if necessary. Anything to provoke David.

Turning to the guard standing straight-faced at the door, Saul commanded, "Send word to every city in Israel of these glad tidings. I would that every soul know of my daughter's betrothal. Let it be

---

[7] Ruth 4:11.

known that I am well-pleased with my son-in-law, Adriel. He adds much honor to my house."

The guard saluted and ducked out of the room.

Jonathan, his face a study in warring emotions, moved over to his sister and new brother-in-law. Betrothals could not be broken without a bill of divorcement, and the fact that Merab had so readily taken Adriel's ring was evidence that she favored the match. Saul knew that Jonathan could do nothing about this. He had to accept it.

Jonathan looked into his sister's eyes. "I am happy for you, my sister. I pray that your womb will be fruitful. May the Lord bless you in the days to come."

Merab's eyes swam with tears, and she kissed her brother affectionately on the cheek, forgetting that her veil was in the way. "Thank you, my brother. I am content."

Jonathan shifted to Adriel. "We have been friends for many years. I am honored to call you brother."

Adriel suddenly looked apprehensive. He lowered his voice, but Saul could still hear him as he asked, "And what of the son of Jesse?"

Jonathan's lips tightened momentarily. "We will find other ways to reward your captain."

The armorbearer sighed. "As long as it does not involve my head."

"Aye. It may be best if you stay well away from his sight."

"It is not his sight I fear," Adriel muttered.

Merab grasped his hand. "Let not this upset my lord. David is a loyal servant and will abide by the king's will."

Adriel raised an eyebrow. "And if he does not? He may feel justly slighted—" He cut off, glancing at King Saul who merely smiled, pretending he hadn't overheard. Saul didn't mind where this conversation was going. Adriel cleared his throat and tried again. "He may find occasion to contest the issue. And I still remain his armorbearer."

Saul watched his daughter's hand tighten, and her voice rose so that all could hear. "What can he do? We are now betrothed. By the law, you may not fight in battle.[8] The son of Jesse will need to release you from your duties." She turned to her father. "Is this not so?"

"Aye, my daughter. I would have Adriel remain here, by my side. It is only fitting, seeing as he is now the king's son-in-law."

Michal let out her breath in a huff. Until this point, Saul's youngest daughter had remained silent, but her eyes had narrowed to thin slits, a clear sign of her calculation.

"I too congratulate you, sister," she said. Saul detected disdain and something else in her voice…glee, perhaps? She kissed her sister, remembering to lift her veil to do so and then turned to her father. "This has been a joyous occasion, but I would like to offer a sacrifice on Merab's behalf. May I take my leave?"

Saul frowned. He'd never taken Michal for being overly religious, but he certainly couldn't refuse this request. "Aye. You have my leave."

Michal gave a half bow and left. Jonathan took that as his cue. He pushed Adriel and Merab ahead of him. "We too will take your leave, Father—with your permission, of course. There are many things that need discussing, the details of which I am sure you would not find interesting."

Not the least of which is David, Saul thought. "I am always interested, my son. But you have my leave to go."

Saul watched his family leave, his face frozen in a patronizing smile. When he was alone but for his other son and the remaining guard, he turned to Ishui, gesturing for him to step closer. He didn't want the guard to overhear and spread unnecessary rumors.

"Yes, my Father?" Ishui asked curiously.

"I have need of you. Find for me the herdsman, one Doeg the Edomite." He grinned at his son. "Heed me well, my son, for I have a task for you well-suited to your nature."

---

[8] Deuteronomy 20:7.

And Saul told his impetuous son his plan. As he talked, Ishui's smile grew to match his father's.

14

David strummed the harp strings, losing himself in the music that drifted off in the stiff breeze of a cooling evening. He needed the soothing sounds more and more these days. As responsibilities piled up, David found himself relying upon these moments of peaceful solitude where he could praise and worship his God. David enjoyed the composition of prayers, voicing his thoughts and heart through songs and psalms.

He sang softly, baring his soul to Jehovah, and trying to ease his tortured mind. Below him, the camp of the Indebted stretched out along the gentle slope of a forested hill. Less than four hundred men remained of his original thousand. There had been recruits over the last three years, but nowhere near enough to replenish his thinning ranks. His total force now numbered just short of seven hundred men.

For the last three years since he was given command of the Indebted, he had given his entire life to obeying his king's command to be valiant and to fight the LORD's battles. He bore a multitude of scars now, not a few of which marred his soul. He was no longer a wide-eyed, uncertain lad eager to please.

At twenty-one years of age, David had become a warrior in his own right. His skill in battle had become renowned. He'd slain hundreds of Philistines, so much so that women often sang of his prowess, echoing those words he'd first heard when returning from the slaughter of Goliath...*David has slain his tens of thousands.* He'd led his men into battle scores of times in defense of the cities, towns, villages, and farms up and down the fringes of the Shephelah plain.

He'd even gained a name among his enemies. The Philistines' bounty on his head had grown over the years so much so that he had grown wary of men of Belial,[1] Hebrews who had forsaken the yoke of God and who may harbor enough greed to try and collect the bounty. Worrying about the Philistines was one matter, but it was another completely to worry about his own countrymen.

David smiled grimly at the thought. He'd become a magnet during a battle. The Philistines had come to believe that only David's death would reverse their ill fortunes. They would attack him without reason, often in disorganized, insane rushes that allowed David and his now incredibly disciplined fighting force to cut them down with ease.

David sighed deeply, allowing the cares of command to run off his shoulders. He strummed the harp, trying out a few lines of verse. He didn't struggle to compose songs. Words came to him with ease, the accompanying notes springing forth from his fingers seemingly of their own accord.

Tears came, and his chin quivered with emotion as he stared up into the darkening sky. He needed Elohim then, his need like a burning flame that sat atop his heart trying to consume what was already consumed. And for the next hour, he worshiped his God, allowing his passions, his fears, and his love to pour out before the LORD.

At length, he was interrupted by Shammah who came puffing heavily as he climbed the hill to where David sat under the stars. He seemed grim, though he offered nothing except to say, "A messenger, my lord Captain. From the king."

David's fingers stilled, the last notes drifted off with the breeze that tugged at David's beard. It had been three long years since a messenger from the king had come directly to David. He received his orders from Abner, but the king had been mysteriously silent.

---

[1] Deuteronomy 13:13; 1 Samuel 30:22.

The last messenger from the king had ignored David altogether, instead going to Adriel and informing David's armorbearer that he was being recalled back to Gibeah.

David sorely missed his friend. Over the last years, they had practically been inseparable. They had fought side by side so often that having him gone felt like a missing arm. Adriel served not only as David's friend, but as a tie to a deeper friendship—Jonathan. Some of the most joyous occasions for David had been when Jonathan had contrived some excuse to visit David. The three of them would go apart and renew their friendship. They were as brothers, their bond strong—and Adriel was part of that bond.

"What tidings does he bring?" David asked.

The large man shrugged, still wheezing from his rapid climb. The man needed to lay off the wine, but David doubted that would ever happen. "We know not," Shammah replied, gasping between words and scowling. "His words are for you alone. I like it not."

David stood then and slung his harp around his shoulders by a leather strap. "Then we should hear the man." He eyed Shammah. "You were elected to fetch me?"

The bald man fixed a glare upon the tents below. "Aye. Curse the lot. They did it on purpose, surely."

"My lieutenants have ever been lazy and good for nothing," David agreed, deadpan.

Without thinking, Shammah said, "Aye! That's the truth of it! You should scourge the whole lot..." He trailed off, eyeing David with displeasure as realization struck.

"Good advice," David agreed seriously. "Find me a man willing to administer the floggings and we will see it done after I hear the messenger's tidings." Still keeping a straight face, he strode away down the hill.

Behind him, the thickly bearded man muttered, "Insolent captain. T'will be an armless man that I find to administer the flogging, be assured of that!"

David grinned. He had developed a rapport with his men that had been strengthened through battle beyond anything words could adequately express. The Indebted had developed into a highly skilled and discipline fighting unit. David's pleasure at their growth and newfound camaraderie knew no bounds. He saw each man as his brother, and many had saved David's life.

The young captain found his other lieutenants gathered around a nervous-looking messenger just inside the pool of light of a central cooking fire. No doubt his men had been plying the man with insults and threats, trying to pry the tidings from his lips. Typical of soldiers the world over, news from home held particular importance for each man.

"Make way," David called, shoving between two of his men.

They grudgingly made room for him, but crowded close, eager to hear what the man had to say. Upon seeing David, the messenger bowed. "My lord Captain. I bring word from the king."

"Directly from the king?" David asked.

The man hesitated. "Nay, my lord. Not directly. I am but one sent throughout all Israel to announce these tidings. We were instructed to seek out each captain and the elders of each city."

David frowned. Typically, such a thing meant good tidings—though not always. Mostly, this happened when the king would call Israel together to one of the yearly feast days or to relay word of a great victory—such as when David had killed Goliath those years ago. But sometimes it was to warn of an invasion or of a new tax levy.

"Then say on," Eleazar said, his face screwed up impatiently. "Our captain is here, man. Withhold your words no longer!"

Clearing his throat, the man said, "Let all Israel rejoice! The king has betrothed his beloved daughter, Merab, to Adriel, son of Barzillai. The king is well-pleased with his son-in-law, Adriel, and much honor has been added to the house of Saul. All are to rejoice in this." This last phrase was said in a whisper. Clearly, the messenger knew to whom he spoke and knew what his words would mean.

David stared at the messenger in stunned disbelief. Adriel? Merab? How could this be? What cruelty was this?

Adino, his lanky form looking much like the spear he leaned upon, put a hand on David's shoulder. "I am sorry, my lord. I can't—"

David shrugged off the hand. "These are false words," he spat out. "A trick of my enemies."

The messenger reddened at being called a liar. "These are the words I was tasked with speaking, my lord."

David glared at him so harshly that the messenger flinched. "Did the king, of his own tongue, bid you to say these words?"

"Nay. We were told by the captain of Saul's personal guard. He bade us to say these words."

"Then they are false," David spat out, barely able to keep his temper in check. He wanted nothing more than to remove the messenger's head for speaking such cruel words. "The king has promised his daughter to me."

Seeing the dangerous glint in David's eyes, Shammah intervened. "David, he would not knowingly speak false words."

With tremendous effort, David kept his temper in check, but his left hand gripped his sword's pommel so tightly that the knuckles showed pure white. "You have delivered your tidings, messenger. Leave."

The poor man scrambled away, no doubt offering prayers of thanks to Jehovah for being able to leave in one piece.

David stood trembling, all the peace and calm of only minutes before having been shattered by the messenger's words. "Break camp!" he bellowed. "We march for Gibeah this night!"

His lieutenants exchanged worried glances. "It is not meet to travel at night," Adino drawled. "Perhaps the morning would suffice?"

David's eyes glinted dangerously. "I would be in Gibeah as quickly as may be, Adino. I would know the truth of these tidings from the king's own tongue."

"And what then, my captain, if they be true?"

David hesitated. He hadn't thought that far ahead. But then he shook his head. "Nay. Adriel would never betray me. This I know. The tidings must be false."

Adino looked doubtful. He too liked Adriel, but all knew that the king's messengers would not speak falsely. To do so would mean death. "Then if it be not true, let us wait until morning, my lord."

David pulled at his beard in frustration. Adriel should have returned by this time. The fact that he had not left a seed of doubt in his mind. He wanted—needed—to discover the truth of the matter. Still, traveling by night would not be wise. He relented. "Very well. But we leave at first light."

But at dawn, the situation changed yet again, and not for the better.

Two men entered the camp shortly before first light as David's men were stirring in preparation to march toward Gibeah. One wore the royal armband around his upper right arm. David did not know this man well and had met him only once at the feast following his triumph over Goliath. This was Ishui, son of Saul. The other man was well-known to David, and the instant the young captain laid eyes on the redheaded man, he had to suppress a violent urge to draw his sword and run the man through.

Gripping his sword tightly with his left hand, David bowed low to Ishui. "My lord, this is an unexpected visit. What may your servant do for you? David ignored the Edomite completely, and not without cause. For Doeg the Edomite was no friend of David's.

Ishui, tall like his father, but wearing a haughty smirk, didn't even bother to look at David. Instead, he swept his eyes over the camp as the men began the process of preparing to march. He pointed. "What goes on here? Where do you march?"

David's lips tightened. He didn't want to say, so he lied. "We seek the LORD's enemies wherever they may be, my lord. This is the task your father, the king, has set for me."

Ishui grunted. By this time, most of David's lieutenants had gathered around. They stood in stony silence, instinctively understanding that something ominous was occurring and not liking it. The king's son finally looked at David, dismissing the rest of the men as easily as one would lose interest in a slug. "That time has passed," he announced. "You are to return to my father, the king. I will take command of these men and lead them into battle where I may."

Shocked, David almost let his mouth fall open. "My lord! This is unseemly. Your father—"

Ishui stepped right up to David, so close that his nose nearly poked David in the eye. Since he stood several finger-widths taller, Ishui looked down at David and sneered. "My father has commanded, harper. You will do as you are told. Are you not Saul's servant? Are you not bound to obey?"

David's natural obstinance to such behavior began to assert itself. He stood rock still, refusing to back away so much as a toe. His fingers curled into a fist, and only Adino's hand coming to rest on his shoulder prevented him from punching the impudent prince right in the gut.

"You do our captain an injustice," the spearman drawled as if the air around the two men was not already filled with violent tension. "You know well that he will obey the king's command."

"I would hear it from his tongue, Indebted."

David realized then that Ishui was trying to provoke him into a fight. The prince's nostrils flared in anticipation, and his eyes smoldered in contempt. And if it hadn't been for Adino, David would have gladly traded blows with the pompous prince. Throttling his anger, David stepped back carefully. "Then listen well, son of Saul. I am the king's man and will obey."

Ishui's lips curled in disdain, but his eyes reflected disappointment. He had been prepared for a fight and when one had not developed, he seemed not to know what to do. The prince floundered for words, the scars on his face and arms whitening as his blood pumped. At length, his eyes hardened as he came to a decision.

"You have lifted yourself above your station, shepherd," he said, eyeing David with apparent glee. "My father knows the truth of this and has given my sister, Merab, to a better man than you."

This confirmation that Saul had broken the marriage promise hit David like a dagger in the gut. His entire body stiffened as the implications struck him all at once. So, King Saul had disdained David, and Adriel had betrayed him. His body shook with emotion, and his mind seemed to shut down.

It might have stayed like that, but Ishui seeing the pain in David's eyes had to push it further. "Your armorbearer was most pleased to be betrothed to my sister, and Merab was grateful not to be betrothed to a lowly dog. I too am well pleased to have Adriel as brother-in-law." He looked David up and down. "Much more so than you, shepherd."

David's eyes snapped into focus, boring into Saul's second-born son like an awl through leather. His body went perfectly still, and his muscles relaxed. In the last few years, he had discovered this island of calm right before the enemy engaged him. It allowed him to cast aside all emotion, to focus on one action, one purpose.

To kill.

Ishui had no idea how close he was to death at that very moment, and if it wasn't for Shammah, who no doubt recognized the signs, David would have beheaded Saul's son in one lightning quick draw and swing of his sword. But the huge man interposed himself between the two men, causing David to take a long step back lest he be bowled over by the large man. Adino steadied him, while at the same time pulling him even farther back.

"For our part," Shammah said to Ishui, "we are glad to have the fool Adriel gone from our midst. He talked overmuch, so we too are pleased with this betrothal, and we are most happy that you have brought such joyous tidings. We thank you, prince."

Ishui's natural inclination was to attack the impudent man who had dared to insert himself between him and his victim, but one look at the muscular bald man and his great size caused the prince to hesitate. He was doubtless a bully at heart, and bullies were cowardly when faced with a fight where the end was in doubt.

Finally, he snarled and stepped to one side to glare at David. "I dislike your face, son of Jesse," Ishui snapped, losing patience with the whole affair. "I wish it removed from my presence. You will leave now to present yourself to my father within two days. My servant Doeg will accompany you, and you will be chargeable to him in all matters. His task is to see that you go straightway to my father. Two days, son of Jesse. You must present yourself to my father in two days."

David still wanted to draw his sword and wage war upon the son of Saul, to see his blood spilled upon the ground and his lifeless carcass hung upon a tree.[2] But Shammah's intervention had reminded him that this man was the son of the Lord's anointed and to injure Saul's son would be to injure the king himself. That was something David could not bring himself to do.

He bowed to Ishui, a formality only. There was no real deference in the gesture. "As you command, my lord."

Hardly mollified, Ishui grunted and then looked at the lieutenants. "Stand the men down. We stay here until I give leave. Let no man who draws sword depart the camp upon pain of death. Things have been entirely too lax here, and I will not allow it to proceed further." He glared about, but no one said a word. "Any family in camp must leave immediately. You are indebted, and it is time you remember your place."

Quite some time had passed since the Indebted had been so threatened. David had relaxed many of the restrictions placed upon his men, knowing that they would fight better if they had something to fight for. Ishui seemed determined to undo all of that.

The lieutenants stared stony-faced back at the king's son, looks David was all too familiar with. He had seen the same expressions when he had first been given command of these men.

---

[2] Deuteronomy 21:23.

Ishui glanced at David. "Why are you still here, son of Jesse?"

Biting back a scathing retort, David bowed again, turned and went to his tent. He moved quickly to gather his things. He was anxious to be off. He needed to learn the truth of the tidings regarding Merab and to set things right for the Indebted. Only the king could do that.

He found an ass, bound his things to it, and led the animal to the outskirts of the camp where Doeg was lounging against a tired-looking ass laden down with supplies.

"I am ready," he said curtly to the redheaded man. "Let us go."

Doeg's curly red hair bounced as he swayed his head around to peer at David. It had been some years, but David recognized the man's perpetual sneer, one he seemed to wear around anyone he felt was beneath him. He was a stout man, muscled, but with much of it going to fat. His red beard was unkempt, ragged, and untamed. Crumbs of his last meal clung to the red bristles tenaciously. Wrinkles ringed his eyes, giving him a squinting appearance that only enhanced the disdain his sneer affected.

"Took long enough, shepherd." He lazily reached over to take hold of the guide rope and stepped away from his animal. "Come along then. We can't keep the king waiting overlong."

He began walking then, but at an infuriatingly slow pace. David matched it, brimming with impatience, but knowing that the time was not right to hasten the Edomite along—for standing on the fringes of the camp with his arms crossed was Ishui. He watched David until he was out of sight.

15

The first day of their journey back to Gibeah took them into the hills north of the Elah Valley. It was an odd route to follow, but when David questioned his companion, the surly Edomite simply shrugged and said that he knew of a shorter way than the traditional one.

David didn't believe him, but Ishui had commanded David to travel with the herdsman, and he'd come to believe that if he didn't do as Ishui had commanded, there would be repercussions. Not that David feared for himself, but he worried for his men. He had no doubt that Ishui would take vengeance upon the Indebted if his orders weren't obeyed.

"What do you know of the betrothal of the king's daughter?" David asked at one point as they slowly descended a steep hill. He probably should've remained silent on this topic, but he couldn't help himself. He'd put a lot of thought and energy into fulfilling the dowry that Saul had tasked him with. He'd thought he'd done all that his king had wanted. He needed to know why things had changed.

The Edomite glanced around at him and grinned maliciously. "I know little more than you. This Adriel, son of Barzillai, if I remember his name correctly, pleased our master and was rewarded with the king's daughter to wife." He paused, still grinning. "Is not this daughter the one you sought as wife?"

"Aye. I do not understand what has taken place."

The Edomite shrugged. "The ways of kings are beyond such simple men as ourselves."

That, as far as it went, was certainly true. David continued to struggle with his disappointment. Already early signs of depression were beginning to creep around the edges of his mind. He decided to change the subject. "Why did King Saul call upon you to be my escort? I could make this journey alone."

"Perhaps. But then perhaps you have done something displeasing to the king, and he wants someone he trusts to watch over you."

"And you are a man to trust?" David asked sardonically. The two men had never gotten along all that well. Doeg was the one who had told Saul of David's anointing by Samuel. For a time, that revelation had created tension between David and the king, but that had largely been smoothed over—no thanks to Doeg.

The redheaded man scowled. "You doubt my integrity?"

David snorted softly. "Aye. I do, herdsman. Would you like to make something of it?"

Doeg glared at David, but David just stared back, smiling confidently and letting the full weight of his well-earned reputation come to bear on the Edomite. If the herdsman wanted to press the issue, David would be more than happy to solve their differences with fist or iron.

The Edomite did not rise to the bait. He turned away, jerking the lead rope of his ass. The animal brayed in protest, but the redhead would have none of it and cursed the beast, jerking harder. They fell silent then, both lost in their own thoughts, though David could hear the herdsman muttering to himself from time to time. The silence suited David just fine.

Along about sunset, Doeg stopped. "We'll camp here."

David looked around. "Here" was nowhere. By his reckoning, they were somewhere west of Jerusalem near the Valley of Rephaim. He couldn't see the valley from his location or spot the light of a single town or village. It seemed fitting that they would be lost in the wilderness. It matched his mood.

"We would've been in Bethlehem by now if we'd taken the established routes," David pointed out.

Doeg shrugged. David was starting to hate that gesture. The slovenly man said, "We'll still make it in time. There is no need for haste."

Deciding that there was no point in arguing, David went about preparing the camp. He pitched his tent on a patch of smooth ground and unbuckled some of his armor, laying it aside. He sighed as he flexed his muscles, freed from the armor's weight.

He then saw to his ass, giving the animal a portion of grain he kept in a sack tied to the animal's back. The ass would graze on the autumn grass to supplement the grain.

The stars began to poke out through the clouds, and the moment David could see three stars in the sky, he knew the day had ended and another had begun—not that he minded. The previous day was one he wanted to forget. Somewhere, what might have been the sound of a trumpet or a ram's horn carried faintly to his ears like a soft tone he couldn't quite identify, but one he knew subconsciously he'd heard.

Doeg began to kindle a fire. Once the small flame was well fed, he produced some salted meat which he set to cooking. The sizzling meat tickled David's nostrils and caused his stomach to rumble alarmingly. He suddenly realized he had hardly eaten since that morning. For his own part, he had brought some jerked meat, and some Elah nuts that Adino had forced on him, but little else.

The Edomite gestured to the fire. "Come. Sit. Eat with me."

David turned a suspicious eye on the man, wondering why the man was suddenly so friendly. He studied the redhead for a time but detected nothing untoward. Finding a flat stone near the fire, he sat down. The warmth of the fire felt good against the chilling air.

"Hungry?" Doeg asked?

"Aye. I have not eaten much this day."

"Good. The meat will be ready soon."

David frowned. The man was not talking like himself. He was being overly pleasant—almost subservient. The man only acted that way when he thought there was some advantage to himself. Perhaps he was worried that David might harm him in some way. But no, the sly redhead thought his position superior to David's. He wouldn't push it to the point where it turned violent, but he would not refrain from belittling David when and where he could. Something about all this set David's senses to tingle alarmingly, but he couldn't quite determine the source of his unease.

The two men sat in relative silence for a time, the only sound being the crackling of the fire and the sizzling sound of the meat as it roasted. David's stomach growled yet again.

Finally, the meat was finished, and the Edomite speared it with his dagger. He tore the meat in half and proffered a still sizzling portion to David. The young captain took it, handling it by Doeg's dagger and smelling the rich aroma that set his stomach to growling like a bear warning another predator to stay away from its kill. He licked his lips and lifted the meat to rip off a chunk with his teeth.

And something made him hesitate.

Some instinct warned him that what he was about to do was wrong. He examined the meat carefully and could detect nothing untoward. He wouldn't put it past the Edomite to poison David's food if the opportunity presented itself, but that wouldn't be within the herdsman's character. The Edomite might stab someone in the back, but poison was too subtle, too sophisticated for the herdsman.

So what had made David hesitate?

"What means this delay?" Doeg demanded. "Eat."

"Why so hasty?" David demanded in turn.

"The food is good. I would not see my efforts wasted." So saying, the herdsman took a large bite of the meat himself, chewing and swallowing in apparent bliss.

"Is this goat?" David despised goat meat. And giving David something he hated *would be* within the Edomite's character.

"Nay. It is lamb. Eat."

Lamb. A memory stirred in David's mind. Just a short time ago, a sound had reached his ears, a sound he had dismissed. A trumpet. A sudden chill of apprehension swept over David. He hastily counted the days in his mind. This was the seventh month. The Feast of Trumpets[1] had been observed how many days ago? Ten.

Today was the Day of Atonement, the holiest day of the year to any devote Hebrew.[2] On this day, the high priest would make atonement for the sins of Israel.[3] More so, this was the only holy day where Elohim commanded each Hebrew to afflict their souls by fasting the entire day![4] In addition, no one was allowed to do any work.[5] Violators of these holy commands would be cut off from Israel or assuredly destroyed by God Himself.[6]

David threw the meat into the fire and rose to his feet in a tower of anger. "You knew this day to be holy!" he roared, hand searching for his sword hilt. The cursed weapon was not there, lying well out of reach beside his tent.

Doeg scrambled back, his face ashen even in the firelight. "What is this that you say?"

"This is the Day of Atonement, vile dog! This is a day to afflict our souls with fasting. You would have me break this most holy commandment! You would have me cut off and destroyed in Israel!" David quivered in unsuppressed rage. He knew in his heart that this had been Doeg's plan from the beginning, to lead David far into the wilderness where he could not hear the trumpets that announced the Day of Atonement to all Israel,[7] where he would eat and thus violate the most sacred of days.

"I know not what you mean, Hebrew," Doeg sputtered. "This is as any other day!"

David had enough. He strode around the fire and kicked the meat out of the Edomite's hand. The man squeaked in shock and scrambled back, but not quick enough. David snatched him by the front of his tunic and jerked him to within an inch of his face. "Do

---

[1] Leviticus 23:24.
[2] Leviticus 23:27.
[3] Leviticus 16:29-31.
[4] Leviticus 16:31, 23:27.
[5] Leviticus 16:29, 23:30-31.
[6] Leviticus 23:29-30.
[7] Leviticus 25:9.

not speak false words to me, you lying jackal. By the God of my fathers, Doeg, you are worthy of death for the deeds you have done this day."

The herdsman's eyes grew round in fear as he struggled against David's grip, but nearly four years of warfare had hardened David's muscles and his rage would not be thwarted.

"I did not know!" Doeg whispered in a hoarse voice, thick with fear. "I did not know!"

"You are in Israel, dog, and here, even a stranger must obey this holiest of commands.[8] We will rest this day and fast. Seek my God, Edomite, lest He strike you down for your sin this day. If you so much as eat another bite, I will slay you. Say that you understand!"

"I understand!"

David shoved the man away in disgust, his heart still racing. He had just narrowly avoided a tremendous blunder. The events of the day before had shaken him, and he'd lost sight of the fact that he had stood on the eve of the Day of Atonement.

Doeg scrambled back out of David's reach. He stared at the captain who had been within a moment of ending his life, and still he dared to ask, "And what of the king's command to present yourself to him this day?"

"Fool. The king cannot command a man to break the Sabbath[9] of this day. There will be no traveling. We rest. Do not presume to speak for the king, dog."

The words struck the herdsman like whips. He flinched violently at the anger that still laced each word and wisely fell silent, backing away from David even more.

David ignored him. He needed to compose himself and prepare to seek God's mercy for his sins this year past. David knew that it was impossible to be right with himself until he was first right with his God. This was the ultimate purpose of the Day of

---

[8] Leviticus 16:29.
[9] Leviticus 23:32.

Atonement and the necessity of afflicting one's soul. On this day, a man could renew both his heart and mind.

The high priest would be doing the same, though to a much more severe degree as he prepared himself to offer the necessary holy sacrifices. David didn't know how exactly the high priest would keep the Day of Atonement in a traditional manner since for years now the Ark of the Covenant resided in Kirjath-jearim[10] and the tabernacle resided at Nob with the high priest.[11] That, however, was not David's problem. For this day, he would afflict his soul and seek God's mercy for his sins.

Turning his back on the herdsman, David retired to his tent. There, he fell on his face and bowed himself to the earth. He would remain in this position for most of the day, rising only to see to basic needs and to the needs of his beast of burden.

For David, the Day of Atonement was a cleansing time for his soul. He both dreaded the day and looked forward to it with great eagerness. The contradiction in his emotions was not lost on him. He dreaded having to face his sins, how he had disappointed his God, how he had failed in his love for Jehovah. But he loved the cleansing aspect, how he felt renewed, refreshed, and reinvigorated. There was nothing like it. He would always end the day with a sense of completeness and oneness with Elohim.

So, for this day, David set aside every other concern, problem, or burden. This day was to renew his spirit in his God.

---

[10] 1 Samuel 7:2.
[11] 1 Samuel 21:1; 22:19.

16

King Saul paced back and forth through the length of his court. Ishui had failed. And that dog of an Edomite had failed. How hard could it possibly be to provoke the son of Jesse into some unseemly behavior? David hadn't taken the bait and hadn't struck Saul's son. Such an act alone would have been justification enough to hang David for treason. And Ishui could provoke a rabbit into attacking a wolf. So how had David refrained?

But even then, the Edomite should've succeeded. If provoking David hadn't worked, then Doeg was to cause David to violate the holiest day of the year, the Day of Atonement. The plan was foolproof. But David had seen through the artifice, and worse, when word had gotten around how David had treated the Edomite for his lack of reverence for the Day of Atonement, it was Doeg and not David that the people spoke of stoning. Saul was forced to dismiss the herdsman back to his herds where he could cower among the cattle until the furor had faded.

Yesterday had been the final day of the Feast of Tabernacles, the last holy day of the year.[1] It was the most festive time of the year for Israel, but Saul had found little to rejoice in. The harvest had been particularly bountiful, but the people attributed such blessings to Lord's hand upon David. David was the one who had kept the

---

[1] Leviticus 23:33-44.

Philistines from burning the crops. David had driven the enemy away from Israelite cities and towns. It was David, David, David!

Saul growled in the back of his throat, and the two guards looked over at him apprehensively. All knew of his mental and physical spells and what it did to his temper when the evil spirit of the LORD was upon him.[2] The king ignored them.

The only other three men in the room were Jonathan, Ishui, and Adriel. Saul's other sons had departed on various administrative tasks throughout the coasts of Israel. Ishui's presence here troubled Saul. He turned to his second born and said, "I am glad that you have returned, my son, but what of the company of Indebted that I gave you charge of?"

Ishui shrugged. "They were an unruly lot, Father. Undisciplined and lazy. I flogged many, but even that failed to motivate them. It seemed prudent to disband them."

Saul blinked in surprise and sat down heavily on his chair. "You disbanded them?"

"I dispersed them into other companies."

The king considered this apprehensively. Over the last three years, the company of Indebted under David's command had become the most celebrated and famous of Saul's fighting forces. It didn't surprise Saul that his second son couldn't command David's former comrades. Few people liked or trusted Ishui, a fact that Ishui was completely oblivious to.

Ishui's lack of leadership ability was one of the reasons Saul still hoped to win over Jonathan. His eldest son would make a wise and goodly king and would preserve the family name and honor. Saul doubted that Ishui was even remotely capable of such behavior. Only David stood between Saul and Jonathan. Only David stood between Saul and his legacy.

Jonathan was shaking his head. "This was most unseemly, brother. The Indebted should be honored for their service. If anything, they should be given their freedom!"

---

[2] 1 Samuel 16:14, 23, 18:10, 19:9.

Ishui snorted. "They deserve it not. They were lazy in their obedience and walked the line of treason. We are well rid of them, I say."

"Father," Jonathan appealed, "you know what the Indebted have done. We should be honoring them with their freedom."

Saul knew that this wasn't a fight he could win, but in granting the Indebted their freedom, it would be the same as disbanding them. In this, Saul saw a glimmer of an idea. If they were dispersed, David would be further isolated. Saul knew now that making David a captain had been a mistake.

He nodded to his stricken eldest son. "You are right, my son. These men deserve our gratitude. Prepare a messenger. We will make them free in Israel and let them go home to their families."

Jonathan grinned. "Thank you, Father!"

Ishui's face betrayed his displeasure. He didn't like having his will thwarted, but he rarely made an issue of it. He liked to push his authority upon others in more direct ways. "All except the fifty I brought with me," he countered.

"What fifty?" Saul asked.

"They are the most troublesome of the Indebted. They should not be granted their freedom."

"Who is among them?"

"All the lieutenants. I've had each flogged at least twice. By my word, Father, most should be slain."

Jonathan stepped up to protest again, but Saul held up a hand to forestall him. "We will not slay valiant men," Saul told Ishui. "But as you say, I will not free them. Not yet. Have them camp without the city. I will see to them at another time."

Saul saw relief in both Jonathan's and Adriel's eyes. He remembered then that Adriel had been a comrade-in-arms with most of the Indebted for a number of years. This thought gave birth to another. He motioned for Adriel to approach. "Have you yet seen David, my son?"

"Not of late, my lord," the good-looking man said, his face full of apprehension.

"Does he begrudge you then?"

Adriel pulled at his left thumb nervously. "I believe so, my king. My betrothal has pierced him to the quick."

That too had been part of Saul's plan. He'd hoped that by hurting David, the young captain would behave unseemly. But thus far, David had acted wisely.[3] It was a constant source of irritation for the king.

"I would not that there be enmity between you two," Saul lied to Adriel. "It would be well to make sure your friend."

"The enmity is not between us, my lord. I fear it surrounds us. I would not have it so, but it may not be otherwise." Adriel pulled harder at his thumb. "May I speak my mind, my lord?"

Something in his tone arrested Saul's attention. "Aye. Speak."

"The matter of my betrothal to your daughter is the source of this enmity. Yet there may still be a way. Your second daughter, Michal, loves David.[4] Could we not give David her in the stead?"

Saul sat up straighter. "This is so? Michal loves David?"

Jonathan, seeing a solution to bring David back into his father's favor, stepped up next to his new brother-in-law. "This is so, Father. Michal has so said at least once."

Knowing Jonathan's tendency to under-exaggerate matters, this meant that Saul's daughter had been outright vocal about her feelings on a number of occasions. Saul let a smile grace his lips, pleased.[5] *This could work.* "Aye, this is well. I will give him her."[6] Mentally, Saul added almost gleefully, *That she may be a snare to him.*[7]

He would try one more time to pit the hand of the Philistines against David.[8] If it failed, he would have to resort to more direct methods, but the best scenario would be if David were to die by

---

[3] 1 Samuel 18:5, 14, 15, and 30.
[4] 1 Samuel 18:20.
[5] 1 Samuel 18:20.
[6] 1 Samuel 18:21.
[7] 1 Samuel 18:21.
[8] 1 Samuel 18:21.

other hands than his. Michal would be a snare all right—in more ways than one.

"Adriel, go. Seek David and bring him to me."

"Is that wise, Father?" Jonathan asked. "Perhaps it would be best if I call him."

"Nay. Whatever problems lay between Adriel and the son of Jesse must be put aside. I would not have this among my most favored servants." Saul speared Adriel with a steely glance. "Make it right, my son, and bring him to me. Say nothing on the matter of Michal. I wish to be the one to tell him."

Adriel bowed stiffly. "I will do as you command, my lord. Where do I seek the son of Jesse?"

Jonathan pointed toward one of the walls. "He is in his house and has so abided since his return."

"I know it." Adriel bowed once more, turned and left.

Saul watched him go. He didn't much care if Adriel and David patched things up. In fact, it would serve Saul well if they did not. Regardless, if David had been truly offended at losing Merab, then what would he do to win Michal? Thank Jehovah for Michal's misplaced infatuation!

David instantly recognized the voice of the man hailing him from outside his house. For an instant, intense anger and pain flared up like a seething volcano, but David clamped down hard on it. He'd had more than twelve days to get used to the fact that King Saul had given Merab to one of his good friends. He didn't like it, but he had come to accept it.

Still, knowing that Adriel stood without brought back all the original pain and anger like a flashflood. He took a long moment to regain control of himself. He then went to the door of his small house and opened it. A small courtyard had been built in front of the two-story abode. Brick walls separated David's house from his neighbors, but it remained open in the front, which is where Adriel stood looking like a rabbit cornered by a wolf.

"Adriel," David acknowledged. He somehow made it sound like both a greeting and an accusation.

His former armorbearer winced. "I am unworthy, my lord."

David regarded the man, trying to determine a proper response. Adriel's words were not an apology, and David, thinking about it, realized he would not receive one. Jonathan had warned David that Adriel had long desired Merab, so when the opportunity had come, it should not have been surprising that he had jumped at the chance. David couldn't very well blame him for that.

It wasn't that David loved Merab. He didn't, at least not in the same sense that Adriel did. For David, it had been more about being the king's son-in-law. It had hurt that Saul had so disdained him and all his work to fulfill the vaguely worded terms of the dowry that had been imposed upon him. He'd spent over three years of his life trying to please Saul, and clearly, he had somehow failed.

None of that made it easier for David to resist smashing his fist down Adriel's throat. His words, however, belied his feelings. "It is done, Adriel. There is no undoing it. Perchance, we should move on from this ill state of affairs?"

"Most gladly, my lord."

"I perceive that you are come for another reason as well. What would you have of me?"

"The king commands you to come and stand before him."

David sucked in his breath. He hadn't seen the king in over three years. He knew in his heart that he had somehow offended King Saul, but he didn't understand how. When he had returned with Doeg after the Day of Atonement, he had presented himself to Saul's court as commanded by Ishui, but he had been refused entry. A messenger had ordered him to return to his house—a house given to him by King Saul—and to await the king's pleasure. That had been nearly two weeks ago.

"Then let us go," David said, his heart a bit lighter. All he wanted was a chance to make things right with his king.

Though the bond would never again be the same between the two men, they walked side by side to the king's house.

Saul felt nervous, and this angered him. Why should he be anxious in the presence of the son of Jesse? For years now, Saul had been hearing of David's exploits, his prowess, and his uncanny ability to be victorious in the face of certain defeat.

I am still king, he shouted into the vaults of his mind. A shout that was also a prayer. Would that Jehovah Elohim would be with him once more!

Saul swallowed hard and sat straighter in his chair. He effected an air of vaguely displeased interest, an aura he had perfected long ago.

The door opened, and David strode through followed by Adriel. Saul's eyes narrowed as his fears were instantly justified. This was no boy that had come before his king. This was a warrior, a man who had shed much blood. The boyish face had long since faded in favor of a leaner, more rugged appearance. The scraggly beard had filled out and was well-trimmed and reflected the strength of the man beneath. David had added a handbreadth to his height, and his body had swelled with well-toned muscles. Saul could pick out battle scars; one in particular ran raggedly from David's left ear and disappeared into his beard, leaving a white line that the beard would never be able to fully hide.

It was more than David's appearance that grabbed Saul's attention. It was his presence, the air of command and self-assurance that clung to him like a well-used cloak. David was truly a leader of men on par with Saul himself. Here stood a true challenger to Saul's throne—not an upstart boy with delusions of grandeur. And the Spirit of the LORD was so obviously upon David that it sent a cold spike of dread deep into Saul's heart, like a death knell that would forever ring in his ears.

David strode up before his king and bowed deeply. Then he did an astonishing thing. He fell to his knees and bowed with his face to the earth. "My king!" David cried, his voice deeper and stronger than Saul remembered. "I am here at your command. Command your servant, and I will obey."

Saul kept his eyes on David, ignoring all the others in the room. The next few moments might save Saul's house. "Rise, son of Jesse. Know that I am well pleased with you."

Hesitantly, David rose to his feet, his body seemingly to unfold from the floor. Saul stood then too. He was still noticeably taller than David,[9] and he didn't much like looking up at the younger man from his chair.

"I feared it to be otherwise, my lord," David said. "Have I not been valiant for you?"

Saul read a touch of rebuke into the question, and his heart hardened further. "You have been most valiant, my servant."

"Then if I may be bold, my lord, why then have you given Merab to another?"

"It was meet to do so, son of Jesse." Saul had no intention of explaining himself to one of his servants. "It is not for you to question, however."

David immediately bowed again. "Forgive me, my lord."

Saul waved the apology away. "It is naught. But know that I am truly pleased with you, and your service should not go unrewarded." He gestured toward where Merab and Michal stood. Merab looked understandably nervous, but Michal looked hungrily at her father. Saul had not told her his plan, but she was an intelligent girl and had no doubt figured out part of it. "Know that you will this day be my son-in-law in the one of the twain.[10] Behold my daughter Michal. She I will give you to wife. What say you, son of Jesse?"

David took his time to answer. He looked first at Michal and their eyes met. An understanding passed between them, though

---

[9] 1 Samuel 9:2.
[10] 1 Samuel 18:21.

exactly what, Saul could not say. For Michal, David would be the best match she would find. That she loved him was beside the point and played only a small, yet significant, factor in Saul's decision. For David, this meant he would become the king's son-in-law, something any man would desire. For Saul, David would be bound to his family, true, but more importantly, Saul could lay a snare for David's life.

David turned his eyes back to Saul. "I thank my lord most humbly. I am unworthy of this gift. It is too much."

Saul froze. That was unexpected. "Say it not. You have been most valiant, my servant. Accept your reward."

"Allow me leave to afflict my soul and seek the will of Elohim, my lord."

Saul cursed under his breath. He could not in good conscience refuse such a request. What was wrong with the man? Why wouldn't he accept the offer? Saul softened his voice, trying to sound fatherly. "My son, this is well said. Take leave then. Seek our God's face and know His will. I doubt not that Jehovah would refuse you the daughter of the LORD's anointed." He threw this last at David like an invisible dart.

David's face twitched at the words, but he did not change his mind. He bowed yet again. "Thank you, my king. I will do this thing."

Saul waved his hand. "You may go."

David turned and walked from the room. His gait lacked the determined swagger evident when he'd first arrived. No, Saul judged David to be uncertain. *Good.*

But a seed of doubt had grown in Saul's mind. *What if David refuses?* He gnawed on this fear, turning it over in his mind and examining it. No, he could not take that chance. He needed this betrothal between David and Michal or it would be more difficult to arrange the harper's death.

He looked at Jonathan and Adriel. "Go, commune with David secretly, and say, 'Behold, the king hath delight in you, and all his servants love you: now therefore be the king's son in law.'"[11]

His son looked worried. "Why must this be done?"

"I don't want David to refuse out of some misunderstanding or act of pride. Make sure he knows that he has his king's favor." Saul gestured to Michal. "Do it for your sister."

Jonathan looked at his sister and saw the hope that so obviously filled her eyes. "Would you have me speak thus, sister?"

"Aye," she said breathlessly. "I would. I would be wife to David."

Saul's eldest son straightened. "Then I shall." He nodded to Adriel. "Come, my friend, let us seek out David."

King Saul watched as they left. If rubbing his hands together in glee were a kingly gesture, he would have done it.

---

[11] 1 Samuel 18:22.

17

"Why this unseemly hesitation, my brother?" Jonathan said to David. David fingered the strings of his harp, letting the chords fill the room. The soothing sounds helped him think. When he was most confused or unsure, he would compose a song. It was amazing how setting words to music could so mimic his heart.

His refusal to give King Saul an immediate answer confused him. He had almost accepted. He should've accepted. Only a doubt clung to his heart like a canker sore.

Adriel chimed in. "Aye, my friend, Jonathan has the right of it. There is no need to hesitate here. The king has said that he delights in you."[1]

All three sat on mats in David's house. Light from the open door illuminated the three of them and murmuring voices discussing one matter or another could be heard as men and women passed by outside.

David spoke his doubt aloud, "Do you think it is a light thing to be the king's son-in-law, seeing that I am a poor man and lightly esteemed?"[2]

"What nonsense is this?" Jonathan scoffed. "Wait. Nay, perhaps it is true. Your father is among the poorest I've ever seen.

---

[1] 1 Samuel 18:23.
[2] 1 Samuel 18:23.

His house is akin to an ant hill in size. His fields like sparse patches of weeds. 'Tis true."

David winced and then grinned. "Nay, my father is wealthy, but I am the eighth son. My inheritance will be naught."

Jonathan waved that aside. "It is not your wealth my father seeks."

"But I am lightly esteemed," David insisted. He took in Adriel with a raised eyebrow. "Why else would your father disdain me and give Merab to Adriel?"

Adriel's voice filled with sadness. "Do you so desire her?"

"Nay," David replied sharply. "She is pleasant to the eyes, 'tis true, but so is Michal. I question the manner of it. I do not begrudge you her."

"It seems that Michal finds you easy on the eyes too, my friend," Jonathan teased.

"Truly?"

"Aye."

David heaved another sigh. "Still, I fear this is all some ruse, for what purpose I know not. What can I give in the way of dowry?"

"Have you not given enough?" Jonathan asked. "All Israel is indebted to you, and once, years ago, my father promised his daughter to the one who slays Goliath. You have the right."

David sighed. "The Philistines yet abide in their coasts and cities…"

The other two men looked at him in astonishment.

"You think you must utterly destroy the Philistines?" Jonathan asked.

"Is that not what your father wishes?"

"You think my father's decision was based on this?"

Doubt still rattled around in David's head. "I know not what lies within your father's mind, Jonathan. I know only that I am unworthy of your sister and unworthy to be the king's son-in-law. I fear what your father wishes is beyond my power to give."

And there was really nothing more anyone could say to that. Jonathan sighed and shook his head. "I think you are mistaken."

David nodded soberly. "Perhaps. But only time will tell."

Saul listened to his son's report of his conversation with David.[3] Adriel added a bit more insight to David's mind, but in general, it seemed clear that David didn't think Saul would ever let him marry one of his daughters. He didn't believe Saul would ever ask for a dowry he could fulfill.

In many ways, Saul agreed. But if it was a matter of being worthy, then the answer would be simple. Unfortunately, David was a rival, one created by Samuel. David must be put to death and preferably by the hands of the Philistines.[4]

Time to put the rest of his plan into action. "Clearly, the son of Jesse will not agree unless he feels worthy. He needs to fulfill my dowry request. Tell David that the king desires not any dowry, but a hundred foreskins of the Philistines to be avenged of the king's enemies."[5]

Jonathan frowned. "Truly, Father? This seems overmuch. His company has been disbanded. Only a few of his men are encamped nearby."

Saul knew this of course and was why he had said it. To claim a hundred foreskins meant David would need to engage a much larger force than merely a hundred men—one large enough to overwhelm David and see the end of the son of Jesse's interference. There was another way to meet the requirement though. David could do it piecemeal, over time. So he added, "Should not such a dowry be difficult, my son? Should not the son of Jesse show himself truly worthy? Let him acquire the foreskins if he may, but he must do so within a fortnight's time. No more."

"Father—"

---

[3] 1 Samuel 18:24.
[4] 1 Samuel 18:25.
[5] 1 Samuel 18:25.

Saul cut him off. "Enough said, my son! Take my dowry offer to David. Let him decide if he is worthy or not."

Jonathan bowed stiffly, turned on his heel, and stalked out of the room. Saul sighed deep in his soul. His son didn't yet understand the dangers that the son of Jesse posed to their house and future. He would one day, but until then, Saul's duty was to destroy any threat to his house. He grieved for his son's blindness, though, and wondered how his son could be a proper king unless he could see more clearly.

There was yet time. Time to slay David. Time to turn Jonathan's heart.

"A hundred foreskins?" David repeated, his mind working furiously.

"Aye," Jonathan said, "within a fortnight's time."

David shrugged. He could do it in two weeks surely. During the last few years, there had been several times when he and his men had slain more than a hundred Philistines. True, David had had a thousand men under his command at the time. Now he had only fifty. But these fifty included his lieutenants.

"The condition is acceptable," he told his friend. "I can do this." He became excited. All he had to do was slay a hundred of the uncircumcised Philistines, and he could be the king's son-in-law. Pleased,[6] he couldn't help but let a grin spread across his face.

Jonathan and Adriel exchanged a glance. "Aye, 'tis simple, much like skinning a lion while it is yet alive and vigorous." Jonathan mimicked David's shrug. "Simple."

"Do you doubt my prowess in battle?"

"Nay. May I suggest that you leave your sword behind? I think you'll need naught but a pile of rocks to throw. Your aim must surely be equal to the task, and we would not want to give you an unfair

---

[6] 1 Samuel 18:26.

advantage when you face the mighty host of the cowardly Philistines."

David smirked, finding his friend's droll humor pointed if nothing else. "I take your meaning, my brother. But if it be Jehovah's will, none shall stand before me. And I would be your brother in more than one manner. Dissuade me not from this course."

"Then I shall go with you," Jonathan declared. "I would see this dowry paid in full so that you may be my brother-in-law."

Adriel looked somewhat startled at this announcement, but David's heart warmed at the words. Still, it would not be wise. "Nay, my brother. Only men under my command may go. This is my task. Let it not be said that another man paid David's dowry." David glanced at Adriel who also seemed on the verge of volunteering. "You must abide here as well, Adriel. You are betrothed and should not risk your life in battle until you are well wed."

The handsome man nodded glumly.

"But there is something I would ask of you," David continued. "Please call my lieutenants. I would meet with them and plan our action."

Adriel stood up, grateful to be able to serve. "I will do as you request, my lord." He hesitated. "And thank you."

Turning, he left David's house. A small weight lifted from David's shoulders when the other man had left. He had forgiven the man, but that didn't mean he no longer felt some measure of pain every time he was in his former armorbearer's presence.

"He's a good man," Jonathan said after Adriel had disappeared out the door.

"Can you now read my mind?" David inquired.

"'Tis not hard. Your muscles do not relax while he is around."

David grunted softly. "I know he is a good man, but knowing he betrayed me in accepting Merab is hard to take."

"My father gave him little choice, my friend. The mind of my father was set on this, and nothing would dissuade him. Do not bear any further ill will against Adriel."

"I will try."

"Good enough, then!" Jonathan clapped David on the shoulder. "What plan do you have for collecting these foreskins?"

"The Philistines have a garrison at Timnath[7] of around four hundred men. I will draw them out by burning some of the farms and villages in the vicinity."

"Timnath? I do not much like that city. 'Tis where Samson's troubles began."[8]

"Aye," David agreed, "but Samson mightily discomfited the Philistines, did he not?"

"And lost his life in the process,"[9] Jonathan pointed out. "How will you avoid the same fate?"

"By trusting in Jehovah Elohim. What else can I do?"

"Be wise. We trust in our God, David, but He trusts us to behave and act with wisdom. You know this. Consult with a priest first, I beg. Know Elohim's will before you act."

David rose to his feet, his eyes gleaming. "Aye! This is well spoken. I will do so without delay."

He left an astonished Jonathan sitting on the floor and immediately strode out of the house, bent on having the consultation done with before his lieutenants returned with Adriel.

The local priest was Amzi, an aging man of nearly eighty years. He received David into his house with the crusty attitude that some elderly men obtained when the years weighed heavily upon their shoulders. He used a staff to get around, and he peered at David through eyes that no longer saw clearly.

"David, eh?" He grunted in displeasure. "Never heard of you. What do you want, young one?"

David placed some gold coins in the priest's hand. "For you, honored one, to help ease your latter years."

The priest sniffed in disdain, but he quickly pocketed the coins. "Very well, young one, I thank you for thinking of an old man. Few seek me out these days. Not that I'm complaining, mind you. I like

---

[7] Also spelled Timnah.
[8] Judges 14:1.
[9] Judges 16:30.

my peace. But King Saul seems to have forgotten the old ways. I am surprised that one so young has come to see me. What is it that you want?"

The man's memory was failing, David noted. This was not the first time David had sought the LORD's will from Amzi. Clearing his throat, he said, "I would know Jehovah's will, my lord. Should I go up against the region of Timnath? Will the LORD deliver the garrison there into my hand?"

The old man gripped his staff tightly. He wore the linen ephod, an apron-like garment with an embroidered front that depicted stones representing all the tribes of Israel. The ephod worn by the high priest contained real stones, but most priests abroad wore a facsimile of the original that was not nearly as ornate. The ephod represented the office of the priest and his right to commune with Jehovah Elohim. Amzi was undoubtedly related in some way to Aaron, the original high priest. Only men of Aaron's line wore the ephod.

Growing serious, the man nodded. "Very well, young one. I will inquire of the LORD for you. Stand still."

The old man dropped painfully to his knees and bowed his head. For a long moment nothing happened, then Amzi said is his crackly voice, "Speak. The LORD hears."

David sucked in his breath. No matter how often he did this, the holiness of what he was doing—communing with the God of the universe—always awed him. How could Jehovah be mindful of man? Knowing he must speak, he asked, "Should I go against the garrison at Timnath? Will they be delivered into my hand?"

Amzi's voice changed, growing deeper and less broken. "Go. Thou shalt prevail, and the daughter of Saul shall be thy wife."

David shuddered. He wondered if this was how the high priest felt when he stepped into the most holy place within the tabernacle. Amzi coughed, regaining his cackling, broken voice, and struggled to stand upright. David hastily helped the old man to his feet.

"Did you hear what you wanted, young man?" the priest asked.

"Aye. The LORD will deliver the garrison into my hand. It is well."

"Is it then?" the priest asked, wheezing in near silent laughter. "Be warned, not always do men hear what was truly said, nor do men always get what they truly wanted or needed."

David looked questioning at the old priest. "I understand not."

The man wheezed again. "Most young ones do not," he agreed. "We ask what we will of the LORD, but do we ask what the LORD wills?"

"You speak in riddles. The LORD spoke. I will be victorious."

"There are many types of victories, young one. Sometimes, our greatest defeats come at the hands of our greatest victories. The end may be different than you envision."

David struggled to decipher the man's riddles. How could defeat come through victory? It was a contradiction in terms. He shook his head. Clearly, the old man's wits had deserted him.

He bowed to the priest. "I thank you for your time…and your words."

The old man laughed wheezily and turned, hobbling away. "Words are spoken cheaply. It is the heeding of them that costs." He cackled again. "So, we shall see. Aye, we shall see."

18

David watched as the smoke billowed black and high into the air. The fields burned well, and if the garrison at Timnath could not see this, then they were blind. An autumn mist had gathered in the early morning dawn, hovering low in the valley like a blanket and obscuring much of the surrounding terrain. But the billowing smoke rose above this and would be visible to the garrison which lay beyond the cloaking mist.

"It is done, Captain," Shammah said, stepping up beside him. The bald man had woven dried lizard tails into his beard, which added a macabre aspect to his appearance. As long as David lived, he would never understand the huge man's penchant for weaving parts of dead animals into his beard before entering battle.

"The farmers?" David asked.

"Dead."

David nodded. This was the cruel side of what he did. Mercy and compassion were unknown between enemy nations, and even a hint of kindness would be exploited and turned against the enemy. More so, fraternizing with the idolatrous nations was strictly forbidden and punishable by death.[1] Israel had already learned the hard way how easy it was to be led astray by the seemingly glamorous and pleasurable ways of living that appeared so attractive in heathen cultures.[2]

---

[1] Numbers 25:5-9.
[2] Numbers 25:1-9.

Elohim was holy, and He expected His people to live holy.[3] Other nations knew this, and they set out to deliberately corrupt Israel when they could, knowing that the easiest way to enslave Israel or destroy her was to first corrupt her. David ruefully reflected that corruption was historically an easier method of conquering Israel than warfare.[4]

David was taking no chances with this dilemma. When facing seemingly harmless Philistine farmers, they were still slain. This was the way of the world in which David lived.

Nearly fifty of David's men hovered nearby, awaiting his next orders. "The Philistines will be upon us soon," he said for all to hear. "They must answer what we have done here." He looked at Adino who seemed nearly asleep as he leaned against his spear. "Move west through the valley and take up a position where we can ambush the garrison."

Timnath had been built in the middle of the Sorek Valley, almost due east of Ekron. The valley was popular among farmers for the rich soil and the stream that rarely ran dry. Incidentally, it was the same stream that flowed through the ravine in which Adino had killed nearly three hundred Philistines three years before. Wistfully, David wished he would've harvested the foreskins back then, making this entire raid into Philistia unnecessary.

No. Not unnecessary. Philistia was ever a thorn in Israel's side. Now or later, this battle would be necessary.

Adino gestured to Mahli, one of the lieutenants that David had won over during the last few years. "Make for that spur to the north. Keep the men quiet. No noise."

Letting Mahli lead, the men slipped nearly soundlessly through the trees of the valley toward where they would ambush the Philistines coming from Timnath. Only the jingling sound of armor and weapons could be heard.

---

[3] Leviticus 11:44-45.
[4] The entire book of Judges.

David looked around at the hills. Somewhere around here, Samson had burned the Philistine vineyards and destroyed their crops.[5] The irony of what David was doing was not lost upon him in following Samson's footsteps. Samson had afflicted the Philistines because the woman who was supposed to be his wife had been given to another.[6] The similarities in their situations was uncanny.

David and his men moved up the slope where they could see the entire valley floor. Somewhere toward the west lay Timnath and the Philistine garrison.

They waited. But not for long. First, a few fleet-footed scouts scampered ahead, appearing and then disappearing in the mist like wraiths. David let them go unmolested. He was after the bigger prize.

Then, out of the mist, vague shapes could be seen marching in order. Colorful headdresses caught the eye while the duller banded leather armor seemed almost indistinct in the fog. The iron heads of spears, like a forest of branchless saplings poked out of the low hanging mist.

David held his men at the ready. He wanted the bulk of the Philistine garrison to pass him so that he could hit any of the bowmen or chariots they may have brought along. In the resulting chaos, David's men should have an easy time killing at least a hundred of the enemy warriors.

When the time was right, David gestured, and his fifty men slipped down the slope as silently as spirits. They did not yell, shout war cries, or otherwise let the enemy know they were there. Over the last few years, David and his men had almost become extensions of each other. They knew instinctively what their captain wanted and moved as if of one thought through the early morning mist.

They fell upon the Philistines like a pack of wolves attacking larger prey. They never uttered a word, knowing that the silence of their mist-shrouded attack would completely unnerve the

---

[5] Judges 15:5.
[6] Judges 14:20, 15:6.

superstitious heathens. Screams of pain and then screams of terror began to fill the misty air. The Hebrews moved like wraiths, killing one man and then pulling back into the shadowy fog only to strike again in a completely different location.

David wielded his sword with a hybrid technique taken from Eleazar's fluid almost dance-like movements, Shammah's brutal straightforward attacks, and Adino's lightning fast stabs and spins. He killed two men in rapid succession, their blood staining the ground in muted red as seen through the fog.

Grimly, he stalked into the Philistine ranks like the death angel of lore. A Philistine materialized out of the midst, his eyes wide and terror stricken. He saw David and flinched violently, lifting his spear in a weak defense. David batted it aside and stabbed the man in the chest, the heavy iron point of his sword parting the leather bands and slipping between the metal studs to take him in the heart.

The Philistine gurgled in stupefied terror, clawing at the sword before falling limply to the dewy grass. David dismissed him from his mind and went hunting for another.

Adino bounded by, startling David. The lazy man lost all his slothful demeanor once the battle had begun and seemed almost like a boy at play. He twirled and stabbed, leaving a trail of bodies in his wake. He, more than the others, had been often flogged by Ishui. The lazy man's bearing had naturally irked the second son of Saul. When questioned about it, Adino had merely shrugged the matter aside in favor of the Elah nuts David had brought with him.

David growled—more a chuckle really—and headed off in a different direction, knowing it was probably useless to follow the deadly Adino. And for this battle, David wanted to be intimately involved. This was his dowry to fulfill, so it was his task more so than for the others.

A Philistine body flew through the air and landed at David's feet. The man's skull had been caved in by a heavy club. Shammah stalked out of the fog, his huge form frightening even David. For a moment, he saw Goliath, the giant he had killed in the Valley of Elah.

Then he saw the lizard tails in Shammah's beard and breathed out in relief as his lieutenant took on more normal proportions.

"These Philistines are scurrying around like rats, Captain!" he boomed, no longer even trying to remain quiet. "They're as slippery as eels!"

David grunted and pushed past his lieutenant. Shammah happily let his captain pass and went off in his own direction, whistling tunelessly in a macabre parody of Eleazar's habit.

And so it went. The Hebrews destroyed the Philistine garrison with a great slaughter. When the sun finally burned away the fog, revealing the valley floor in its entirety, over two hundred Philistine warriors lay dead, about half of the entire Timnath garrison.

Adino and Eleazar, both grinning broadly, approached David. "It is a great victory," Adino admitted, already looking bored despite his grin.

Eleazar's sudden frown was obligatory, however. He whistled a sharp contradictory tune and added, "Mark my words, the Philistines will retaliate for this."

David shrugged. "The Philistines need no excuse. They despise us. We will be ready for them when they return."

Eleazar looked doubtful, but then he always looked that way. David surveyed the field, stretching tired muscles. He had taken no wound from this battle, a rarity, and one for which he silently praised Jehovah. "How many did we lose?"

Adino, once again leaning lazily on his staff, frowned sadly. "Eleven, Captain, including Mahli. Some Philistine dog skewered him from behind with a spear."

David winced. Eleven was a tolerable casualty rate when compared to the two hundred dead Philistines, but each man had been with David for a long time. He would grieve deeply for these men. He remembered Mahli. The man had questioned David's ability when David had first taken commanded of the company of Indebted. Despite that, they had grown close over the years, and he would be sorely missed.

"Gather our dead," he told Adino. "I would not leave them behind for the Philistine vultures." Glancing at Eleazar and Shammah, he said, "Let's harvest the foreskins. I want two hundred to give to the king, and I would be away from here quickly before the Philistines realize that we are truly few in number."

"Aye. The fog served us well," Shammah rumbled. The man was blood-spattered and sported a few minor wounds which he seemed not to notice.

David fingered the long scar on his cheek. Not one of them would ever be the same for the battles they had fought. They were all changed. It had yet to be revealed whether or not the change was good.

Sighing, David set about to collect the foreskins.

Reverently, knowing what it would mean, David set the two bags, stained with blood, on the ground in front of King Saul's chair. He stood, offering his king a deep bow, before stepping back. "Two hundred Philistine foreskins," he announced to the silent onlookers. "To fulfill the dowry of a hundred foreskins and make Michal my wife."

Saul's court was filled nearly to overflowing for David's audience with the king. But David had eyes only for King Saul and Michal who stood slightly behind her father. Michal's eyes above her veil looked proud as she gazed at David.

Few believed that David could achieve the feat of acquiring one hundred foreskins in so short a time. But a week and a half after Saul's challenge, David had not only accomplished the deed, he had doubled the dowry price. Tales of the battle spread quickly, and as usual, had raced ahead of David and his men. So it was, that when David arrived in Gibeah, Saul and his entire court were waiting.

Jonathan, Abner, and other commanders of the army stood in silent ranks against one wall. Scribes gathered in a corner, writing furiously on stretched parchment with long feathered quills.

Saul stared impassively at David. The young captain wished he could read the king's face to know his thoughts, but as ever, Saul revealed little. The king stood and stepped over the two bags. He didn't bother counting them, even though there were exactly two hundred[7]—David had made the count himself three times.

"You are well come to our court, son of Jesse," the king said, his deep voice able to penetrate to the furthest corners of the large room with ease. "And you have purchased my daughter, Michal, with the foreskins of these, my enemies. Do you have a token to give her?"

David had come prepared for this. He pulled out a gold chain from a pouch at his side. The chain ended in a gold medallion studded with precious jewels. He had plundered it off a dead Philistine lord that he'd slain in battle some time ago. It was worth more than most people would ever see in their lifetime. It was the only thing David had ever kept, giving the rest to his men. Originally, the piece had been meant for Merab, but its purpose would be served just as well for Michal.

Taking a deep breath, he moved to stand before Michal. She smelled of flowers, he noted, and his knees suddenly went weak and he had to lock them firmly in place. Michal had dressed in all white silk, and the soft cloth rustled around her ankles as she turned to face David. Her eyes smoldered triumphantly as she looked at the gold chain.

Unlike her sister, David knew that Michal cared not for jewelry, but the token of their betrothal far surpassed what Adriel had given to her sister. This, she no doubt believed, was a proper betrothal token.

David held it forth and said the ritual words, "By this token, you are set apart for me, according to the law of Moses and Israel. By this covenant you are mine."

---

[7] 1 Samuel 18:27.

She took the medallion with stately grace befitting the daughter of a king. "By this token," she said, her voice ringing throughout the room, "let all know that I belong to the son of Jesse to be his wife."

"It is done!"[8] Saul declared, his deep voice sending echoes of sound through the room. He moved next to his daughter and uttered the traditional benediction, "The LORD make my daughter as Rachel which did help build the house of Israel."[9] He then turned and kissed David's cheeks. "And let all know that this is my son, that the house of Saul and the house of David have been joined by covenant this day."

A cheer rose from the crowd, mostly from David's lieutenants who stood in two ranks at the back of the court, but he could see pride and joy reflected in the eyes of everyone in the room. David took Michal's hand and they moved to the center of the room to receive the well wishes of the court members.

The wedding itself would not take place for a year or so. But in Hebrew custom, the betrothal was just as binding as the wedding. So, by any measure of the law, David was married and had a wife.

He couldn't keep a foolish grin from spreading across his face, and he was more than conscious of his wife standing at his side. More than that, he was now the king's son-in-law at last. He, David, a shepherd from the hills of Bethlehem had somehow found favor with the king and had become his son-in-law. Truly, the LORD had blessed him.

Adino, appeared before the couple. He looked strangely naked without his spear, but his eyes were wide and glittering with joy as he kissed his captain. "With this betrothal, I suppose you will no longer be our captain."

David was exempt from military service for at least a year according to the law of Moses. There were exceptions of course, but generally speaking, Adino was right. He clasped the lanky man's

---

[8] 1 Samuel 18:27.
[9] Ruth 4:11.

shoulder. "Then you will need to take my place until after the wedding."

Adino lost his grin. "Ah, no, my captain. Such a thing requires much effort."

"You were captain of the company before I came," David pointed out.

"Not by choice."

David smiled maliciously. "Then your fate has once again caught you, my friend, for I too give you no choice. You are in command."

Adino sighed. "Eleazar foretold that this betrothal was ill conceived and would doom our company. I see now that he was right."

David grinned, letting his gaze wander to Michal. They were espoused now. Her eyes twinkled as they looked upon him.

"Are you joyful, my lord?" she asked.

"Aye," he replied. "I am."

"It is well that I can please my lord." She gestured to the two forgotten bags of Philistine foreskins. "You have done your duty admiringly. Truly, the LORD is with you."

"It is well that He is."

She nodded and squeezed his hand. Her skin felt soft against his rougher, calloused hand. He took a deep breath and offered a silent prayer of thanksgiving to Elohim. All was well with the world right then. What more could a man ask?

19

King Achish's scowl could easily curdle milk. He stood before his throne, glaring at the roomful of courtiers. "This cannot stand!" he shouted, his mind filled with anger. He raised a crumpled piece of parchment above his head. "The son of Jesse has slaughtered the Timnath garrison. Over two hundred lay dead on the field of battle, mutilated by the hand of Jesse, their foreskins harvested like so much wheat!"

Gasps and exclamations of rage rose from the audience. They had been called to attend Achish, and the Philistine lord would only call the council together if he had a matter of import to lay before his advisers.

Ahuzzath, high priest of Dagon, took a step forward, commanding attention. "This unholy circumcision of our dead must be answered, my king. This David must die. Dagon demands his blood and heart be sacrificed in the flame."

Achish's portly frame jiggled as he nodded. "Aye! The lord of Ekron is already on his way here. Send messengers to the other three Philistine lords. I would call a convocation. What we do concerns all the tribes of Philistia." A roar of approval greeted those words. Achish scanned the room. "Where is the one called Maon who once claimed kinship with this David?"

A muttered rumble of anger spread through the crowd and Maon was pushed forward. The Hebrew fell to his knees and bowed with his face to the floor. "Here is your servant, O mighty king!" Maon cried.

Achish plopped back down in his throne with a grunt. "What is meant by this unholy mutilation of our dead?" he demanded of Maon. "Is this some wretched desire of your Hebrew God?"

Maon looked appropriately worried. "Nay, mighty king. Never have I heard the like. This may be a message by David's hand, one meant to weaken our hands and erode our resolve for the true gods of Philistia!"

It was a pretty speech, Achish admitted to himself. Ever the pragmatist, Achish could appreciate the clever use of the tongue. And the Philistine lord had learned long ago never to cast aside talent when it could be exploited instead. In fact, if he knew a way to turn David to the Philistines, he would jump upon the chance in a heartbeat. Right now, however, indignation and anger were the needed weapons. David's attack on the Timnath garrison and subsequent mutilation had stung, and Achish wanted to capitalize on the raw emotions of his people.

"You think this unholy mutilation is a message from David then?" Achish demanded.

"Aye, my king. David seeks to provoke you and the other Philistine lords into rash action that he might destroy you."

Shock and awe was not an unfamiliar tactic to Achish. He'd utilized it on a number of occasions himself. He thought about it for a moment, trying to see if there was a way to turn it to his advantage. An idea came to him. "Stand, Maon. I have a task for you."

Maon stood warily to his feet. "Speak and I will obey."

"I will compose a message for the king of Israel, Maon. We will demand that the king turn David the son of Jesse over to us so that our gods may exact just retribution for this foul deed. You, Maon, will deliver it."

"Me?" Maon squeaked.

"Aye. You know their vile tongue and can convey our true intent. Besides," he added, looking around, "no true Philistine should sully his soul by coming into the presence of a worshiper of Jehovah. You, therefore, will be our messenger."

Maon visibly swallowed. "Must I go into the presence of King Saul?"

"Nay. Give it to the first captain of his armies you can find and then hasten back to my side."

The former Jew sighed. "Thank you, my king."

The high priest of Dagon spoke. "Do not be yet hasty, king of Gath. We will need time to gather our strength, offer the proper blood sacrifices, and prepare the warriors. I counsel patience."

The portly king considered the request. It might be best to wait some months. If King Saul refused to hand David over, then the Philistines would be obligated to invade in force. "You are wise," he told the priest. "We will await the outcome of our conclave and do as you bid. Offer the sacrifices." He glanced at Maon. "But do not give this one to our gods. I will require him to deliver the message at the appointed time."

"As you say," the priest agreed. "The power of our gods will give us victory." The wily priest's eyes glittered darkly. "Indeed, king of Gath, we have among us those who have made a holy vow to slay this evil demon from the barren rocks of Israel." He gestured, and three men stood forth.

Achish was impressed.

He'd not seen their like since Goliath had stood within this very throne room. The first man, though not as large as Goliath, must have possessed the blood of the giants somewhere in his ancestry. He loomed large, and the gigantic axe he held casually over one shoulder looked able to cleave a man in two. The other two, one a spearman and the other a swordsman, held themselves with the quiet confidence of warriors who knew no equal.

Achish knew them, of course. He'd seen them in battle and knew they had no equal. The swordsman had once singlehandedly slain thirty Amalekite warriors. And Achish had witnessed the spearman once throw his spear two hundred and fifty cubits with enough force to completely skewer a wild boar on the run.

It was mention of a vow that surprised him. "What vow have they taken?"

The high priest straightened, his white hair seeming to glow. "They have vowed to keep themselves from women, to say no word, and to slay none other until the heart of David has been cast into Dagon's fire. They have but one purpose now—to slay David." The priest glanced at the gathered throng, reveling in the attention and power he had over the people. Raising his voice, he added, "Assemble your conclave, king of Gath, and then send your message to the weak king of Israel. But we adjure you by the gods of our forefathers to arrange matters so that these, our champions, are made to face the son of Jesse."

The lord of Gath nodded and then looked at the wide-eyed Hebrew. "Do you understand what is required?"

"Aye," Maon said softly. "And I thank you again for the opportunity to serve."

Achish waved the thanks off. He didn't really believe any of what he had said to either the priest or the rebel Hebrew, but he needed to pacify the priest of Dagon and find a use for the Israelite, so he had said what needed to be said. And looking upon the priest's tattooed head and radiant, oblivious smile, he felt he had accomplished his goal.

In truth, other interesting rumors had been reported by Philistine spies regarding the state of affairs among Saul's court. Achish saw an opportunity here to create further discord in the ranks of the Hebrews. This David, it seemed, had been anointed to ascend to the Israelite throne. Achish doubted that King Saul had taken such news with easy grace.

Aye, there was a path here, one hovering just at the edge of his mental vision, a path that could culminate in the destruction of Israel, the death of King Saul, and the enslaving of this talented warrior known as the son of Jesse. That would be the ideal end to all this, but if David could not be turned, then he would die at the hands of these new champions.

"He must be slain!" King Saul shouted at his advisors. The time for subtlety had passed. Saul had tried to orchestrate David's death by the hands of the Philistines, but that plan had not worked. Now, more direct means must be employed to see the son of Jesse dead.

He glared at his counselors. "We must slay David afore he conspires to take the kingdom."[1]

Abner, a look of confusion dominating his typically implacable face, stepped forward. "Wherefore, my lord? Has not David served you well?"

Saul slammed his fist into his chair, sending it skittering violently across to the floor. "He is in league with Samuel," he bellowed. "Between the twain, they seek to rend the kingdom from my hand."

Now Jonathan stepped forward. "Not so, my father!"

Saul turned on his son and grabbed a fistful of Jonathan's tunic and jerked his eldest son within a fingerbreadth of his face. "You are blind, my son. The son of Jesse has somehow enchanted you. Can you not see?" He shoved his son away, looking about him. "Can none of you truly see? A conspiracy has been strongly made against me, and I alone am able to see it?"

There could be no doubt. Everything Saul had tried to do to see David dead had failed. There could only be one reason for these failures: there was a conspiracy. What else could explain the son of Jesse's ability not only to evade death at every turn, but to flourish? Saul wasn't certain of who all was involved in this conspiracy to replace him as king, but he knew Samuel, the Great Seer, was among those who supported David. Even Jonathan was suspect, but Saul wasn't yet prepared to cut off his son.

"He is your son-in-law," protested another of the counselors, cutting deeply into Saul's private musings.

---

[1] 1 Samuel 19:1.

But this fact only fanned the fires of the king's anger. "Aye, and by what trickery did he gain my daughter to wife?" Saul flourished his javelin, swiping it about him in anger. Two days had passed since that ill event. Saul had made a calculated mistake. He should've demanded a thousand foreskins instead of merely a hundred. He bristled at the thought. "He is now one step closer to taking the kingdom. This was all planned. He and Samuel have planned this!"

Everyone stared at the king—most in shock. Saul knew that David's exploits had endeared the young warrior to many of Saul's servants.[2] How could Saul rule when even his own servants loved his enemy? His rage built into a towering crescendo. "David must be slain! Find him, slay him!"

"But, my lord—" Jonathan again tried to intercede.

"Slay him!" Saul shouted again. "You will slay him! This is my command!"

Jonathan, his own face a mask of matching anger, stared at his father, his posture exuding rebelliousness. Snarling, the king's son turned on heel and stalked out of the court, slamming the heavy oak door closed as he left.

Saul let him go. He had given the command that would make him a murderer, and he had no intention of withdrawing it. David must die. The future of Saul's house depended upon this one fact. This he knew deep in his heart. If David continued to live, he would do so to the ultimate destruction of Saul's house.

He scowled at Abner. "You will instruct the army that if any man come upon David, he is to be slain."

Abner carefully schooled his face into his typical emotionless expression. "As you command, my lord."

At last. Finally, someone who would heed him.

"See it done," Saul said, feeling he must get the last word in.

---

[2] 1 Samuel 18:5.

"David! David!"

Startled, David rushed to his door and yanked it open to find a worried Jonathan standing there looking over his shoulder. The prince, without looking, reached up to bang on the door again and David had to catch the other's wrist lest he be smacked in the face.

Jonathan whirled around, saw David, and grabbed his arm. "Come with me now!"

The urgency in the prince's voice brokered no argument. David let himself be drawn out of his house and into the narrow street. Jonathan began walking rapidly toward the main gate.

"What is wrong?" David finally managed to demand.

"My father seeks to slay you."[3]

"What?"

"It is the evil spirit. Of this I have no doubt, but you must hide yourself—somewhere secret."

David yanked his arm free and came to a full stop, his heart pounding. His greatest fear had been realized. "Why, Jonathan? Am I not in his favor? What have I now done?"

Scowling, Jonathan grabbed David's arm and pulled him forward again. "It is the evil spirit. I'll try to sort it out, but I beg you, until I do, you must take heed to yourself at least until the morning."[4]

"I don't understand," David fairly wailed. Everything had been going so smooth, so perfect. What had happened?

"Neither do I," Jonathan admitted. "There is a grove of trees at the edge of the western meadow where a rock spire rises. Do you know this place?"

"Aye. It lies to the south of the meadow."[5]

Jonathan nodded. "My father loves to walk near there. On the morrow, I will prevail upon him to visit this place, and I will commune with him of you. What I see, I will tell you."[6]

---

[3] 1 Samuel 19:2.
[4] 1 Samuel 19:2.
[5] 1 Samuel 20:19, 41.
[6] 1 Samuel 19:3.

As they approached the gate, Jonathan hesitated. "Word may have gone before us." He pulled a hooded cloak out of his satchel. "Put this on and hide your face."

David did as instructed. Through the narrow opening, he could see the guards at the gate. They lounged, looking bored. Perhaps they watched those going in and out of the city a bit more carefully than usual. Perhaps that was David's imagination.

"Take this also," Jonathan said, handing David the satchel. "There is enough food for a day or two. You will have to abide in the field until I call you."

David had not thought of that. He took the satchel gratefully and slung the strap over his shoulder. Then together, they walked casually toward the gate. In his haste, David had not taken any weapons with him, but in truth, he didn't know what he would do if the guards tried to stop him. They may have instructions to kill David on sight, and though he would not easily be taken, he harbored no rancor against Saul's servants who were simply following the king's command.

As they neared the gate, David's heart began to race and sweat formed on his forehead. He had no wish to fight his own countrymen.

"I'll commune with them," Jonathan whispered. "Leave the city and heed not their commands to stop."

David nodded and took a deep breath, letting it out slowly and trying to affect a natural and casual walk. When they neared the men, Jonathan pulled ahead and approached the guards, hailing them loudly and bringing to bear the full weight of his commanding presence.

His hood pulled low, David continued to walk sedately, trying everything to avoid calling attention to himself. One of the guards still spotted him and called, "You there! Halt!"

But Jonathan pulled the guard's arm, jerking him back around. "I am speaking to you, soldier. What ill manners is this? Am I a slug that you so ignore me?"

The guard sputtered, trying to apologize to the prince, but Jonathan would have none of it. He started shouting at the man, gesturing furiously, and threatening all kinds of everlasting dooms if the man so much as ever again dared to ignore the prince.

In the confusion, David slipped away and turned west toward the meadow and out of the guards' line of sight.

He could still hear Jonathan yelling at the guard. *Bless him!* But soon, even the raised voice of his friend faded away with the early evening air. David shivered, grateful for the cloak. Winter was approaching, and the nights were growing colder.

Even the birds were largely quiet as if in respect for the turmoil that raged in David's heart and spirit. Once again, the man David had set out to please had determined to kill him. Once, years before, the king had cast a javelin at David's heart. The issue had been quickly and quietly dismissed as the result of the evil spirit that had come upon the king. Perhaps Jonathan was right. Maybe this latest threat was but the result of the evil spirit that plagued Saul. The king still had those moments of intense rage and depression. Maybe that was all it was, but if so, why was David so often the target of these rages? The pain in David's heart bit like a poisonous snake.

His thoughts became jumbled, confused. He had no idea what this would mean for his betrothal to the king's daughter—or if one had anything to do with the other. Saul had a history of reneging on his promises in that regard. Did the king truly not want David for a son-in-law?

Unsure and sick to his stomach, David hurried over the uneven ground of the south side of the meadow. Illuminated by the fading sun was a spire of rocks that rose above the trees. David would hide there and see what would happen in the morning.

Sleep didn't come easy. In fact, it didn't come at all. He missed his harp and the soothing notes that often allowed him to find his center and focus in his God. But this night, he could not. It was a lonely night in which David felt that even Elohim was ignoring him.

When morning finally arrived, he felt stiff and sore. The cold had seeped through the cloak during the night, invading his muscles and bones like some insidious disease. How he had longed for a fire, but he had dared not attempt it—even if he had had the means to kindle one. He walked around for a time, trying to work the kinks out of his muscles and trying to fight away the drowsiness of a sleepless night. He ate some, but the dried meat and fruit tasted bland. His stomach rebelled, and he eventually put away the food.

With nothing to do, he slipped down to the edge of the trees and peered into the rising sun to see if he could spot Jonathan and his father. He didn't know if his friend could prevail upon his father to take this early morning walk. The king seemed less inclined to listen to those around him, but David desperately needed for this to happen, so he prayed fervently for Jonathan's success.

Several hours later, two men, followed by a small squad of guards, made their way through the meadow. Dew hung heavily on the browning grass, and so the group skirted the edge to keep out of the taller stalks. David watched carefully, trying to mark their passage and predict where they would pass so that he might overhear the conversation.

Jonathan had clearly indicated the rocky spire as the place he intended to bring his father, so hiding among the rocks there would be his best option. He slipped deeper into the trees and made his way stealthily to the rocks. Finding a hidden niche nearest the side where Saul and Jonathan would come, he squeezed inside and waited.

A short time later, his ears picked up muted voices drawing closer. It took time, but eventually he began to distinguish the words.

"You do him wrong, Father." That was Jonathan.

"He would take the kingdom, son." Saul's voice, deeper and reflecting both disapproval and weariness, floated to David's ears.

Those words caught David's attention like a knife point aimed at his eye. Perhaps this wasn't about Michal after all. It was about David's anointing by Samuel. He'd thought that issue long ago settled. Apparently not.

"Where did this rumor spring from, Father? What has he ever done to teach you this fear?"

"Samuel—"

"The Great Seer resides in Ramah, my lord. You know this. He has not ventured forth in years."

"Except to anoint David to become king in my place."

"But you have bound him to our family, my father. He is betrothed to Michal, and she does love him. I too love the son of Jesse, and he harbors the same love for me. He would not lift his hand against us, so you have nothing to fear. Do not sin against him, for he has not sinned against you."[7]

Silence followed that remark, and David strained his ears trying to hear.

"It is hard to see otherwise," Saul said. "All Israel loves David. Even my own servants love him—as you have so pointed out. What more can he have but the kingdom?"

"He does not seek the kingdom, Father. Surely you know this. Everything he has ever done has been for you. His works for you have ever been good![8] He put his life in his hand and slew the Philistine, Goliath, and the LORD wrought a great salvation for *all* Israel. You saw this and did rejoice. Why will you sin against innocent blood and slay David without a cause?"[9]

David held his breath, listening for the king's response. When it came, it was tinged with a sadness and softness that David had rarely heard from the king. "You think this to be the right course, my son? You truly think me in error?"

"I do. The son of Jesse has ever been a loyal and trustworthy servant. Name one instance where he has not. Was he not valiant for you, for our people, and for our God? He has only ever done that which you have commanded him to do."

Another pause. Then Saul said, "Very well. As the LORD lives, he shall not be slain."[10]

---

[7] 1 Samuel 19:4.
[8] 1 Samuel 19:4.
[9] 1 Samuel 19:5.
[10] 1 Samuel 19:6.

David slumped weakly against the rocks, his relief palpable. If it weren't for the tightness of the cramped quarters, he would have no doubt fallen to the ground. Saul had sworn by God not to kill him. Few vows were stronger.

"Call the son of Jesse," Saul continued. "Let him stand in my presence as afore. Tell him…tell him to bring his harp."

David could hear the thick emotion that carried each word. David didn't doubt the king's sincerity.

"I will tell him, Father."

Their voices drifted off. After a time, David pried himself out of the crevasse in which he'd hidden and sat down heavily on a nearby rock. Sometime later, Jonathan approached after having made some excuse not to return to the city.

David looked up as Jonathan moved through the trees. The kings' son saw him and then sat down next to him.

"Did you hear?" Jonathan asked.

"I did. Thank you, Jonathan. Your care of me is most appreciated."

"Our hearts are knit. We are brothers. It will ever be thus."

"What of the others? Will Saul's servants seek to slay me if I enter the city?"

"Nay. The king has rescinded the order. All is well. Come. Let us go. We'll stop by your house and retrieve your harp. It would do my ears well to hear you play in my father's court once again."

"This is truly good tidings," David said, letting out a long breath and relaxing. His stomach growled, and a smile lit his face. "My stomach cries for food, my friend, and that which you gave me in the satchel is ill suited for such glad tidings."

Jonathan clapped him on the shoulder. "Aye! Such a feast must consist of a few cakes and goat meat, your favorite."

David shuddered. "'Tis a foul beast, I tell you truly."

The prince grinned. "But you are worthy of such great honor."

Suddenly, the dried meat in his satchel seemed much more appetizing.

20

The harp strings thrummed gently, the notes, surprisingly, setting King Saul at ease. He glanced at David, no longer a boy, but a warrior true, sitting against the wall and plucking at his harp.[1] The man's eyes were closed, which was a good thing, for Saul was unable to keep the venomous look off his face.

The whole world conspired against Saul. He had finally admitted that even Elohim had abandoned him. For clearly, the LORD was with David, the enemy of Saul.[2] He so desperately wanted to kill the son of Jesse, to end this agony of heart and mind. The source of all his woes could be laid squarely at the feet of David. Saul would have done it…he'd have killed David if it hadn't been for Jonathan. His son had maneuvered him into a corner, charging that murdering David would only make matters worse. Saul had to admit the truth of that, but he was on the verge of simply not caring.

He knew in his heart that the first opportunity he had to kill David, he would take it—murder or not. But Jonathan had helped make one thing abundantly clear. The time wasn't right, and the best thing to do when you knew an enemy plotted against you was to keep them close.

So, for the last seven months, Saul had to endure his enemy's presence in his very court and at his own table.[3] During the hours

---

[1] 1 Samuel 19:7.
[2] 1 Samuel 18:29.
[3] 1 Samuel 20:18, 24-25.

spent administering his kingdom, David's harp would alternatively irritate him and soothe him. If he could avoid looking at David, then he could let the music ease his tortured soul, but then he would conclude that such peace was a device meant to lull him into a false sense of security so that David could find some hidden advantage in his plot to snatch the kingdom to himself. Saul meant to stay vigilant against his enemy, so he resisted the heavenly music.

During meals, he had to endure David's laughter and association with his own family. He hated how his son so thoroughly trusted the son of Jesse. Saul despised how Michal would wait hand and foot on the young captain. He found it infuriating that David could so easily get along with the king's other sons.

Abner strode in snapping Saul out of his musings. The general brushed past the guards as if they didn't exist. Saul had expected his cousin's entrance. Word had been sent ahead of the general's arrival. The tidings would be bad if it had brought Abner back from the Philistine border.

Without preamble or greeting—other than a bow—Abner spoke, "The Philistine lords are stirring yet again, my king![4] They are gathering near Ekron and speak of vengeance for the Timnath garrison."

Saul raised a hand to still the sudden burst of muttered conversation that sprang up around the court. "Do you think they mean to invade?"

"Aye, my king. Their intentions are no secret for they sent a messenger."

This was new and might explain why Abner himself had come to see Saul instead of sending someone. The Philistines had never sent a messenger before. "What word did he bring?"

Abner looked troubled. "The messenger was a Hebrew of the tribe of Judah. He brought word from the five lords of the Philistines. They demand that we deliver David, the son of Jesse, into their hands. Their gods have demanded his shed blood and his

---

[4] 1 Samuel 18:30, 19:8.

heart thrown to the flame of their idols. All this in retribution for the so-called abomination of harvesting two hundred foreskins."

Saul had known that something like this would happen. Slaying men on the battlefield was one thing, but it was another matter to mutilate their bodies—particularly in the manner in which David had done so. It mattered not to the Philistines that Saul had requested such gory trophies as proof of David's dowry. All the Philistines knew was that circumcision was a solely Hebrew religious custom, and to have it done to their dead was an insult they could not abide.

Saul had made David odious to the Philistines, and that was something the king intended to use. If nothing else, he could blame any further Philistine depredations on David. It might even give him the pretext he needed to slay the shepherd.

The music had stopped upon Abner's words, and Saul noted that David was listening intently to the conversation. "Is that the entire word," he asked his cousin.

Abner shook his head. "They have given us a month to deliver him into their hands, my lord, else they will invade our coasts and do to us as David did to them."

The temptation to grant this request washed over King Saul like a flash flood. He nearly drowned in his desire to be rid of his enemy. But no. Giving David to the Philistines would undermine his own rule in the eyes of all Israel. They loved David, and if there was one thing Saul wanted more than David's death it was the good will of his people.

"What say you, son of Jesse?" Saul asked, turning to David. "Shall we give you into their hands?"

"If that is my lord's wish," the shepherd replied slowly.

Good. Saul enjoyed David's uncertainty. "And what course do you counsel, Captain?"

"Give me my thousand, my lord. Let me go forth against them. I will teach them not to make demands of the LORD's anointed."

He certainly sounded eager. Saul considered the request. It might be the best course, and since the Philistines were so set on

1 Samuel 19:8

killing David, it might be best to hope one final time that David would fall at their hands. "But you are yet betrothed," he pointed out to the harper.

David rose to his feet and set aside the harp. He bowed to Saul. "Then let us in haste prepare the marriage feast, my lord. Let me be wed to my wife, and then I will go and destroy these, your enemies."

Abner nodded. "This is well, my lord the king. We must teach the heathen dogs that they are unworthy to spill the least of Hebrew blood." He glanced at David approvingly before adding to Saul, "Have the marriage feast, my king. Then I will take David and destroy the princes of Philistia."

Saul didn't care much for what he heard. It bothered him that his general and cousin sought to work so closely with David, his enemy. But he couldn't rightly refuse this advice. It was the best option to deal with both David and the Philistines. "Then in five days, we shall have the marriage feast. Call my daughter. Let her prepare to be taken to her new home." He looked at David. "Call your family to attend you. Prepare yourself and your home, my son. For in five days' time, you will be wed."

The Hebrew wedding involved a certain amount of pageantry. For that one day, the bride and groom would be treated as royalty. It began with David's walk to Saul's house to claim his bride. David wore an elaborate robe, scented in frankincense and myrrh, and trimmed in gold. A wreath of new flowers adorned his head, and his sandals, borrowed from his father, were laced high up his calves. He wore two silver armbands on each upper arm, and they glittered sharply in the lamplight of the early evening.[5]

His hair and beard had been neatly trimmed, and effort had been made to hide the variety of scars on his face and hands.

---

[5] Isaiah 61:10.

Along with two of his brothers, he walked down the narrow streets and up the hill to Saul's house. His brothers carried lamps by which to see, and they too had dressed in their most stately outfits, lacking only the flowered crown and royal armbands. David's parents would wait at his house for him to return with his bride.

He arrived at Saul's house just as the sun disappeared behind the hills to the west. King Saul, resplendent in his royal robes, stood in the courtyard, his sons arrayed behind him. The women waited within to be called forth only at Saul's word.

"Who comes to the door of my house? What seek you here?" Saul demanded.

David took a step forward and bowed. "I am David, son of Jesse the Bethlehemite. I come to claim my wife, Michal, whom I purchased for a hundred foreskins of the Philistines."

Saul nodded. "You are well come, then, my son. Behold, your bride." He turned and gestured to the door. One of his sons opened it. The first woman through was Saul's wife, a stately if somewhat troubled woman. And then Michal followed, and David caught his breath in amazement.

Michal wore a silk halug that glowed golden in the lamplight. Her long, silken hair had been braided and was adorned with pearls. A gold tiara had been placed upon her brow, and diamonds glittered and danced upon a pendant that hung directly upon her forehead.[6]

David remembered to breathe after what seemed an eternity. He let his breath out explosively and found his mouth dry. Michal's beauty far surpassed his wildest imagination.

They had done something to her skin so that it had taken on the shining texture and luster of polished marble.[7] She looked so delicate, so queenly.

Her family formed a line, and as she passed each one, they whispered a benediction to her. When she reached her father, Saul took her hands and kissed her brow. "You are our flesh and blood.

---

[6] Jeremiah 2:32.
[7] Psalms 144:12.

May you be the mother of thousands and may your seed sit in the gates of their enemies and rule them."[8]

David waited as the final benediction was given by her father. Saul then walked Michal to David and put her hand in his. "Your wife, my son," he said, his face strangely emotionless. "You are of our family now. May your sons be strong and valiant."

David bowed to his king, and then smiling at his bride, he turned and walked stately out of the courtyard—well, almost stately. There was a bounce to his step that he couldn't quite control.

Michal reached up and touched her veil. She would not remove it until she entered her new house, but the gesture and what mysteries may lay beneath nearly made David stumble. She turned an upturned face to him. "Am I pleasing to my lord?" she asked in a trembling voice.

David swallowed hard. "You are," he said. She was his. His wife.

"Come, my lord," she urged him, "the feast awaits, and I would that all Gibeah see me."

David's mother had coached him carefully on this. The wedding procession to his house was the most important part of the ceremony for the bride. For this brief time, she was a queen. Everyone would want to see her. The talk of the city would center around Michal for the next day or two, and most brides wanted to get the most out of this special time.

The young captain, enjoying the feel of her hand, led her from the courtyard and out into the street beyond. Her family followed, and for a moment, Jonathan clasped David's shoulder as he passed, and that gesture, more than anything, settled him down.

A crowd waited outside the courtyard, torches and lamps were held high on poles to shed light on the bride and bridegroom. Virgins, still wearing their veils, lined the street on both sides. David and Michal would pass through them. The moment they stepped through the gate, music sprang into existence, laughter and cries of

---

[8] A similar benediction was given Rebekah in Genesis 24:60.

benediction were lifted up. Men ran before them, playing on instruments, and dancing preceded the happy couple.

The route to David's house was well known, and everyone had heard that David's father would set a wondrous feast for his popular son, so most of Gibeah had turned out for the wedding processional.

At one point, Michal grabbed his arm with both hands and pulled him nearly to a stop. "Slower," she hissed. "You're going too fast."

David blinked. He had already been walking at a slower pace than normal. He looked down at his wife, but her eyes were not on him. They were on the crowd. Indeed, she was truly enjoying this—even more so because her older sister had yet to have her wedding to Adriel.

And so they went, walking at a snail's pace. Men and women danced ahead of them, men to the front and women just behind, their movements graceful and joyful. Other men played popular songs of joy and praise on a variety of musical instruments. A few servants even walked ahead of the procession, handing out grain to the children, who scampered about laughing and playing.

Eventually, they arrived at David's house. The house had been cleaned and decorated from top to bottom by David's mother, sisters, and sisters-in-law. Flowers had been woven into long chains and draped around the door and windows. The air smelled of frankincense mingled with the mouthwatering smells of cooked foods.

Nearly as important as the wedding procession through the streets was the moment Michal would enter her new home. The moment they crossed the threshold, the wedding would be complete, and they would be truly and well married.

A pathway opened before them leading to the open door. Here Michal pulled David to a stop, and breaking tradition, she turned to him. "My lord husband, giant-slayer, do me the honor of escorting me into my house." For Hebrew woman, the home would be her domain, her place of rule. In those walls, she would ever be a queen.

The pause outside the door to the house was artfully done. David had planned on escorting her into the house all along, but the pause and the words—particularly reminding everyone of who she had married—created a rising cheer that rolled around them like a cacophony of thunder. Whatever else Michal might be, she certainly had a flair for the dramatic. David would be wise to remember that.

"Of course, my lady," David said in a ringing voice. "The house is yours."

Even the veil couldn't hide the wide smile that obviously spread across Michal's lips. It didn't matter to her that the house was obviously smaller than her father's. She clearly enjoyed that she had married the most well-known man in Israel. David's fame had spread far and wide, but she was the one who had married him.

Slowly, they approached the door and just at the entrance, she hesitated just enough for another cheer to rise into the night from behind her. Then with David a half a step ahead of her, they entered the house.

David's mother and older sisters met Michal there. "My daughter," Natzbet, the older matronly woman, exclaimed, converging on the new bride. "You are well come to your new house."

They removed her veil and attached it to the back of her hair. When Michal turned, David beheld her face for only the second time. He sucked in his breath. Michal was truly a more beautiful woman than he remembered. The first time he had beheld her face, she had done so just outside her father's court in a moment of anger some years before. Her face, now devoid of such anger, looked angelic to the smitten captain. Her nose might be a little too long and narrow and a mole growing off to one side of said nose might be unappealing to some men, but her full lips, stately cheeks, and a dimple arrested David's attention fully.

He swallowed hard and held out his hands to receive her. When she took them, Jesse stepped forward, his aged and rugged skin looked strangely soft in the lamplight. "My house is honored, Michal, daughter of Saul, to welcome you into our family. May your seed last for a hundred generations."

Michal bowed formally to her father-in-law. "I thank you, and may the LORD's blessing be upon this house."

Jesse smiled in a fatherly manner at her. "Then take your places so that we may begin the feast!"

A canopy of blue silk had been placed in the middle of the dirt floor of the house. The house wasn't very large, so most of the crowd stayed in the streets or in the small courtyard out front. But under the canopy, two solid-looking oak chairs, like thrones, had been placed. David led his bride to the chairs, and together they sat, much like a king and queen would, to hear more benedictions and well wishes from those coming in to partake of the feast Jesse had prepared.

The line stretched long, and it seemed as if the entire city had turned out for the wedding. Michal glowed under all the attention, and at one point, she turned to David and said, "This is as it should be."

David frowned at her, not quite understanding.

She gave him a tight smile. "It may be that the LORD will make you king after my father," she explained in a soft voice that only he could hear. "And I will be at your side. We will start a new dynasty, you and I. One greater than my father."

Her words sent a cold shiver through his body, and he stared at her uncertainly. *What is this?* The rest of the festivities made no impression on David at all. Michal's nearly treasonous words echoed endlessly in his mind. Faces appeared before him. Words were said. He smiled, nodded, and said words back. But it was all a blur. He saw none of it and heard none of it.

Even after the last person had left and David found himself alone with his wife for the first time, he felt numb. All his excitement and anticipation of this night evaporated into nothingness. His new wife had hinted at a coup, the usurpation of her own father. Now what should he do?

21

Traditionally, the wedding festivities lasted a whole week.[1] But two days after David had escorted his bride to her new house, Saul gave him command once again of a newly formed company of Indebted.

"You must confront the Philistines," Saul had charged him. "They seek your life for the deeds done to them. It is your duty to turn them back and chastise them for their impertinence."

So, not long after, David found himself leading a column of largely fearful and inexperienced men through the hills and mountains of western Israel toward Ekron where the lords of the Philistines had gathered with their armies.[2]

"This will end in disaster," Eleazar predicted. "These men are untrained and untried."

Adino, walking beside him with easy strides and chewing absently on Elah nuts, shrugged. "What does it matter? The Lord God of our fathers is with David. We will prevail."

The swordsman grimaced and whistled a short melancholy tune. "Aye. That is true, but the king could've given us our men back."

---

[1] Judges 14:7.
[2] 1 Samuel 18:30, 19:8 (Chronologically, the two verses could be referring to the same event or to two or more separate events. I chose to treat them as a singular event for the purposes of this novel.).

"Most of them were freed of their debt," the spearman pointed out. "Should we call them again from their homes?"

"They would've come."

David, listening intently, sighed. Eleazar was right. The men in his old company would've come in a heartbeat if he had asked. But he had not. They had earned their freedom and unless the king saw fit to recall them to battle, David was content to let them remain home.

Half of his lieutenants had remained with him, including Eleazar—which surprised David. The man complained so much that David had always believed the experienced swordsman would jump at the opportunity to go home.

These new men were not the same as David's original group he'd been given command over—undisciplined, fearful, unruly. These new men were simply young and inexperienced. But they would have to do. He'd molded men into an effective fighting force before, and there seemed no reason why he couldn't do it again.

Shammah, walking on David's other side grunted and ran his hand over his shiny bald head. "We don't need them. Just you and I could handle this lot of mangy dogs."

"These are the Philistine lords," Eleazar disagreed, punctuating his words with a sharp whistle. "They won't just run away because we show our faces."

"Didn't plan on it. Thought I'd let my club do the talking." Shammah swung his huge war club around his head for emphasis.

"Typical," Eleazar muttered. He glanced at David. "Other than our big friend's overly optimistic solution, what is your plan? The men will break and run the moment the battle swings against them. You know this."

David gave the swordsman a mollifying nod. "Aye."

"Then what is your plan?"

The young captain thought for a moment. "I thought I would just challenge them in the same manner Goliath once challenged us."

Eleazar stared at his captain in horror. Finally, he put his hand over his eyes and whistled a dreadful tune. "We're doomed," he moaned.

Shammah's ringing laugh echoed off the hills.

A spur of rock and an ancient ruined wall provided David with the perfect platform to issue his challenge to the Philistine lords. Before him stretched the Shephelah plain and the Philistine hosts, tens of thousands strong. Not as great as they once had been, the Philistine numbers were still respectable enough to cause David a measure of alarm. If they decided to invade, Israel would be hard pressed to hold them back.

The Philistines' colorful headdresses danced in a stiff wind, like swaying swashes of colored grain. The measured beats of the Philistine drums reverberated around David and his men. The hill David had chosen to make his stand sloped steeply to the west, providing a formidable barrier to the front, but if the enemy decided to outflank him either to the south or north, there wouldn't be much David could do to stop them.

This day had been coming for some time. David more than even Saul before him had become a thorn in the Philistine's side. His constant victories in battle had assaulted the very core of their national identity and religious fervor. The harvesting of the foreskins had been the last straw as their rather peculiar sense of honor had been violated and nothing short of David's death would satisfy them.

In a way, David had created the current crisis. So it was up to him to end it.

The wind blew in from the east, which was perfect for David's purposes. He raised his sword high and bellowed, "Lords of the Philistines! Harken to my voice! I am David, son of Jesse. It is I who have defied your gods and slain your warriors. It is I whom you seek to slay. Come! Stand forth and hear my challenge!"

David's challenge was reckless and foolhardy at best, but something in his spirit had moved him to make it. He didn't have much confidence in his men, true, so he hoped that such an unprecedented challenge by a Hebrew would move the Philistines to curiosity at the very least.

Out of character or not, it felt right to do. In essence, he was pitting his God against the gods of the Philistines. In this, he had all the confidence in the world as to the outcome.

David watched as his words were relayed through the ranks of Philistines. A ripple, not unlike what a stone would cause to the calm waters of a pond, radiated through the ranks and five men, each wearing a gold crown instead of the standard colored headdress stood forth from the host.

Each man was arrayed for battle, wearing more bronze armor than was typical for the average Philistine soldier. They moved out from the ranks and stood just beyond bow range.

"We are the Philistine lords," one shouted. He was a somewhat pudgy man with a round face and small eyes. "I am Achish, king of Gath."

"Do you speak for all?" David yelled back.

"I do."

"Then hear my challenge. You come forth to avenge upon my blood the deaths of your brothers and sons. Here I am. Choose a man from among you to fight with me. Let us see whose God is greater. If I prevail, then you will no more seek my blood. You will take your armies and return to your homes. If your champion prevails, then you may pour out my blood upon the altars of your gods."

The five kings conversed for several long minutes. Finally, the slightly pudgy form of King Achish stepped forward again. "If you lose, son of Jesse, it will be more than your blood that we will require. We will burn your heart in the fires of our gods. Only then will we be at peace. Is this fate not blasphemous to you?"

David shrugged, though it was doubtful the men would notice the gesture from that distance. "My God will not permit it. Come!

Let us see whose God is greater. Is it the bestial gods of the Philistines? Or is it the one true God, Creator of heaven and earth? I fear not any man among you. Did I not fell your champion Goliath?"

David smirked, knowing that this was a challenge the Philistine lords could little afford to ignore. They would have to field a champion to fight David or else lose face with their own people. Their power rested squarely in what they did right now.

After a moment's consultation, Achish bellowed, "Your words are good, Hebrew! But the gods of the Philistines are three: Dagon,[3] Baalzebub[4] his son, and Ashtaroth,[5] his mistress. It is fitting therefore that you face three of our champions at once to prove which gods be true and which be false." Even from where David stood, he could see the sly grin that overtook the king of Gath's face. "If your God is the one true God as you claim, then what have you to fear?"

David silently cursed himself for stupidity. He'd been outmaneuvered. He had fully expected to take on one man, but not three—and not three at once either.

From behind David, Eleazar hissed sharply. "Do this not, David. This won't be like when you faced Goliath."

Shammah's deep voice overrode his fellow lieutenant. "We can't withdraw. We have issued the challenge. Yet, I pray you, let me go in your stead, my captain. I will bash their heads in for you. I will be your champion."

If the truth was known, David was sorely tempted. Facing three of the Philistines' very best would not be a simple fight. Yet, David had invoked Elohim's power. What was he if he did not trust in his God? In his heart, he knew the answer to that question. He would be nothing. No, this was his fight. His battle. He would trust in Jehovah to guide his arm and prove Jehovah Elohim as the only true God.

---

[3] Judges 16:23.
[4] 2 Kings 1:2-3, 16.
[5] 1 Samuel 31:10.

"Nay, my brothers, but this is a battle I face with but Jehovah as my right arm."

A long silence followed this announcement. Finally, Adino's laconic voice corrected, "Or, my captain, you are but His right arm. So go with Jehovah and prove their folly upon their foul bodies. Once the deed is done, we will make haste to meet you upon the field of battle and slay any unwise enough to remain."

"It will be well then," David said, smiling. Then lifting his voice, he cried, "Abide there, lords of Philistia, while I come down to you. Choose your three men 'ere I come, for I would not wait upon you. Let us do battle, and let our shed blood be proof of whose God is greater."

David jumped off the crumbling rock wall and set his shoulders. He looked back only once. His three lieutenants and friends regarded him with a mixture of dread, regret, and confidence. He bowed to them. "It has been my honor to serve with such noble men as you. I thank you for these last years. I have truly found a home among you."

Eleazar, normally so pessimistic in everything, straightened and saluted his captain. "Nay, the honor is ours. Go slay these braggarts and uplift our God upon their bodies. You have become our champion, my Captain. Go and be valiant for us once more."

Valiant. That word rang in David's mind. That was the same word Saul had used when commanding him to fight the LORD's battles. Be valiant. Be valiant for me. That's what King Saul had said. He'd asked David to champion him in battle. For the last four years or so, David had done exactly that. Now, at last, he understood it.

His true task was not to be valiant for the human king of Israel, but to be valiant for Jehovah Elohim, the God of Israel.

At various times throughout the history of the Hebrew people, Elohim had called upon a man to represent Him to the nations, a champion that stood firm against the unrighteousness of a world ignorant of the One True God. Abraham had been such a man. Moses had been such a man. And Joshua had been such a man.

There had been others, many others, but in all cases, God chose them and asked them to stand before Him and before His people.

David recalled that day so long ago when Samuel had anointed him. The Great Seer's words had been burned into David's heart. He could not forget them even if he wanted to: *"The LORD has chosen you, David, son of Jesse, to be captain over the people of Israel, His inheritance."* Most, including King Saul, understood the anointing to be about becoming a king. True enough—though David was uncertain if that was the intent—but more than a leader of men, it meant that David was to be the LORD's champion, to be valiant for Jehovah.

His resolve strengthened, David adjusted his armor and strode down the southern slope to reach the base of the hill. There, he walked alone to face the mighty host of the Philistine army.

Achish, the king of Gath, left the group of Philistine lords and walked up to David, standing just outside sword-striking distance. Not that it mattered. David could kill the portly king easily at this distance if he so desired.

Achish nodded. "You speak our tongue passably well, Hebrew," he said in the Hebrew tongue.

David gave the barest hint of a shrug. "And you, my lord king, speak the holy tongue passably well."

The Philistine king smiled. "You are pert, young captain. It is a shame that my fellow kings feel you must die. Under other circumstances, I would've liked to have known you. You've caused us no end of trouble, and many a widow sits alone this night because of you, but I feel there is something greater about you...something that we two may discover together."

David regarded the Philistine king levelly. "I accept your praise."

The king started, staring at David, and then he let loose with a belly laugh that rang out far and wide. "Ah! You are a bold one! If I had a hundred men like you, I would be invincible!" His eyes glittered. "I offer you another way, Hebrew. If you renounce your king, I could persuade these others to leave off and spare your life. Serve me, young David. I will make you a god! Nations will tremble at your coming! At the very least, I will aid you in the overthrow of King Saul so that you may take his place. Are you not nearly king of the land already? It would not take much to complete the task."

David felt his jaw dropping and hurriedly snapped it shut. This was the last thing he'd expected from the Philistine king. "What of what I did to the Timnath garrison? Is that not why you seek my blood? To avenge those mutilated men?"

Achish smirked. "It was truly offensive, young one. You know how to enrage us. Three of my brother kings nearly died of the fits when they found out." He sighed. "But alas, they recovered. It would have gone well with me if they had choked fatally on their anger." He gave David a cynical grin. "I, for one, understand. You know how to strike fear and anger into your enemy's heart. I like that. I like your methods, and I could make you feared by all, my young captain. The kingdom of the Hebrews would be but the beginning. You have but to serve me and all that you wish will be yours."

There was no way. No way in heaven and earth would David ever serve the Philistines. Surely, the chubby man understood this. But no, the man was in earnest. David could see it in the lord's greedy eyes. The king saw a way to become chief among his brother kings, and he lost nothing in presenting the possibility to David.

"And what of my God?" David asked more out of curiosity than of any desire to serve the heathen king.

"He serves you well," Achish said, shrugging. "I see no reason to ask you to bow before any other. Keep Him if you will. It is naught to me."

David chuckled low under his breath. "That is where you are wrong, my lord. My God does not serve me. I serve Him. I cannot betray my people or my God."

King Achish studied David for a long moment, obviously hoping to see something other than the steely determination that stared back at him. At length, he sucked in a deep breath and let it out slowly. "It does not have to be this way, young captain. Behold!" He turned and gestured, and from the ranks of Philistine warriors walked forth a man David knew.

Maon.

David nearly swallowed his tongue in surprise. He half took a step toward his wayward brother, but Maon stopped and folded his arms in a universal gesture of rebellion. "Maon?" David called. "What means this?"

It was Achish that answered. "Your brother serves me, son of Jesse. He has found a place of honor among us. It was he who delivered the message to your king. It was he who helped bring you to this place. He has seen the truth of our gods and our people. Will not you? Serve me, David, as your brother does."

Unsettled now unlike he'd been at any time since issuing his challenge, David could only shake his head, staring fixedly at his lost brother.

"I could only but try," the king of Gath said mostly to himself. "It was destined to be no other way. So be it." He pointed. "Behold, son of Jesse, our champions!"

Three warriors stepped forth to pass Maon and set themselves against David. The middle one grabbed David's attention first. He must've been born with Anakim blood in him, for he stood a good cubit taller than David, taller even than King Saul, but not nearly as tall as their former champion, Goliath. He was huge, however, larger than Shammah by a significant amount. This man wielded an axe, an unusual weapon for the Philistines and may have accounted for why he was chosen. David had no idea how to defend against such a weapon.

The warrior on the left wore no armor, only a battle skirt and flexible leather sandals that wrapped nearly up to the knees. He carried a long spear and the way he held it reminded David of Adino. His muscles gleamed in the sun light, much like Shammah's bald head did after he oiled the skin.

The last warrior was armored in traditional Philistine garb, ribbed armor wrapping around his chest, blue headdress, shield, and sword. He twirled his blade in a casual blur, and David instantly recognized that even Eleazar would be hard pressed to defeat this man in one-on-one combat. David had been at war long enough now to recognize skilled combatants, and there was little doubt that David now faced the Philistines' very best.

And he had to fight all three at the same time.

His confidence up to that point had carried him forward when nothing else would, but now, having seen Maon, his lost brother, standing against him with the Philistines and facing three formidable warriors, a sliver of doubt stabbed deep into his heart, and he was reminded that not all of Jehovah's champions had survived when called upon. Samson had died at the last, single-handedly giving the Philistines their greatest defeat ever.

He might win this battle, but he also might lose his life doing so. And the problem with that was that David didn't want to die.

22

David hefted his shield and peered intently over the top as the three Philistine champions spread out to surround him. He couldn't do anything to stop them, so he let it happen. They did so silently, not saying a word, which he found eerie. He slowly began to turn, keeping at least two in his vision at any given moment.

This brought him around to face the axe-wielder. The huge man attacked immediately to the approving roar of the Philistine host watching. David raised his shield to catch the brunt of the swinging axe and immediately regretted it. The axe wasn't a typical weapon, and the shield, made to turn arrows, spears, or swords, nearly folded with the impact. The wooden frame built behind the heavy bronze shield to which David clung, splintered and snapped alarmingly, and his arm nearly broke under the assault.

David hissed in pain and danced away, his arm numb from the massive blow. If the other two men had attacked David at that moment, he would've died. There was no way he could have avoided all three attackers. But strangely, the other two men hadn't moved in yet. They stood at a distance and watched in total silence. Instead of speaking, the spear wielder began to drum his spear against the hard ground in a slow beat while the swordsman drummed his sword against his shield in the same measure. The sound thus produced reminded David of a death watch—and he realized suddenly, it *was* a death watch—his. The rest of the Philistine host took up the drumming beat and the sound slammed into David like a spiritual disease.

Still off balance from finding his brother among the Philistine host, the drumming further eroded David's spirit. David leaped away from another tremendous swing of the axe and barely avoided being split in two.

He discarded the shield, now practically useless, and took a doublehanded grip on his sword. The axe-wielder charged in a third time, swinging another massive overhand blow with both hands. David jumped back, and the axe head whizzed by, smashing into the rocky ground and sending sparks flying. Seeing the warrior off balance, he thrust with his sword and succeeded in nicking the Philistine's arm.

The warrior grunted, but uttered not a word as he jerked his axe up and then cut horizontally. David brought his sword up desperately, but not to block directly, for that would've been foolish. The axe clanged against the sword and slid along its angled length to pass over his head within a handspan of his hair.

David flicked his sword out again, scoring another nick. The giant Philistine's eyes narrowed, and he responded by unexpectedly jabbing straight out with the axe. The move caught David unprepared, and the blunt end of the axe smashed into his mail shirt, bruising his ribs and sending him flying backward to land heavily on the rocks, gasping for breath. He couldn't believe the strength of the Philistine warrior!

A roar from the Philistine host accompanied David's fall, momentarily drowning out the slow drumming of weapons. Still not having gathered his breath completely, he rolled away just in time. The axe head buried itself in the ground where David's neck had been. Sparks and gravel stabbed at his face from the near fatal blow.

Instinctively, he reversed his roll as soon as the axe hit the ground and stabbed with his sword. The sword point took the Philistine in the belly, but David failed to inflict a serious wound as he didn't have the strength or leverage to thrust further.

The Philistine's mouth tightened in pain, and he staggered back, tearing his axe out of the ground as he did so. David, still gasping, leveraged himself up to his feet with his sword and stood panting, watching warily as the axe-wielder examined his wound with hate-filled eyes.

Faintly, above the encompassing drumming, David detected the sound of sandals scuffing on the rocks. He twisted to the side as a spear was stabbed through the space he'd just occupied. The bladed spear still caught David a glancing blow, however, leaving a wicked-looking cut along his sword arm. He spun away from the attack, gasping for breath. Blood ran down his arm and soaked his hand. The sword became slick in his grasp.

The Philistine spearman retreated, twirling his spear as his eyes danced with vicious mirth. The remaining champion, the swordsman, still stood to one side, watching and pounding his sword against his shield. He too said nothing, but his eyes were narrowed with malicious mirth as he regarded David coldly, like some dead fish. The man never blinked. Not once. David swallowed as fear rose in his heart. If both the other Philistine champions had attacked while David was occupied with the axe-wielder, he would have been killed easily.

They were toying with him.

The spearman stepped back and then casually licked David's blood off his spear. He gave the young captain a predatory grin, his teeth red with David's blood.

The axe-wielder threw himself back into the fray. The axe seemed to come from every angle imaginable, and only the many years of sparring with Eleazar, Adino, and Shammah kept David alive in the next few moments.

He acquired two more cuts, and he struggled mightily to retain his hold on his slick sword. He retreated frantically, desperately trying to get away from that swinging axe. And nearly died because of it.

The swordsman, who until that moment, had been content to watch, darted forward, his sword a blur of rapid thrusts and strikes that David had no defense for. The blade sliced into his mail shirt, splitting metal links and tearing a gash in David's side. He gasped and fell heavily to one knee. Blood from a cut on his brow seeped into his eye, half blinding him.

Instinct saved him. He flung himself forward, surprising both the swordsman and the axe-wielder as he slipped between the two Philistine champions. He stumbled away, half-blinded, and his heart beating rapidly.

The three Philistine champions watched him silently, though their eyes mocked him even as the Philistine host roared their approval and began cursing both David and his God while continuing that infernal drumming. Spreading out, the three enemy champions began to circle him like a pack of jackals watching their prey as it slowly died. He had no place to go. No way out.

He was going to die. He was no match for these three Philistine warriors—not all three at once. They would wear him down, toying with him, perhaps even keeping him alive long enough to sacrifice him upon one of their abominable altars to Dagon.

"Where is your God now?" Maon shouted from where he watched. His voice carried over the drumming racket and struck David like physical blows.

Through blurry eyes, David looked at his brother. Maon stood with arms crossed, a look of regret and determination filling his face.

"Will He save you from their weapons, brother?"

King Achish stood beside Maon near the other Philistine lords. One of the lords, a gaunt man with a long nose said, "Look upon him, my brothers! Behold a weak and broken man. This is the Hebrew champion. This is the man their God chooses to represent Him." He spat. "Pitiful!"

"Pour his blood upon the altars of Dagon!" someone suggested.

"Burn his heart in Dagon's fires!" another shouted.

The words washed over David driven into his heart by the drumming tempo of the enemy warriors. Each word stabbed more deeply than any spear or sword could ever penetrate, pained beyond anything he'd ever experienced, he fell to one knee as despair caught up to him and tried to burrow its way into his heart.

No.

A stillness fell over the young captain then, and in the vaults of his soul he wondered what it was he was truly fighting for. Up until that moment, he had been fighting the Philistines because they had come out against him—against David—for what he'd done to their dead. He'd been fighting to stay alive, for above all things at that moment, he did not want to die.

But why should he fear death or its shadow? Though he walk through the valley of the shadow of death, his only true fear, he admitted to himself, was that he would walk it alone. But he wasn't alone. He'd never been alone. Jehovah Elohim walked by his side. All he must do is trust in His guidance, in His shepherding. What else would he need? What else would he ever need? He need not fear any evil.[1]

Strength infused his body as he fully accepted his role in this battle. It was no longer for his own life that he fought. He fought for the LORD. He fought to cast down false gods and idols and to uplift Jehovah God to all nations and to all people.

Giving himself wholly over to the Spirit of the LORD, he stood slowly upright, his mind and body yielded to the LORD's direction. He may die, but so be it. He would die in service to his God. No greater end could man achieve if that is what Jehovah so desired.

Pain fled his body, and clarity filled his mind and vision. He saw the carrion birds flying overhead, already anticipating their next meal. He saw the grasshoppers skipping from rock to rock. He heard the faint buzz of insects, mostly stilled into silence by the presence of man. He could sense the Hebrew soldiers watching from the hill above. He could feel their fear, their anxiety as they watched the battle of champions unfold below them. And the drumming sound faded in his ears, purged from his spirit as the LORD's Spirit took control.

---

[1] Thoughts taken from Psalm 23, which David wrote.

He took a single step to the side. He didn't consciously decide to do so, his body simply reacted. The spearman had darted in from behind David and sought to stab the young captain in the back. He hadn't reckoned on the Holy Spirit of God to guide the Hebrew's body. The spear darted like a striking snake between his arm and torso, missing him by the merest of hairbreadths. He caught the spear shaft in his left hand behind the bladed head and jerked, pulling the spearman forward and off balance.

David whipped his sword around behind his head, again without looking. It whirled through the air, singing as it zipped behind his head. He brought the weapon to rest, still holding the spear with his left hand, but his eyes were locked on the axe-wielder and the swordsman. He had never once even looked at the spearman, and now there was no need.

The Philistine army fell abruptly silent, the drumming ceasing abruptly as they stared aghast at what had just happened. Most gaped in stupefied astonishment, unsure of what they'd witnessed.

Behind David, the spearman stood for a long swaying moment, then collapsed to the ground, his throat sliced nearly all the way through by David's twirling sword.

The moment, David felt the dead man's grip on the spear loosen, he took two hopping steps and threw it with all his strength—lefthanded. The axe-wielder, still standing in dumbfounded amazement never flinched as the spear slammed into his chest and sliced his heart in two. He fell like a folded piece of parchment into a sitting position, quite dead, but propped up by the spear shaft sticking out of his body.

That left the swordsman.

Turning, David, still quite calm and with a clarity that came only from being infused with the Spirit of the LORD, moved to meet the last Philistine champion.

So quickly had David killed the other two that the Hebrews watching the battle didn't even have opportunity to cheer. They simply stared in amazement. Even the Philistines hadn't completely registered the quick elimination of two of their most skilled and battle-hardened warriors.

The last champion stared in awe at David. But the Philistine was no coward. He met David with a flurry of thrusts and strikes, his hand whipping about like a viper. Never had David encountered such finesse in a swordsman. Eleazar's style relied heavily on sweeping cuts and slashes with brutal efficient use of the shield, but this Philistine used swift thrusts and lightning-quick parries to attack his enemy.

It didn't matter.

David parried two of the sword strikes and then neatly sidestepped a third thrust, catching the man's sword hand in an iron grip with his free hand, almost casually then, as if his mind were but a spectator, he cut off the man's head.

As before when David had slain the giant Goliath, the Philistines arrayed before him stood in profound silence for the space of twenty heartbeats.

Then a roar of victory shattered the stillness, and David's thousand came streaming off the hill in a full-on charge at the Philistine host that outnumbered them many times over. But the LORD fought for Israel that day, and the Philistines knew it.

As one man, they turned and ran. The kings and Maon were the first to disappear. Many others were not so fortunate, and there followed a great slaughter that day of Philistine warriors.[2] As inexperienced as David's company was, the Philistines were overcome with an unconquerable terror. David's men had little to fear from the enemy that day, and they wreaked havoc and ruin among them.

David would have followed, but his strength gave out suddenly, and the pain of his wounds crowded back into his consciousness. He fell to one knee, gritting his teeth in fierce pain. The wound to his side flared up insidiously, sending waves of agony to his brain. He

---

[2] 1 Samuel 19:8.

dropped his sword and would have fallen altogether except that Adino caught him and gently settled him into a sitting position.

"You did well, my Captain. Rest easy now and let me look at your wounds."

Two other shadows fell across David. He blinked, looking up, and saw Shammah and Eleazar staring down at him. Both wore awed expressions that made him feel somewhat uncomfortable.

Shammah cleared his throat. "Jehovah was surely with you, my Captain. I have never seen its like before."

David grunted painfully and decided that he had no real answer for that statement. These three men, his favored lieutenants, had seen more than their share of miracles. The only problem with constant miracles was that eventually they would no longer seem miraculous. Was the sun rising and setting not a miracle? But the sun never failed in its trek across the sky, so the miracle and wonder of it became commonplace—an everyday event and hardly miraculous.

Eleazar finally allowed a sloppy smile to cross his face. "Aye, it was a truly masterful display of martial skill. But I do have a question, my Captain."

"Ask," David granted magnanimously. He then hissed in pain. Even speaking that word caused his cracked and broken ribs to rebel and the gash in his side to flare insidiously.

"Why wait until the end to dispatch yon champions? Why take wounds first?"

David stared at his lieutenant, and then weakly began to laugh. Oh, how the laughter hurt his broken ribs! But oh, how it refreshed his weakened spirit too. The others joined in, and their laughter echoed off the hills, mixing with the faint cries of the receding battle that was being carried on in the distance.

David looked up toward heaven, and in the hidden recesses of his spirit, he asked his God, "Was I not valiant for You?"

Epilogue

Adriel's heart was conflicted. After all these years, he'd finally won his heart's desire. He was married to Merab, the king's daughter. Since the very first time he'd laid eyes on her, he'd known that she was the one for him.

Now he had her. The wedding had taken place a week past. He had his heart's desire.

But at what cost? His friend David, though amiable toward him, was nonetheless distant. He keenly felt the rift between them, an ache that refused to ease. He hated it. But he didn't know what he could do about it.

He turned his eyes on David who sat on a stool against the wall playing his ever-present harp. White cloth had been wrapped around his wounds, and though only a few weeks had passed since his stunning victory over the Philistines, he was healing rapidly. Adriel had never met a man who could heal as quickly as David.

That last battle between champions had been one that Adriel had missed. He had been at David's side for the last four years, fighting at his left hand, but on that last battle, Adriel had not been allowed to go. David hadn't even bothered asking if he wanted to go.

A great sadness welled up inside his heart. He missed the easy friendship with David. But he had won Merab. It would have to suffice. With that thought, Adriel glanced at his father-in-law, King Saul. The tall king sat hunched over in his chair while David played the harp.[1] The king had awarded Merab to Adriel for his service, and Adriel had accepted. This meant that for better or for worse, he had tied his future to the king.

He knew the rumors about David—about his anointing. He and his former captain had even talked about it a few times while he'd served as David's armorbearer. In a way, he felt as if Saul had somehow maneuvered him into the position where he had had to choose between the woman he loved and the friend he loved. But he'd chosen. And by choosing, he had chosen a side.

Adriel was a highly perceptive individual, a trait he hid behind his wry humor. So he knew. He saw the hateful looks the king had directed toward David when he thought no one was watching. He'd seen the scorn Saul held for David—and the fear. Saul greatly feared David[2] for some reason. And after hearing of the great slaughter and David's victory over the Philistine champions, he understood the king's fear.

David was a very real danger to Saul's kingdom.

Adriel pulled at his nose, trying to understand the dynamics of the situation.

The atmosphere in the court hovered somewhere between jovial and anxious anticipation. Reports had begun to trickle in regarding the aftermath of David's last battle. The Philistines were in disarray. The unity between the Philistine lords had crumbled, at least for the time being, and they were bickering violently with each other—always good for Israel.

David's reputation had grown with each telling of the story. The song that Saul had slain his thousands and David his tens of thousands was once again being sung by girls and women throughout Israel.

Indeed, Adriel had no doubts at all that it was due to David's exploits that Ziba, a man of means who had been brought in to serve Saul's household,[3] admitted an ambassador from the Moabite king

---

[1] 1 Samuel 19:9.
[2] 1 Samuel 18:29.
[3] 2 Samuel 9:2, 10.

to stand before King Saul. There was no love lost between the two nations,[4] and so the ambassador abandoned diplomacy for the direct approach, asking his question—a question that would without fail enrage any king—immediately upon being admitted to King Saul's presence.

"My lord," the ambassador began with an overly smug smile, "the king of Moab, requests to know whom is truly king in Israel. Is it Saul, son of Kish, or David, son of Jesse?"

Saul shot to his feet, his body quivering, and the javelin in his hand poised at the ambassador like a spear. David immediately stopped playing his harp, and the ambassador took a prudent step back.

"What means this question, ambassador?" Saul demanded. "Does your master seek to insult me?"

The ambassador, possessing an oily slick tongue, bowed low in apparent deference. "Not so, my lord. My liege seeks only clarification. We hear David's name being sung from the hilltops. Our spies in Philistia speak of this man—this man named David—as king of Israel." He shrugged. "We are but confused. We would know who rules in Israel."

The king's face turned livid, and Adriel shrank back against the wall as did most everyone else in the room. They had seen this uncontrollable wrath come upon the king before. They knew the signs. An evil spirit had descended upon the king.[5]

Trembling, Saul shouted, "Then let your confusion be no more!" Twirling around, he launched the javelin with terrible force straight at David.

Adriel's former captain flung himself to the side just in time. The javelin slammed into the wooden wall with a terrific impact, a report that resounded around the room.[6]

David, his reflexes honed by years of constant battle, rolled to his feet and darted toward the door in a blur. He slammed into the

---

[4] 1 Samuel 14:47.
[5] 1 Samuel 19:9.
[6] 1 Samuel 19:10.

two guards who belatedly tried to step in front of the door, supposing that the king would wish to bar David's escape. They were bowled aside like twigs before a club.

And David was gone, fled into the night.[7]

Saul raised his hands to the ceiling and cried, "Slay him! Slay him! I want him dead by morning!"

For a long while, no one moved, no one dared. King Saul spotted Adriel. "Take men. Wait for him at his house. In the morning, slay him."[8]

Adriel gaped at his king, scarcely believing the words he had heard. "My lord?"

"You heard me. Go! Bring me his head by morning!"

Gulping and trembling himself, Adriel fled the court, taking five guards with him.

He had no choice. He had chosen a side, and so he set out resolutely to kill a friend.

The End

Thus ends book two of the Davidic Chronicles. In book three, Fugitive, *David must survive a vengeful and wrathful king bent on hunting him down and slaying him.*

---

[7] 1 Samuel 19:10.
[8] 1 Samuel 19:11.

Additional Biblical and Historical Explanations

Facts Versus Interpretation to Discover Truth

Stating a fact and interpreting that fact are not the same. By themselves, facts do not represent truth; they are merely facts. Truth is a fact that has purpose and meaning—often what is called a *philosophy*—that gives the fact a means to interact with your life and become relevant and meaningful to you. This then becomes a truth for you.

For example, take a fact: dinosaur bones. This fact coupled with either the philosophy of evolution or creationism will present two entirely different and opposing truths. Each side considers theirs to be true and their opposite to be false. But the core "fact" is still a bone. The interpretation of that fact leads to our perspective, views, understanding, and ultimately the truth to which we cling.

Jesus said that He is truth, which means that when we see life through His eyes, we find purpose and meaning that cannot be found unless we can view that perspective. Jesus is indeed truth—my truth, and I trust your truth as well. But even among Christian circles, that perspective varies enough that our "truths" are often not quite aligned with someone else's. Welcome to individual soul liberty.

I say this to explain that though I try to incorporate *all* the facts that the Bible speaks of in this series of novels, I am still going to interpret what those facts mean for the characters and events described. Not everyone will agree with my conclusions. For example, a fact: David took five smooth stones with him to fight Goliath. Why five? This is where we begin to interpret the fact. Was it because Goliath had four brothers, and he possibly would need one stone for each? Or did David merely want extra ammunition, thinking it would take more than one shot to bring down Goliath?

When you interpret the fact, your "truth" of the event shifts. Your understanding of it changes, and how you relate to the fact and how it becomes meaningful to your life also changes. This becomes your truth of the story mentioned in the Bible. Preachers do this all the time.

These novels represent my interpretation of those facts into a cohesive and, hopefully, noncontradictory story that will entertain but also spark your fascination for the Bible, the characters, God's interaction with men, and ultimately your own relationship with Him.

I do not expect everyone to agree. But I do hope these novels will inspire you to delve into God's Word in a much more personal way and to see that the characters in the Bible had real lives and that it is those lives to whom God wanted to introduce you.

Scripture and the Law

The Hebrews of David's day had only the first five books of our Bible to guide them—and possibly whatever Samuel wrote, though it is doubtful that Samuel's writings would've been considered scriptural canon in his day. Right and wrong, therefore, were based on their understanding of the Law—the Torah.

Only the priesthood and the king had an actual written copy of the Law. Most families taught their children by oral tradition or by what the priests would have taught. Religious understanding would have been firmly wrapped in ceremony as a means of passing down truth from one generation to another. What David knew would have been delivered from his father and from the local priests living in Bethlehem. Occasionally, pilgrimages to the tabernacle would have been made, but this would likely happen no more than twice a year for a religious holiday such as the Passover and the Feast of Tabernacles.

Physical copies of the Law were rare and expensive to produce. In fact, not so long after Solomon's death, all copies of the Law disappeared and weren't discovered again until Hilkiah the high priest found one in the temple (2 Kings 22:8).

Monuments, markers, ceremony, and oral tradition would have been the primary educational methods employed to inform the next generation about God and the Law.

Fictional Characters and Events

I try to use characters that the Bible already mentions. The story is already in place, and I believe the main characters should remain the main characters of the story.

But there are still several fictional characters introduced into this story. One such is Mahli, one of David's lieutenants. Also, although David obviously had a real mother, her name is never mentioned in the Bible. Jewish tradition holds that her name was Natzbet, so I borrowed that name for her. In a similar sense, Jonathan had a wife, but her name is never mentioned, so Naarah is a fictional name for a real person. The priest in Gibeah, Amzi, is also fictional as is the high priest of Dagon. Likely, there were such individuals, but their names are not mentioned.

Many of the real people also performed fictional roles. In effect, they constitute my best guess as to how a person could logically get from point A (a biblical fact) to point B (another biblical fact). The fictional part is often what happens between point A and point B.

For example, David's lieutenants, Adino, Shammah, and Eleazar were all listed among David's mighty men. Clearly, these men could very well have known David when he was captain over a thousand, but if these men were truly among that company assigned to David by Saul is merely speculation. Their roles as David's lieutenants in the company of the Indebted are fictional.

Adriel's roles as David's friend and as Jonathan's former armorbearer are also fictional. It seems clear that David would have known Adriel in some capacity, and if Saul was indeed trying to hurt

David, then it would make sense he'd give his daughter either to David's friend or enemy. I chose the friendship role for this novel.

The role of Saul's son, Ishui, is purely fictional. In Scripture, his name is mentioned once, and we know he was killed along with his father. Other than that, we know nothing about him.

Timelines and Timeframes

The biblical account is often vague on the actual timeline of events presented in this novel. Perhaps if there is any area that I take the most liberties, it would be with the timeline. For example, 1 Samuel 18:5 has a shroud of confusion surrounding it. In the verse, we are told that David went out wherever Saul commanded him to go, that he was placed over the men of war, and that David behaved himself wisely. However, the verse could either be a summary of the following verses (6-30) or it might be relating events that happened *before* verses 6 through 30. For various reasons, I chose the former interpretation instead of the latter. It appears as if the verse is merely a summary and then gives further explanation of the summary in the following verses, something the Bible does often (compare Judges 2, which is a summary of the rest of the book).

The two lists of David's Mighty Men are another timeline anomaly. In the Samuels, the list of Mighty Men is given right at the end of David's life (2 Samuel 23). However, the same list is given in 1 Chronicles 11 at the beginning of David's reign as king. It is not out of reach to suppose that the deeds of these men spanned much of David's life, even from as early as when David was captain over a thousand under King Saul. In this novel, I include the first three men on the list and put them in David's command when he was captain over a thousand. The timelines fit, but without more evidence, it is merely a guess on my part.

When reading the story in 1 Samuel 18, there is little evidence of a significant passing of time, except for verse 19 which says, "But it came to pass at the time when Merab Saul's daughter should have been given to David, that she was given unto Adriel the Meholathite to wife." This is the only place that really hints that possibly years had passed. Hebrew betrothals often lasted for a year and David was still under the age of twenty, so it is possible that Saul dangled Merab in front of David for quite some time, possibly a year or two, before giving her to Adriel.

Outside of that verse, there is no real indicator that much time had passed. However, most scholars agree that David became king in Hebron no sooner than thirty years of age. This means at least thirteen years pass from David's victory over Goliath to when he becomes king. But where those thirteen years lie is not clear. The only other timeframe given is found in 1 Samuel 27:7, which states that David was in Philistia for one year and four months when he was hiding from Saul. These novels, therefore, must account for another twelve years or so. I give my best guess where that time passed.

I leave it to the reader to decide what is right and pray you have mercy on my decisions.

Violence and Warfare
Life was cheap in David's day, and violence a part of everyday life. The early kings of Israel did not maintain prisons as we understand them today. In many cases, an infraction resulted in a physical punishment—the-eye-for-an-eye, the-tooth-for-a-tooth principle. More serious infractions or violations often resulted in death. Saul and then David often executed people for even minor violations of disloyalty. The Indebted, the men David commands in this novel, is an example of minor infractions being punished in severe ways. Many Hebrews were enslaved because of debt (though there were provisions to free them at the year of Jubilee and after six years of service). However, many of these men represent what we would consider petty criminals or rebels in our day. These are the type of men who came to David later because they saw a way to become free (1 Samuel 22:2).

But as stated, life was cheap. King Saul, for example, killed all the priests of Nob for the simple fact that they had helped David. Saul felt that such a drastic action was well within his rights as king, and no one chastised him for it either. David killed an Amalekite man who had admitted that he'd helped King Saul commit suicide.

The man was lying, but David didn't take the time to find out the truth of the matter. He let the man's mouth be his judge and ordered him killed. On another occasion, David set out to kill every person associated with Nabal because he felt slighted and insulted by the man. Only Nabal's wife, Abigail, succeeded in turning away David's wrath just in the nick of time. When Nabal died a little later, David felt no remorse and saw it as vindication of God's favor.

These examples were not exceptions. They were the norm for that period. Violence and death were common bedfellows, and a simple way to eradicate any malcontent was to kill the malcontented. I tried to keep this aspect of common society in the story. David was a bloody man according to God, and death and violence followed him.

Warfare was also part of everyday life which I tried to portray in this story. I studied the arms and armaments of the period along with common tactics and strategies. I did my best to keep them as accurate as possible in the story. The slaughter of farmers and common folk was a routine occurrence, a practice in which David no doubt participated. As stated in the novel, sympathy and mercy were simply not offered to the enemy, particularly those people viewed as enemies of the LORD. The opposite was true. Israel never expected mercy from their enemies.

Overall, I hope to have portrayed an accurate way of life that reflected the character and life views of the period.

Marriage and Love

For the ancient Hebrews of David's day, marriage and love was viewed entirely different than what we understand today in most cultures. David married Michal, not out of love, but for his love for King Saul and Jonathan. Being the king's son-in-law more than being Michal's husband was what was important to David.

Although love did happen *before* marriage, it was not common back then. Michal loved David before they were wed, but there is no indication at all that David loved Michal. Marriage was an arranged relationship, not often one that was chosen. The arrangement was meant to benefit both families. It was a familial duty to marry well.

Therefore, it was expected that a husband and a wife would love their spouses *after* marriage—in much the same way as one would love one's parents or siblings. No one chooses their parents and siblings. Yet they were expected to love them nonetheless. A wife or a husband was seen in the same manner. Love came, if it came, after the wedding.

Polygamy was common only among the rich and powerful. It was not forbidden—except to kings, and even then, the Bible says not to multiply wives (Deuteronomy 17:17) in order to avoid having one's heart turned away from Him—as what happened to Solomon. So most Israelite kings would not see having a "few" Hebrew wives as a violation of this law. Saul had a concubine. David had a minimum of six wives and ten concubines. In most cases, men could not afford to support more than one wife or come up with the dowry, so polygamy happened mostly in the upper class of society.

Sources and References

Much research goes into a novel like this. I wanted to stay true to the biblical account, as well as to the era and times. This meant I had to learn how they built their houses, what their clothes were made of, and many other customs and facts. The sources below represent the majority of the information about customs, manners, and geography that I incorporated into this novel. Those not mentioned only corroborated what I found in the following sources.

Disclaimer: Undoubtedly, I have missed or didn't learn many facts about ancient life, and so the astute reader may discover historical and geographical errors. Feel free to write me about them, as long as you corroborate them with sources, and I will attempt to incorporate them into future editions of the novel.

Sources:
- The King James Bible
- www.biblicalarchaeology.org
- www.ancient-hebrew.org
- www.gci.org/bible/hist/weapons
- www.thattheworldmayknow.com/the-philistines
- www.gotquestions.org/Jehovah.html
- www.theoldtestamenttimeline.com
- www.israelbiblicalstudies.com & blog.israelbiblicalstudies.com

- www.jewfaq.org
- www.bible-history.com
- www.biblewalks.com/info/trees.html
- www.biblehub.com/timeline/psalms/1.htm
- www.bibleatlas.org
- Jan H. Negenman, *New Atlas of the Bible* (New York: Doubleday & Company Inc., 1969).
- Rand-McNally Bible Atlas - Published in 1910.
- Smith Bible Atlas - Designed and edited by George Adam Smith, 1915.
- Fred H. Wight, *Manners and Customs of Bible Lands* (Moody Bible Institute of Chicago, 1953).
- A. Van Deursen, *Illustrated Dictionary of Bible Manners and Customs* (Grand Rapids, MI: Zondervan, 1958).
- Boyd Seevers, *Warfare in the Old Testament* (Grand Rapids, MI: Kregel Publications, 2013).
- Chaim Herzog and Mordechai Gichon, *Battles of the Bible – A Military History of Ancient Israel* (Barnes and Noble Publishing, 2006).

Commentaries and Dictionaries:
- James Orr, M.A., D.D., General Editor, *International Standard Bible Encyclopedia.*
- John McClintock and James Strong, *Cyclopedia of Biblical, Theological and Ecclesiastical Literature* (1895).
- Canne, Browne, Blayney, Scott, and others, with introduction by R. A. Torrey, *Treasury of Scriptural Knowledge* (1834; public domain).
- *John Gill's Exposition of the Bible* (1746-1766, 1816; public domain).
- *Jamieson, Fausset and Brown Commentary - A Commentary, Critical and Explanatory, on the Old and New Testaments* (1871; public domain).

- *Adam Clarke's Commentary on the Bible* (1810-1826; public domain).
- *Joseph Benson's Commentary on the Old and New Testaments* (1857; public domain).
- *Albert Barnes' Notes on the Bible* (1847-85; public domain).
- *Matthew Henry's Commentary on the Whole Bible* (1708-1714; public domain).
- W. Robertson Nicoll, *Sermon Bible Commentary* (1888-1893; public domain).
- *John Wesley's Notes on the Bible* (1755-1766; public domain).
- F. B. Meyer, *Through the Bible Day by Day – A Devotional Commentary* (1914; public domain).
- W. Robertson Nicoll (Editor), *Expositor's Bible Commentary* (1887-1896; public domain).

About the Author

Greg S. Baker has been writing novels for over twenty years. His books are widely read and enjoyed. His primary focus lately has been on his stellar Biblical Fiction novels and his engaging young adult adventure novels. He has written a number of other helpful books for the Christian life. He has a passion for expanding the Kingdom of God within the kingdom of men.

He lives in the southwest with his wife, Liberty, and their four boys. Much of his writing has been for them, desiring to provide entertaining stories that teach and inspire.

He attended Bible college in the late 1990s, pastored a Baptist church in Colorado for thirteen years, and now works as a writer, a freelance Christian editor, and a programmer from his house. He remains active in his church, serving God in a variety of capacities, but focusing mainly on teenagers and young single adults.

He loves chess, playing sports, and rearing his teen boys.

You can connect with Greg through his website GregSBaker.com. He loves hearing from people and engaging them as an active part of the writing process for his future books. If you love reading, then stop on by.

Made in the USA
Las Vegas, NV
29 October 2024